THE PIRATE'S WISH

"Unique, heart-wrenching, full of mysteries and twists!"
Tamora Pierce, author of Alanna: The First Adventure

"An exciting and original YA novel with magic, pirates, myth and adventure, *The Assassin's Curse* will hook you in and keep you tugging on the line for the next book in Clarke's series."
USA Today

"Its fluid prose, naturalistic dialogue and pace make *The Assassin's Curse* supremely readable. And in Ananna, the young offspring of pirate stock, we have a heroine both spirited and memorable."
Stan Nicholls, author of the Orcs: First Blood *trilogy*

"An inventive debut with a strong narrative voice, a glimpse of an intriguing new world."
Adrian Tchaikovsky, author of the Shadows of the Apt *series*

"*The Assassin's Curse* is a fantastic debut for Cassandra Rose Clarke. I thought the book was fabulous and I want book two now!"
A Fantastical Librarian

"Ananna of Tanarau is a delightfully irascible heroine, inhabiting a fascinating a ld that I would love to spend more time w-dwelling assassins? Yes "
Celine Kiernan, auth

"Inventive and individual storytelling about engaging and intriguing characters."
  Juliet E McKenna, author of the Tales of the Einarinn *and* The Chronicles of the Lescari Revolution

"An enjoying, compelling read with a strong and competent narrator… a highly satisfying adventure."
  SFX Magazine

"A fun, quite often snarky, action-adventure tale filled with sorcery and elemental magic, political intrigue, strange and sometimes ethereal places, and interesting creatures."
  Popcorn Reads

"*The Assassin's Curse* has a sweet mix of all my favorite things in a rip roaring YA adventure read."
  The Diary of a Bookworm

"Ananna and Naji's world is rich with magic and bursting with the potential for adventure."
  Violin in a Void

"Cassandra Rose Clarke has landed herself on my teeny tiny list of authors to auto-buy."
  Small Review

"*The Assassin's Curse* is what I would shamelessly call 'masterful.'"
  The Authoress

"*The Assassin's Curse* turned out to be one of my favorite surprises of the year, and I closed the back cover grinning like a fool."
  Bookyurt

"I'm a sucker for mystical tales of adventure, pirates at sea, curses, princesses with an attitude and magic, and *The Assassin's Curse* provided this and more."
The Library Mouse

"This book is pure magic."
Reading Under the Willow Tree

"Clarke's writing is pretty evocative stuff, the heat of the desert sands is almost palpable."
The Eloquent Page

"Full of action, adventure, romance, magic *The Assassin's Curse* by Cassandra Rose Clarke is an engrossing and original fantasy debut... and a rollicking good time."
Refracted Light Reviews

"Everything about *The Assassin's Curse* was a pleasant surprise, from the characters, to the romance, to every single plot point."
The Cozy Armchair

"I can't remember the last time I had this much fun reading a book."
www.fantasyliterature.com

"A story that will draw you in with its rich setting filled with assassins, pirates, magic, and two lead characters that you can't help but root for. A highly recommended read!"
Fantasy's Ink

"This is a book like no other YA book I've ever read... Please bring more pirates into YA!"
One Page at a Time

CASSANDRA ROSE CLARKE

The Pirate's Wish

STRANGE
CheMISTRY

STRANGE CHEMISTRY
An Angry Robot imprint
and a member of the Osprey Group

Lace Market House
54-56 High Pavement
Nottingham NG1 1HW
UK

www.strangechemistrybooks.com
Strange Chemistry #11

A Strange Chemistry paperback original 2013
1

A catalogue record for this book is available
from the British Library.

ISBN 978 1 90884 427 9
Ebook ISBN 978 1 90884 429 3

Printed in the UK by CPI Group (UK) Ltd, Croydon CR0 4YY

CHAPTER ONE

"Do you feel that?" Naji asked.

"I feel cold." I rubbed my arms over the worn-down fabric of my coat sleeves. Me and Naji'd been stranded on the Isles of the Sky for longer than I could keep track, thanks to him throwing the *Ayel's Revenge* off course while we were headed to Qilar, and the weather did a number on my clothes. I planned to march down to the Wizard Eirnin's house to see about getting some new things later today.

"You're always cold." Naji leaned forward and squinted out at the sea, his features twisting from the rough scars lining the left side of his face. We were sitting outside the shack the two of us shared, knotting bundles of pine needles to re-thatch the roof. "No, this is... something's on the air. Something disruptive."

"Disruptive?" I tossed my bundle of pine needles on the sand. "The hell does that mean?"

"Are you still wearing your protection charm?"

At that, I gave him a withering look and yanked back

my coat collar to show him. "I ain't never taken it off before. Don't know why I'd start now."

He didn't answer, which wasn't much of a surprise. He'd been in a mood the last few weeks – at least, that's what I would guess, I'd stopped keeping track of the days awhile back – mostly cause him and Eirnin had gotten themselves tangled up in a feud. As near as I could tell, it started when Naji was casting one of his blood magic spells. He had a whole mess of them going: some to protect us from the magic of the Isles and some to keep me hidden from the Mists, that whole other world full of lords and monsters who kept trying to break through to ours.

Now, he'd been casting those spells the whole time we'd been on the island, ever since he got his strength back, but this *particular* spell had mingled with one Eirnin had going and messed it up. Since then, the two of 'em had been at a feud like a pair of noble families in some Empire story.

It went pretty much like this: when his spell failed, Eirnin retaliated against Naji, sending a swarm of droning gnats down to our shack one evening. I managed to get away since they weren't after me, and I sat on the sand and watched 'em swirl in a dark cloud around Naji. Not biting him or anything, just annoying him. It took almost two days before he dispelled 'em completely using magic, and by that point I was sleeping out on the beach just to get away from the noise. Then Naji marched down to Eirnin's house as soon as he was free from the gnats and cast some kind of long-term binding charm that made it pour rain for six days straight. Eirnin cleared it up, thank

Kaol, but who the hell knew what they'd get up to next. Probably ruin my day, whatever it was.

"I don't like this." Naji dropped his pine needle bundle into his lap and stared up at the sky, which was gray and cloudy like always. His sleeves were pushed up to his elbows, revealing the swirl of tattoos on his skin. "Stay close to the shack for the next few days."

Well, blood and saltwater. There went my trip to Eirnin's house. And I really wanted some new clothes.

"Does your head hurt?" I asked.

Naji glanced at me. "No," he said. "It's just... as a precaution."

"Right. A precaution." I nodded. If his head didn't hurt, then that meant the curse wasn't activated and I wasn't in danger, which meant I could sneak off while he was fishing, like I'd planned to originally. "Is it... it's not the Mists, is it?"

"The Mists?" Naji shook his head. "No. This is different. Something with the island."

I shivered. Course, his magic had kept us free of the side effects of living on the Isles of the Sky for awhile now.

"Something's changed," he added.

"Something's always changing on this damn island," I said. "The trees, the path in the woods – the freaking *sunrise*." I finished up the last of my pine needles. "There, done. I'll thatch up the roof while you're fishing."

Naji blinked at me, then pushed aside his own pine needles. "Maybe I shouldn't–"

"What? No! I'm starving. And, last I checked, fish is all we got to eat."

Naji sighed. "Stay in the shack."

"I'll stay *on* the shack."

"Ananna, you know I can't concentrate when you do that."

I frowned at him. "I ain't gonna fall! How many times I got to tell you–"

"As many as it takes." He stood up and dusted the sand from his own clothes, which were worse off than mine, hanging in tatters around his arms and legs. Eirnin was only willing to trade clothes with me. "If I feel the slightest suggestion of pain," Naji said, "I'm coming back to the island. Fish or no."

I slumped up against the shack. "Fine. But we're cooking that fish before I thatch the roof. Don't blame me if it rains."

He didn't say anything, only unhooked his scabbard from around his waist and tossed it to me, then stepped into the shadows of a pine tree and disappeared. I wrapped the scabbard around my hips, the sword a reassuring presence at my side.

For a moment I stood there on the sand, listening to the wind and the sea. Off in the distance the bonfire flickered golden. I didn't look directly at it. Naji'd set it alight when we first arrived, and it was a terrible, magical thing. Blood magic. Sometimes Naji would go out at night and stand in the fire's glow, and the next morning he would wake up with dark circles under his eyes. It must've been draining him, bit by bit. I grew up around magic, though I can't do it much myself, but Mama's magic never hurt her, never kept her up at night. But then, she didn't do blood magic.

At least the fire stayed lit even through the worst of the thunderstorms, and hopefully someday someone would see it. I still hoped that somebody would be Marjani, who'd tried to save us from being marooned in the first place. The captain didn't listen to her reasoning, but she'd leaned in close to my ear that moment before the rowboat dropped me and Naji into the sea and promised she'd find a way to come back for us. The memory was one of the things keeping me going day to day.

I gathered up the pine needles and carted them into the shack, dumping them in a pile in the far corner from the fire. I knew Naji well enough to know that climbing on the roof would really hurt him – that damn curse, thinking me scrambling up on the roof was somehow a danger. His curse was that he had to protect me from harm. As far as I can tell, it was a bit of a joke from the northern witch who cast it after Naji went on a mission to her village. He's an assassin, a member of a secret order called the Jadorr'a, and he was hired to kill me once. I accidentally saved his life and now, thanks to that curse, I had to listen to him nag me every time I wanted to get some work done.

Course, he *had* said the disruption, or whatever it was, hadn't activated the curse at all.

Which meant I should be able to make it to Eirnin's house and back before he returned from fishing.

Now, Naji would know where I'd been, but maybe I could cajole Eirnin into getting me some clothes for Naji. It'd be tough, but I was willing to clean out his hearth again.

I didn't have anything better to do anyway.

So I double-checked my charm – still there, hanging on a loop of fabric, just like I'd shown Naji earlier – and set off into the forest with Naji's sword at my side. The woods shimmered in the gray sunlight. It was cold, the way it always was, but walking helped warm me up some.

It took me shorter than last time to make it to Eirnin's house. I noticed that with him. Each time the path seems to shrink, and I don't know if it's magic or if it's just cause I know my way better. Tough to say with wizards.

Whatever the reason, Eirnin's house appeared quicker than I expected. The garden was blooming, big red and orange flowers bobbing a little in the breeze. The air crackled, like a storm was about to roll in from the ocean.

Something disruptive.

I touched my charm again. After so long on the island I knew danger didn't have to look like what I expected. Naji would probably tell me to turn and run back to the shack, but then, Naji wasn't right about everything all the time. Much as he liked to think otherwise.

So I walked up the stone pathway, my hand curled tight around the sword, and kept watch for anything out of the ordinary: shadows moving through the trees, or a curl of gray mist. I prayed I wouldn't see the gray mist.

I didn't see anything.

I knocked on Eirnin's door. No answer. A chill rippled through me, but then, Eirnin had been known not to answer if the mood didn't suit him. I knocked again, and then shouted, "Eirnin! It's me! I'm here about some clothes!"

Nothing.

At this point, the dread was pooling in the bottom of my stomach, and the forest seemed full of sneaking terrors, though I couldn't see any of them outright. Part of me wanted to turn back and the other part of me didn't want to go anywhere near the woods.

I pounded hard on the door, and this time, it creaked open.

I stopped, lifted the sword a little. A scent like flowers drifted out from inside the house. Dead flowers. Rotting flowers.

"Eirnin?" I called out, nudging the door open further. I stepped inside, sword lifted. It was dark. The air was colder than it was outside, as cold as the ice storms in the north, and it felt wrong somehow – empty, hollow.

When I stepped into the main room, the darkness erupted.

Shapes poured out of the dead hearth, dark shadows that slid and undulated along the walls. Moaning filled up the room, the moaning and wailing of a thousand echoing voices. I couldn't move. The darkness slid around me, thick and oily, smelling of decay and magic.

And then a pale figure moved into the room, transparent and glowing. A ghost.

It looked at me, and although its face was stripped of humanity, like all ghosts, I recognized its features immediately.

"Eirnin," I said.

The ghost opened its mouth and a stream of ululating syllables poured out. It was the language of the dead. I'd heard it once before, when a sea-ghost boarded Papa's boat and tried to pull us all under.

I screamed and found the strength to break through the hold of the angry magic that Eirnin had left behind when he died. I raced out of the house, swinging my sword through the thick shadows. They shrieked when I cut them, and their cuts splattered spots of darkness across my hands and arms.

I burst out into the garden. The forest had stilled. Behind me, I could hear the rattle and screams of creatures in the house, and I didn't stop to contemplate on what had killed Eirnin. I just ran. I ran out of the garden and into the woods, and I wasn't even out of sight of the house when I slammed into Naji's chest.

"I told you to stay at the shack!" he roared, dragging me to my feet.

"I'm trying!" I shouted back.

He dragged me into the shadow of a tree, wrapped his arm across my chest, and melted us both into shadow.

A heartbeat later we stood at the edge of the forest, the beach flowing away from us to the edge of the island. Naji slumped up against a nearby pine tree, and for the first time I noticed how pale and waxy he was, and my heart twisted up and I had to stop myself from running over to him and throwing my arms around his shoulders.

"I didn't take off the charm," I said.

"I see that." Naji closed his eyes and let out a long breath. "You realize what that was, correct? What you felt the need to stumble into?"

"Eirnin's dead." I sat down at the doorway to our shack. "I saw his ghost." I didn't have a lot of love for

Eirnin, truth be told, but the fact that he was no more for this world gave me the shivers.

"What were you doing at his house?"

"Getting new clothes."

Naji glared at me.

"I was gonna try and get some for you!"

His face softened a little at that. "I did warn you."

"No, you didn't. You said something on the island had changed. And what in hell does that mean?" I kicked at the sand. "What was all that stuff, anyway? You know what I'm talking about, right? The shadows pouring out of the hearth–"

"It was his magic, released when he died." Naji straightened up and stepped away from the tree. He looked better, which was something of a relief: it meant I wasn't in danger no more. "It has to burn away before it's safe to go back to his house. Which could take months. I don't know. Years, maybe."

"What killed him?"

"I've no idea." Naji frowned. "Perhaps you should stay in the shack for the next few days. Until we figure out the cause–"

"What about you?" I said. "Why do I got to be locked away like some princess in a story?"

Naji glared at me. "You know why."

I turned away from him, fuming. His damn curse.

"Ain't fair," I muttered.

"None of this is fair," Naji said, and he stopped pacing long enough to collect his sword. "There's a fish in the shack waiting for you to clean it."

That was something, at least.

Naji gave me a dark look. "You might as well get used to it."

"What, fish? Trust me, I'm plenty used to fish."

"No," he said. "Letting me protect you."

"We've had this conversation before." I turned away from him and stepped into the shack. A huge flat halibut was laid out next to the hearth, a single glassy eye staring unseeing up at the ceiling.

"And yet you act as if it's the first time you've heard it every time I remind you that you need to stay safe."

I pulled out my knife – another gift from Eirnin, although this was, admittedly, one he hadn't known he'd given me – and shoved it up under the fish scales. Naji didn't think his curse could be broken, cause he had to complete three impossible tasks in order to do so: hold the princess's starstones skin against stone, create life out of violence, and experience true love's kiss. Thing was, I knew at least one of the three, the last one, wasn't impossible at all. Cause I loved him. I loved him more fiercely than I'd loved anyone. But he didn't love me back, and I ain't one to embarrass myself needlessly.

Naji stepped into the shack behind me and shut the door.

"Maybe we should concern ourselves with figuring out who killed Eirnin," I said, fish scales sticking to my hands.

"Maybe we should," Naji said.

But neither of us got to talking.

••••

I spent the next day or two in the shack, like Naji asked. He strung up strands of tree vines and red berry leaves and muttered his charms while I sulked in the corner and watched him. Just cause I was in love with him didn't mean I wasn't gonna resent him for locking me away like I was useless, or that I wanted to spend every moment of the day hanging around him.

Course, I understood that if he hadn't locked me away he would hurt, a pain in his head or his joints, but I still didn't think I was in as much danger as he believed. Just as long as I stayed away from Eirnin's house, right? And there was no way in the deep blue sea I'd go back there.

Those two days were boring as hell, which was exactly what I expected. Naji left to go fetch water or to catch fish and gather berries for us to eat. I sat in the doorway, my knife balanced on my knee, and tried not to look at the bonfire.

By the third day of imprisonment, I was going batty.

"You ain't seen nothing!" I said to Naji, after a week had passed. He'd let me sit just outside the shack that day, and though the air was colder than usual the sun had managed to burn away most of the clouds. "I ain't seen nothing, either. Probably Eirnin's heart just gave out. He was old."

Naji glanced at me. "His heart didn't give out."

"How do you know?"

"I went to his house."

"What!"

"The day after you found him. I wanted to ensure I wasn't being overly cautious." He looked at me pointedly. "I'm not, by the way."

Despite my irritation, a little prickle of fear trembled down my spine. "What do you mean?"

"I mean," Naji said, "I spoke to his ghost."

I shivered and wrapped my arms around my knees. "Nobody speaks to ghosts."

"The Jadorr'a can."

I knew he was gonna say that. Any pirate would tell you attempting to learn the language of the dead is a grave mistake – about as grave a mistake as sailing to the Isles of the Sky.

Naji had a long history of ignoring pirates' wisdom.

"Well?" I asked.

"He was killed by a monster."

"A monster?" I frowned out at the ocean. "What sort of monster? He couldn't have been more specific?"

"The dead rarely are."

I slumped up against the side of the shack. "You're never gonna let me out again, are you?"

"Not until I determine where the monster is and how to destroy it." Naji glanced at me. "Thank you for understanding."

There was an undercurrent of warmth in his voice that made my toes curl up inside my boots, and I looked away from him, over at the beach curving into the forest. I knew I should speak, but I didn't know what to say, so I muttered something about knowing how much it hurt him. As soon as I spoke I was overwhelmed by that secret I carried, the potential power of my kiss. That happened sometimes. I just got to thinking about it at the wrong moments.

Naji stood up in a shower of sand. "The sun's going behind the clouds," he said.

"Oh, hell."

"But it makes it easier for me move through the woods. We're running low on berries."

"And running high on monsters. Maybe you could see about taking care of that nonsense first?"

Naji's eyes brightened a little, and he said, "I plan on doing that, as well."

I usually liked it when his eyes brightened like that, but today it annoyed me, like my having to spend days in the shack was amusing to him.

"I guess I have to go inside."

"If you want me to actually accomplish anything, then yes."

I sighed, stood up, and did as he asked. The air already felt stale. At least the sun was gone. Nothing worse than wasting those few precious moments of sunlight inside.

Naji hung up a pine cone charm in the doorway but didn't leave his sword, which cheered me up a bit, since it meant he might actually have plans to hunt down this monster. I still had my doubts about a *monster*-monster, some beastie roaming the forest. It seems like we would have seen it already. The isles certainly threw enough horrors our way in those first few days we were stranded, before Naji had his powers back in full – all those eerie overnight transformations, trees into stones and stones into sand, and the weird lights that would blink at us out of the darkness of the woods, and the shimmer on the air that Naji told me was the residue from Mists magic. But not once did the island resort to a proper monster.

I stretched out on the nest of ferns I used for a bed and stared up at the ceiling. This was, I had discovered, the most entertaining way to pass my time. Trying to count the number of damn pine needles I'd used to thatch the roof. I got up to fifty-seven before I gave up.

The sky had turned darker since Naji left, and I could smell the rain on the air, waiting up in the clouds to fall. I sat up, mussing my pallet a little, and paced around the shack once or twice. Then I went to get a drink of water.

The bucket was empty.

"Damn him!" Naji always forgot to fill the bucket. Some Jadorr'a trick of never having to drink anything, apparently.

I scowled and kicked at the bucket. It clanged against the floor. I wondered how long till Naji returned. If he was just fishing, it probably wouldn't be long, but if he was off monster hunting–

How dangerous could it be for me to walk down to the water spring?

I mean, before Eirnin dropped dead in his house I'd gone down to the spring a couple times a day. I'd never run into any trouble. The two biggest dangers had been the Mists and the island itself, and Naji's magic kept us protected from both. Why wouldn't it protect me from some island monster?

And I had my knife, which I could throw well enough if necessary.

And nobody ever died from a headache.

I picked up the bucket and slid it into the crook of my arm. Then I walked over to the door and peered out.

Thickening clouds, a deserted beach.

He probably wouldn't even know I was gone.

I reached up and touched the charm for good luck, and then I stepped outside.

I made it to the spring without incident, which left me feeling more than a little smug. The woods were still and the sky thick with the threat of rain. Nothing moved but me: no shadows, no creeping curls of mist, no beasties watching me from the trees. Even the spring seemed calm, nearly stagnant – just a few faint gurgles let me know it was still running.

I dropped the bucket into the spring and took a long drink. It tasted steely and cold like always. Then I filled the bucket to the brim and stood to walk back to the shack.

Something small and sharp zipped past my head, so close I felt the swish of air from its movement, and impaled itself into a nearby tree. I dropped the bucket, water sloshing over my feet and legs, and slammed against the ground. I was tense and ready to defend myself, but at the same time I couldn't help thinking: damn it, Naji was right.

I scanned the glimmering light-shadows of the chiming woods.

Nothing.

Real slow, I reached back for the knife. My fingers wrapped around the handle. Every muscle in my body was ready for a fight.

"Stop right there, *human*."

I stopped. The voice wasn't like any voice I'd heard, not even from the people of the Mists. It had a rhythm like bells, rippling and cascading, fabric fluttering in the wind, high and chiming. Oddly feminine.

"And kindly remove your hand from your weapon."

I obliged, sticking my hand back under my chest. Everything was so damn still. My lungs didn't want to work.

"Who are you?" I choked out. "You from the Mists?"

Laughter filled up the forest, a deep resonant clanging like the bells on the clock tower of the Empire Palace.

"I'm afraid not, girl-human. I am very much a part of your world."

The monster.

I pushed myself up on my hands, moving as slow as possible, listening for the zip of another dart. I leaned back on my heels, keeping my eye on the woods.

"You gonna let me see you?"

"Perhaps. Are you a friend of the wizard-human?"

"The wizard-human? Uh, you mean Naji or Eirnin?" Sometimes playing dumb is the best course of action.

"Naji? I do not know that name. But Eirnin – aye, that's the one I speak of."

"I know him," I said, not wanting to commit myself as his friend or foe. Who knew with monsters?

A branch broke off in the chiming woods, and I tensed up, ready to grab for my knife.

"That does not answer my question."

"Well, I don't know him *well*, not well enough to say–"

Another dart zoomed past my head. I ducked back down.

"I ain't seen him but a couple times!" I shouted into the dirt. "He gave me some clothes and helped my friend out with his curse – well, not helped exactly, more told him what to do next – and other'n that he might as well not exist to me."

The speaker didn't give me an answer. I kept my head down and tried not to let on how scared I was.

For a second I wondered about Naji, if he was hurting real bad, if he was coming to save me.

I wondered how pissed he was gonna be.

"So you have no loyalties to the wizard-human?"

"Ain't got no loyalties to anybody," I said, even though I knew it to be a lie even as I spoke.

A shadow rippled across the forest, and I heard footsteps, the crackle and snap of a figure moving over the fallen leaves of the forest floor.

"You may sit up, girl-human. I will not shoot again."

I ain't so stupid as to take someone on her word for a claim like that, so I moved slow as I could, inching up a little at a time. I was halfway up to sitting when I caught a glimpse of the creature speaking to me, and it took every ounce of willpower not to curl back up into a ball.

The speaker was a manticore.

Now, I'd seen a manticore or two before, locked away in cages, and those were frightening enough. But I ain't never heard one speak – I didn't even think they could. And this one was bigger than the caged ones, only about a foot shorter than me even though she stood on four legs instead of two.

She padded up close to me and leaned down and sniffed with her pretty human-looking nose, then settled down on her haunches, her scaly wings pressed flat against her back, her tail curling up into a point behind her head. Hadn't been darts she'd flung at me, but spines, and poisonous ones at that, if the stories were anything to go by. I kept my eye on that tail.

"I only shot at you when I thought you were an ally of the wizard-human," she said. "I do not care for the taste of girl-humans."

"Oh. Alright." I stood up, slow and careful. The manticore followed me with her eyes, which were the color of pressed gold.

"Perhaps you can help me," she said.

Well, that stunned me into silence.

"Do you have a way off the island?"

It took me a minute to find my voice, and even when I did all I could do was stammer out the most drawn-out "no" in the history of time.

The manticore looked disappointed.

"What do you need to leave the island for?" I asked, mostly in a whisper.

"I'd like to go home, of course," she said. "The wizard-human had kept me imprisoned for almost three life-cycles. I made my escape four days ago."

She licked at her paw. My stomach twisted around and I stumbled backward, one foot splashing into the spring.

"And how..." I said. "How did you—"

"I ate him."

She said it all matter-of-fact, like we were bartering trade in a day market. Sweat prickled out of my skin.

"I told you, girl-human, I do not care for the taste of your sort's flesh." She sniffed. "If you do not have a way off the island, why did you come here at all?"

"We were marooned." I hadn't meant to tell her, but I was so unnerved it spilled out anyway.

"We? There is another human?" She smiled, which was terrifying, her mouth all full of teeth. "A girl-human or a boy-human?"

I didn't want to answer that. So I changed the subject.

"I may be able to get you off the island," I said, quick as lightning. "But you'll have to wait."

"You said you had no manner of escape."

"I don't. But a friend – a girl-human, like me, she might be bringing a ship and crew."

The manticore's face lit up. She fluffed out her mane. "And this friend-girl-human would be able to take me to the Island of the Sun?"

"Sure." I'd heard of the Island of the Sun. It's in the west, not lined up with any of the major shipping ports so not much use to anybody. Except, apparently, manticores. Papa's crew always said it was a wasteland. "But you'll have to wait till she gets here, like I said. And I don't know when that'll be."

"That is acceptable." The manticore stood up and arched her spine, wings fluttering. Her tail curled above her back. "I shall accompany you back to your dwelling."

Naji. My stomach twisted again. Hopefully he hadn't come back yet, and I could find a way to warn him. At least I didn't seem to really be in danger – that would keep him from swooping in to save me.

"It's small," I said. "It'll remind you of your prison, I'm sure of it. You'd be better to live out in the woods…" I swept my hand around and the trees rustled.

"Don't be absurd, girl-human. You will leave me when the friend-girl-human comes. Show me the way."

My brain spun round and round. All I could think about was Naji skulking in front of the fire, unaware that I was bringing in a monster keen on eating him. Was this how it all ended? Me not being able to out-talk a manticore and Naji winding up as its dinner?

"Why do you dally?" The manticore's voice echoed through my skull.

"Uh, I need to get some clean water. Hold on." I felt around in the underbrush for the water bucket. The manticore regarded me with her big gold eyes. I dipped the bucket into the spring, and watched as the water flooded in. Every now and then I dipped the bucket so the water flowed back out again, blocking the manticore's view with my back while I did it. All the while I scrambled to come up with some way out of this mess. Could you strike a deal with a manticore? Stories always made 'em out as monsters, teeth and claws and nothing else.

"This is taking too long," the manticore said.

"Sorry." My heart pounded. I let the bucket fill completely and then stood up. "Look, you gotta promise me something if I'm gonna help you off the island."

"A promise?" The manticore smiled again, teeth flashing. I regretted my words immediately.

"Look, if we're gonna help you, me and my friend, you can't run around eating every man – uh, every boy-human – we come across, do you understand?"

"No," the manticore said. "You would starve me?"

"Of course not! But you'll have to be, ah, selective."

The manticore unfurled her tail, the tip of the spine glistening. "I'm always selective with my meals," she said. "I only ate the wizard-human out of desperation. I have never cared for the flavor of his sort. Much too stringy."

"Uh, that's not exactly what I meant…"

The manticore curled up her lip into a toothy little sneer.

"Why don't you just ask me before you eat anyone? In exchange for getting you off the island?"

"I can agree to those terms."

"And you have to *not* eat the guy if I say no."

For a moment the manticore pouted. Then she licked a paw and ran it over her mane. "We shall see."

Good enough. And if she didn't like the taste of the Wizard Eirnin, maybe she wouldn't have no interest in eating Naji, neither.

We walked side by side back to the shack on the beach. I sure as hell wasn't letting her walk behind me, though she didn't seem to much care one way or the other. She moved real quick even considering her size, though branches snapped, and leaves and pine cones showered over us every time she knocked into a tree. She made more noise than me or Naji ever did.

When we came to the shack, I smelled fish and wild onions frying on the hearth. I stopped. He came home, found me gone, and started cooking?

And then my heart started pounding again, cause now I had to find a way to warn him.

The manticore stopped outside the shack. "You are correct," she said. "This is much too small for me."

I prayed to Kaol and every other goddess I knew that Naji would stay inside. "Let me go in first, let him know—"

"Him?" One of her eyebrows arched up. She ran her thin pink tongue over her perfect lady's lips.

"You promised you'd ask," I said, and then I bolted inside, slamming the door shut. Naji looked up at me.

"I really expected you to do that sooner," he said.

"What?" My breath was coming too fast, and I tried to rein it so he wouldn't think anything was wrong.

"Run off. I didn't think I could truly keep you locked in the shack." He went back to stirring our meal. "I assume you went to get water? It seems like it was an uneventful trip."

He looked at me again, and I could only stare back at him, stricken.

He frowned, and his eyes darkened. "What's wrong?"

I set the water down in its place beside the hearth and tried to come up with the words. Course, I didn't get the chance, cause the manticore bounded into the shack, damn near knocking the door off the hinges.

Naji was crouched in fighting stance with his knife drawn before I even saw him move.

"Ananna," he hissed. "My *sword*."

I picked the sword up from where it was propped up against the wall and tossed it at him, but I kept my eyes on the manticore. "You *promised*," I said.

Naji whipped his head around at me.

"Yes, but you did not tell me you had a Jadorr'a in your stone-nest."

She said "Jadorr'a" the way I might've said "sweet lime drink" or "sugar-roses".

"Ananna, what have you done?" Naji asked me, his voice low. He sounded angry, which if he was like any other man meant he was scared.

The manticore let out a little grumbly noise and crouched low like a cat about to pounce.

"Kaol, couldn't you just eat some fish like a normal cat?" I shouted.

But both of 'em acted like I hadn't said nothing.

And then the manticore's pretty human face twisted up in a grimace. "Jadorr'a!" she said. "You've been cursed."

Neither me or Naji moved.

"You hide the smell well, but... there, there it is again." She shook her head, mane flying out in a big golden puff.

"You can't eat him if he's cursed?" I said.

"Of course not! It taints the flavor of the meat and will pass onto me, and besides which, from the smell of it, this is not a curse I want to possess." She sniffed the air again.

"So, you're not going to eat him?" I said.

"Not until the curse is lifted." She sniffed once more, her nose wrinkling up at the brow. "Three impossible tasks," she said. She turned to Naji. "I shall help you."

Naji looked at a loss for words, which might've been funny in any other circumstance.

The manticore sat back on her haunches. "It's very warm in your stone-nest."

"We have a fire going," I told her.

Naji shot me a dirty look.

"You promise you ain't gonna eat him till his curse is lifted?"

The manticore shuddered. "I told you, I cannot abide the flavor of cursed flesh. It tastes half-rotted."

Naji stayed in fighting stance.

"Girl-human, you were correct in assuming that I would find your stone-nest too similar to the walls of the wizard-human's prison. I shall make a nest nearby. Is that acceptable?"

I didn't dare look at Naji when I answered "yes".

The manticore nodded and backed out the door, the snap and stomp of her footsteps drifting through the cracked stone walls.

Naji finally let down his knife and sword. He turned toward me. Kaol, I wanted to run out onto the beach and dive into the cold black sea. Anything to get away from the expression on his face.

"What—"

"She bullied me!" I said. "She asked if I knew a way off the island and I was trying to keep her from finding you and – and *eating* you and—"

Naji held up one hand.

"You don't have a way off the island."

"I will when Marjani shows up. Look, she doesn't eat women, alright? And she won't eat you cause of the curse, and we can't break that till we leave. So Marjani takes us to the Island of the Sun and we drop off the manticore and then we fix your curse."

Naji stared at me. "My curse is unbreakable," he said.

"That ain't true." Sadness washed over me, and I wondered what would happen if I kissed him right then, and showed him at least one of the tasks wasn't impossible.

"It is." He sighed. "At least I know I won't die in the jaws of a manticore. Although I can't believe you brought that creature here."

"I didn't have no choice! What the hell was I supposed to do? She kept shooting spines at me."

Naji looked at me sideways. "She wasn't going to hurt you."

"Yeah, but how I was supposed to know that?"

Outside, the manticore roared, and it sounded like a trumpet announcing the winner of the horse races in Lisirra. Naji tossed his sword onto the table and looked defeated.

CHAPTER TWO

I was sick to hell of eating fish. Even onboard Papa's ship we never ate this much fish. There'd be dried salted meats, and fresh seabird, if we were close to land. But here on the Isles of the Sky it was nothing but fish, flaking like paper and just as tasteless.

"Then go hunting," Naji told me one evening when I complained. "I'm sure your pet manticore will be happy to accompany you."

"She ain't my pet." I flung a piece of fish down to the strip of tree bark we used as plates. In truth I'd thought about hunting before, cause I'd seen flashes of these graceful horsy animals through the dappled light of the trees, but I didn't know the first damn thing about hunting game. If I had a pistol, maybe I could do it.

I didn't tell Naji none of that, though, cause I knew he'd make fun of me. He was still sore about me bringing the manticore around.

"Finish your meal," he said, like I was some little kid.

I glared at him and shoved the food away, sending the fish splattering across the floor.

"Finish it for me," I said, and stomped out of the shack.

I walked down to the shore edge to calm down. I made sure not to get too close to the signal fire, but I could see it glimmering off in the distance, golden swirls twisting up toward the sky. And the smell of it was strong, too, on account of either the breeze or the island shifting us downwind: it wasn't so much like wood burning at all, but like blood.

"Girl-human, I am in need of your assistance." The manticore came ambling down the beach, flicking her tail left and right. That tail still gave me the shivers.

"What do you want?"

"There's a burr in my mane." The manticore shook her head. "A great tangle. Would you remove it for me?"

I stared at her.

"The hell would you do if you were on the Island of the Sun?" I asked. "Take it out yourself."

The manticore growled. Growls I didn't mind, but you best believe I had my eyes fixed firmly on the poisoned tip of her tail.

"I would command one of my servant-humans to remove it for me," she said. "And she would remove it without complaint, singing all the while."

"Servant-humans."

"Yes. We fill our palace with your kind and they do our bidding and offer themselves as food whenever we are hungry."

I wasn't sure I believed her. She had a lot of stories about the Island of the Sun, and its great red-sand desert and the great wealth of her family and what an *honor* I'd give them, one they would certainly thank with a *boon*, if only I delivered an uncursed Jadorr'a to their eating table.

She trotted over and sat down beside me, tucking her massive paws underneath her body, sticking her head close to my lap. There was a snarl in her mane, a big knot where something'd gotten stuck.

"Fine," I said. "But I ain't singing."

She sniffed like she wasn't too happy, but then she stuck her chin on my knee. The weight of her head was a lot more than I expected.

I combed my fingers through her mane, which was surprisingly soft, plucking out around the tangle. I moved slow and steady cause the last thing I wanted was to pull too hard and have those big white teeth of hers slice through my leg. Ain't no way it was a burr in that huge mass of fur – a burr's too small – but I felt around with my fingers and I realized she had a pine cone stuck in there.

"This may take a while," I said.

The manticore didn't answer save for that trumpeting sound she made whenever she was content. Everything about her voice sounded like a musical instrument. Even her full name – Ongraygeeomryn – kinda sounded like a bell chiming when she said it. I couldn't say it, which was why I just called her the manticore and left it at that.

When I had the pine cone about halfway untangled from her mane, my stomach growled, and I thought about the fish I'd flung at Naji.

"Hey," I said, plucking at her fur like it was a guitar string. "Would you go hunting with me?"

The manticore lifted her head a little, enough that I got a face full of her mane.

"Hunting?"

"Yeah." I leaned back, wiping her fur from my mouth. "I'm sick of eating fish."

"Fish is not food."

"It is for people. Look, could you help me or not? I just want to bring down one of those horse-animals I've seen in the woods."

"Caribou. That is what the wizard-human called them."

"Fine, the caribou. Could you bring one down for me? Don't use your stinger," I added. "I want to eat it, remember."

The manticore laughed. "To bring down such a clumsy creature will be easy. Tis a shame there are no more humans on this island."

I didn't say nothing to that, just tugged at the pine cone, hoping it'd come free. It didn't.

"If I bring you a caribou," the manticore said, "will you groom me whenever I ask?"

I stopped. "Groom?" There I went, making deals with a manticore again.

"Aye. Brush my mane and coat, and pull the thorns from my feet."

"That all? You want me to wipe your ass, too?"

"Don't be crude, girl-human."

"I'm just checking on the particulars before I agree to anything."

"No, that service I will not require of you. Manticores bathe themselves."

Well, that was something, at least. In truth plucking the pine cone from her mane wasn't that terrible – kind of relaxing, actually. Took my mind off Naji.

"Sure, I'll groom you. But not for one caribou – for any you catch. And you'll catch 'em anytime I ask."

She made a *hmmm* noise of displeasure.

"Look, it'll take me and Naji awhile to get through a whole one of the things."

The manticore sighed. "Yes, I suppose that is true."

"Plus you said it was easy hunting."

I had her there. She got this squished-up look on her face that meant I'd just called her manticore-ness into question.

"I agree to your terms, girl-human. A lifetime of caribou for a lifetime of grooming."

I hope not a lifetime, I thought, but I picked up her paw and shook on it.

The manticore stayed true to her word. I pulled the pine cone from her hair and the next morning I woke to the sound of claws scratching across the shack's door. Naji stirred over in the corner, still asleep. The fire in the hearth had burned down to ash. I stumbled over to the door and opened it.

The manticore sat with a dead caribou at her feet, her face smeared with blood.

"Here is your caribou, girl-human," she said.

A jagged tear ripped across the caribou's throat, and its head hung at an angle. "You didn't sting it, did you?"

"On the spirits of my mothers, no, I did not." The manticore gave me this solemn look. "Enjoy your meat, girl-human." Then she trotted off, wings bouncing, toward the shadow of the forest.

When I turned around, Naji was lurking behind me, sword and knife drawn.

"Kaol!" I shouted. "How long you been standing there?"

"I was in the shadows," he said. "I didn't want the manticore to see me." He walked up to the caribou and poked it with the toe of his boot. "Why did she bring you this?"

I crossed my arms in front of my chest and didn't answer.

Naji turned around. "Ananna, you have no idea how dangerous that creature is–"

"Oh, come on," I said. "She can't eat either of us."

"She *won't* eat either of us," Naji said. "There is a difference."

I scowled at him cause I knew he was right.

"Now answer my question," he said. "Why did she bring this to you?"

I sighed. Naji kept his eyes on me, waiting. And so I told him what happened the night before, with the pine cone and all. His face didn't move while I spoke, though his eyes got darker and darker.

"That was a mistake," he said. "Making a deal with a manticore."

"Well, it got us meat, didn't it? Something that ain't fish." I yanked his sword away from him. "You don't like it, you don't have to eat it."

He didn't say nothing, and I stomped outside and pushed the caribou to its side and stuck the knife into the skin of its belly. I'd cleaned fish before – big fish, too, sharks and monster eels – so I figured a land creature couldn't be much different.

Naji came out and watched me. I could feel him standing there, the weight of his presence. It made my skin prickle up sometimes, having him watch me. Not in a bad way.

"I would still check for spines," he said. "You shouldn't take a manticore on its word."

"Planning on it." I had been, too. I ain't stupid.

It took me close to an hour to skin the caribou and gut it and slice the meat from the bones. I didn't find any spines, and I checked everywhere I could think of – in the stomach and mouth, in case she tried to hide one. Nothing. By then Naji had the hearth fire going, and he roasted some of the meat and we had a right proper meal.

The caribou didn't taste like any meat I'd had before – it was a bit like sheep meat, only wilder and leaner – but it was sure better than another round of fish. Naji ate it without saying nothing, and I figured he was sick of fish too but wasn't gonna admit it.

When we finished eating, Naji told me to start cutting the raw meat into strips.

"Why?" I asked him.

"Because otherwise we're going to wind up with a mountain of rotting caribou carcass," he said. "Which is something I'm guessing you didn't think about when you asked the manticore to hunt for you."

I hadn't, mostly cause I didn't realize how much meat was on 'em, nor how dense it was. So I went outside and started hacking at the caribou with his sword. I laid the strips out on some flat stones, figuring Naji planned on drying 'em out but not sure of the procedure for it.

He disappeared with the water bucket into the tree shadows and returned a few minutes later, the bucket full of seawater. He went into the house, then came back out and started gathering up the meat strips.

"What did you get all that seawater for?"

"We need the salt." Naji draped the meat strips over his forearms. "Keep cutting. We'll probably have to sleep outside while the meat is processing."

I frowned at that, thinking about the rainstorms that stirred up the woods without warning.

By the time I finished cutting up the caribou my arms ached something fierce and the whole front of my coat was stained with blood. And I couldn't run over to Eirnin's house and get a spare, neither.

I carted the sword back into the shack and dumped it next to the hearth for cleaning. Naji was scraping salt out of the bucket, this big pile of it glittering on a piece of tree bark like sand. Another kettle boiled and rattled over the fire, and the air smelled like his magic. He'd already hung up some of the meat strips, hooking 'em to the rafters with little bits of vine from the woods. They swayed a little from the breeze blowing through the open door, looking like dancing snakes.

"How'd you know to do all this?" I asked.

"I learned when I was a child," he said. "Did you finish slicing up the carcass?"

I nodded, wanting to ask him about his childhood, wanting to know everything I could about him. But I figured he'd snap at me if I said anything.

"Good. Start hanging the rest of the meat from the ceiling."

I did what he asked. It was satisfying work – we'd pack the strips in sea salt, let 'em sit, and then lash 'em to the ceiling. Plus, I liked working with Naji, being close to him without having to find anything to say or without having to worry about the stupid curse. It reminded me of the way Mama and Papa used to work together on the rigging, in the early parts of the dawn, clambering over the ropes and shouting instructions at one another. I used to watch 'em from the crow's nest and think about how that must be what it's like to love someone.

When we finished the whole shack smelled like meat and you could hardly walk from one side to the other on account of all the slivers of caribou dangling in the way.

"How long's it gonna take?" I asked. "Till it's all dried out?"

"A few weeks." Naji glanced at me. He was over at the hearth, messing with the fire. "There's a cave not far from here. We should start moving our things."

"The cave!" I said. "The rain'll get in."

"Exactly. It's why we had to hang the caribou up in here." Smoke trickled up from the fire, gray and thick. It made my nose run.

"I know that." I scowled. "Just don't know why we have to live in the cave is all."

Naji stepped away from the hearth. "Would you rather move into Eirnin's house?" He glanced at me. "Spend the next few weeks living side by side with ghosts and magic-homunculi?"

I glared at him. He looked like he wanted to laugh. I knew he had me.

I rolled up my clothes and started the trek down to the cave.

CHAPTER THREE

Living in a cave wasn't so bad, despite the way the dampness flooded in every time the skies opened up with rain. This soft, thick moss grew over the rocks and made for a bed more comfortable than my big pile of ferns back in the shack. We kept a fire burning near the entrance and ate half-cured caribou and berries and the occasional fish to mix it up.

After a few days, the manticore sniffed us out.

"Girl-human," she said. "Did you and the Jadorr'a think you could flee from me?"

It was nighttime, the sky starless from the rainclouds, and Naji was sleeping down deeper in the cave, his tattoos lighting up the darkness. I didn't know if he was dreaming or casting magic in his sleep. He'd told me once he talked to the Order sometimes, though he never told me what about. They would've rescued him weeks ago, when we first landed, but they wouldn't have rescued me. That's why he was still here.

And no one else is crazy enough to sail to the Isles of the Sky. Hadn't seen so much as a sail on the horizon the entire time we'd been on the island.

I popped my head out of the cave's entrance. The manticore sniffed at me and flicked her tail back and forth.

"The shack's filled up with meat," I said.

"Caribou is not *meat*," she told me. "Too gristly, too tough. Like tree bark."

I couldn't imagine the manticore having ever actually tried tree bark, but I didn't say nothing, just shuffled out into the woods. The air was damp and cold like always, and I pulled my coat tight around me.

"Do you need something?"

"May I see your new rock-nest?"

I sighed. "It's just a cave."

"It is larger than your old nest."

"Yeah, I guess."

The manticore trotted past the fire and into the cave's main room, her footsteps silent on the moss. Naji's tattoos turned everything pale blue.

For a minute the manticore stared at him, tongue running over the edges of her teeth. I edged toward the sword.

But the manticore didn't lunge for him or shoot a spine. Instead, she turned around on the moss a few times, like a dog, and then settled in.

Well. Looked like she found a new home.

"Brush my mane, girl-human," the manticore said. "In exchange for catching the caribou."

"I thought the caribou was in exchange for pulling out the pine cone."

She shook her head and I didn't feel much like arguing with her.

"What do you want me to use?" I asked. "My fingers?"

"Don't be silly. A brush will suffice."

"A brush?" I laughed. "I don't have no brush." I pointed at my own hair, which was a tangled, knotted mess from the rainwater and the woods and the wind – even if Naji had been halfway interested in me at some point, he sure as curses wouldn't be now. I'd hacked some of it off with Naji's knife, but it was hair. It grew back. "You think I'd look like this if I owned a brush?"

The manticore frowned. "I thought that was merely the humans' way. You will not tend to your grooming unless commanded by a manticore."

"The hell did you get that idea from?"

The manticore looked genuinely confused.

"You know what?" I said. "Forget it. I don't have a brush, but I'll work it through my fingers, alright? Best I can do."

The manticore heaved a sigh like this was the biggest burden to her, worse than getting trapped on a deserted island in the north, worse than having to eat animals instead of people. Not that she shut up about either of those things.

I sat down beside her and started working through her mane, a few pieces at a time. It was pretty tangled – not as bad as my hair, but bad enough that I could see how someone as prissy as her would want it fixed.

It was boring work, but calming. Once I got the tangles out her mane was soft as spun silk, and it reminded me of the scarfs and dresses we'd pull from Empire trading ships, the ones I used to sleep on as a little girl.

And there, in the darkness of that cave, in the cold damp of that island, I started missing Papa's ship real bad. I combed through the manticore's mane and I thought about the open ocean, the hot breezes blowing across the water and the warmth of the sun. I didn't think I'd ever feel warm again.

I moved to the other side of the manticore's head. I could see Naji, curled up on his side. Seeing him made me sadder still, remembering how miserable he'd been on the *Ayel's Revenge*, how comfortable he'd been in the desert.

Even if he loved me back, we were tied to different parts of the world.

"You should kiss him, girl-human."

I yelped in surprise at the sound of her voice, and my fingers caught on a snag in the manticore's mane. She hissed and yanked her head back.

"What?" I said. "Kiss who?"

"Who else is here?" she said. She rubbed against her scalp with the back of her paw. "The Jadorr'a."

"What would I do that for?"

The manticore giggled. It sounded like a wind chime. "To complete the first impossible task, of course."

I froze, my hand hovering near her mane. Ain't no way she could know that I was in love with him. Did manticores even know what love was? I doubted it.

"I ain't his true love," I said gruffly, shoving my fingers back into her fur.

"Aye, but he's yours," she said. "I can feel it when you're close to him, like a lightning storm."

My face turned hot. "That's the island talking," I muttered. "Don't mean nothing."

"Go on," she said. "While he's sleeping. Don't you want to help him? Your friend?" She smiled, teeth sparkling in the firelight. "Your *true love*?"

"Course I want to help... *my friend*." I pushed away from her and crossed my arms over my chest. "But you're just telling me to do it so as you can eat him."

"In time," she said. "All tasks must still be completed." Her eyes glimmered. "Just one little kiss. He won't even know it was you."

I looked at her and then I looked at Naji, handsome and disfigured all at once. Maybe she was right. If I kissed him softly enough, maybe he wouldn't even know it was me: it had never, in the past month, occurred to me to kiss him while he was asleep. In the soft, velvety haze of the open air, this seemed like the most perfect idea I'd ever heard.

One kiss, just enough to help him on his way. To give him hope again.

"Go on," she said, speaking into my ear, close enough I could smell the carrion on her breath.

I pushed away from her. Naji kept on sleeping. He lay on his side, one arm slung across the pallet of moss. His hair curled around his neck. The lines of his scar looked like the paths a lover's hand would take as she ran her fingers down his face. They were beautiful.

I knelt down beside him. His breath was slow and even. I could feel the manticore staring at us, waiting.

I leaned forward, holding my breath. He didn't move.

I closed my eyes.

I pressed my mouth against his, and his face against mine was rough and soft like falling leaves.

My whole body swelled with light. I felt a crack, like lightning cleaving a tree in two, like a wine glass shattering on a stone floor.

Something breaking

And then I was flat on my back, and Naji's knife was at my throat, his knee digging into my stomach.

"Ananna?"

"What the fuck are you doing?" I shrieked. My face was hot and I could feel this weight behind my eyes and I told myself I wasn't going to cry, not over this. The memory of the kiss was sweet as spun sugar on my tongue, but the rest of me burned with humiliation.

He slid back, dropping the knife away. "What did *you* do? I felt someone attack me–"

The manticore started to laugh.

"I was just walking by!" I shouted. "And you jumped out at me."

"Jadorr'a," the manticore said. "The girl-human *kissed* you."

Apparently manticores knew as much about keeping a secret as they did about humans –not a damn thing.

Naji's face didn't change. I wanted to throw up.

"You can feel it, can't you? I know you can. I can smell it, the change in the curse–" whispered the manticore.

"Shut up!" I scrambled away from Naji. He was still staring at me, but now something had changed in his expression. I couldn't read it, didn't want to read it.

He didn't move except to let his knife drop to the floor. The weight in my eyes built and built, and I jumped to my feet and turned and ran out of the entrance of the cave, into the dark rattling woods. It was cold as the ice-islands, but I was so hot with humiliation – I gave him a kiss and he thought it was an *attack* – that I didn't feel it except in my lungs, burning 'em like fire as I ran into the chiming forest.

I tripped on a fallen tree trunk and went sprawling into the ground, wet from the recent rain. The gossamer dust of the leaves coated my palms, and when I sat back and pushed my hair out of my eyes I could feel it sticking to my skin.

The forest was chiming like crazy, as though a storm was on its way, and I let out this scream cause it was the only thing I could do. I screamed and slammed my fists into the ground. The dampness crept in through my clothes and I didn't care. I just screamed.

"Ananna?"

Naji's voice was soft and hesitant, blending in with the forest's chiming.

"Go away."

He materialized beside me.

"Go. The. Hell. *Away*."

"No."

I wiped at my face, smearing mud across my cheeks. The powder from the leaves came off on the back of my hand. "Fine," I said, and tried to stand up. He grabbed my arm.

"Look at me," he said.

"Let go."

He didn't, and his grip was stronger than I expected. I tried to wriggle away from him but he held me tight.

"Will you stop it?" he said. "I'm trying to thank you."

That stilled me, the kindness in his voice. I slumped against the ground, and he dropped his hand to his side. My arm burned from where he touched me, and not cause it hurt, neither.

"It worked," Naji said. "Your ki... what you did. It worked."

I didn't say nothing, just drew my legs into my body and curled up tight like I could disappear into the shadow.

"It wasn't impossible," Naji said.

"Course it wasn't," I snapped. "What's impossible is somebody loving *me*."

He didn't answer. Part of me had been hoping he'd tell me I was wrong, that he'd at least try and comfort me, but when he didn't my chest got tight and painful. I turned away from him and my skin prickled the way it did when the air was full of magic. But there was no magic here Just another reminder that Naji didn't love me back.

"Thank you," he said after a few moments had passed.

"Whatever." I stood up. He didn't stop me this time. I couldn't stand the closeness to him. I kept thinking about the way his mouth had felt. "I have to go."

"Thank you," he said again, like those were the only words he knew.

I walked away from him, away from the forest and the cave, toward the sea.

●●●●

I woke up the next morning covered in sand, my head pounding like I'd spent the night tossing back rum in some Bone Island drinkhouse. The sunlight, weak as it was, hurt my eyes, and I rolled over onto my stomach and pressed my face against the cold beach.

I thought about Naji. Jackass.

I thought about myself. Idiot.

It took me awhile to work up the willpower to sit up, and longer still to get myself to standing. I didn't know where I was. I couldn't see the smoke from the bonfire, which was a bad sign, but one I chose not to dwell on for the time being.

Somebody said my name.

At first I thought it was Naji, that he'd been lurking in the shadows waiting for me to wake up so he could humiliate me again with his thank yous, but then whoever it was said my name again, and I recognized the ice in the voice.

The Mists lady. Echo.

"Hello again," she said, curling into existence beside me. "I heard you experienced a bit of a disappointment last night."

I couldn't speak. I was too blindsided by her sudden appearance. She slid closer to me, the edges of her body blurred and translucent, as if she wasn't completely in our world, and I skittered backwards a little, not daring to take my eyes off of her. She was after Naji at the behest of her lord, who Naji'd stopped from taking over our world a few years ago. The lord wanted revenge for it, wanted to see Naji dead or enslaved or worse. Naji had hidden himself from the Mists, though, so she always came to me instead.

Except Naji had cast new magic when we came here, magic that was supposed to keep me blocked from the Mists, too. It was supposed to keep me safe–

Unless he'd dismantled it while I slept last night. Like the thought of me loving him was enough to leave me soft and vulnerable out there on the beach. Like it was worth the pain it caused him.

"What do you want?" I asked, pushing myself up to standing. My legs wobbled and the world spun around me like I was drunk. I didn't want to let on that I was supposed to be hidden from her sight.

"My lord would be willing to extend his offer to you a second time. Power. Wealth. *Magic.*" She leered. "All you have to do is hand over the Jadorr'a. It's an excellent arrangement, if you're so inclined."

"I ain't."

I took a few steps backwards across the beach, hoping I was headed in the right direction, hoping that my running away would discourage her somehow. But of course it didn't. Echo followed, sliding up close enough that I could feel the cold dampness from her body. I stopped, paralyzed by fear. Echo curled around me, one hand tracing the outline of my profile. But she didn't touch me. I was still wearing the charm around my neck. I wasn't hidden, but I was protected.

"I know what it's like," she whispered in my ear. "To be hurt by a man. It must be hard for you. It's not the kind of hurt you can heal with violence."

A starburst of anger exploded in my chest, and for a moment my thoughts were filled with an irrational white-hot blaze.

And then I whirled around and punched her square in the face, right at that point where her eyes met her nose.

Pain erupted through my hand like I'd punched bone, but then my fist slid straight on through her head, and she dissolved into smoke, disappearing completely

For a long moment I stood there, my anger consumed by astonishment, and waited for her to return. But there was just the waves crashing up against the bottom part of the island, the wind rattling the pine trees. Nothing.

After a while, I set off down the beach, although I did pull out my knife. Just in case.

I walked for a good hour, working off the soreness in my legs and the ache in my head. I'd split open my hand when I punched Echo, but after a while the sting of that disappeared too.

"Girl-human!"

I stopped. The blaze of anger made a sudden, violent appearance. The damn manticore. She'd started this all, hadn't she? All for a meal.

"Leave me alone!" I shouted.

The manticore trotted out of the woods, flicking up little sprays of sand with her paws.

"The Jadorr'a sent me," she said. "He said you were in danger."

"Not anymore." If I needed any more evidence that I repulsed him enough to undo the protective magic, it was right there: he hadn't come for me himself.

"This is all your fault," I said.

The manticore fell into step beside me.

"I know."

I glanced at her. Her face looked strange. It took me a moment to realize that it was cause she looked guilty.

"He hurt you," she said. "Soul-hurt."

I kicked at the sand.

"As opposed to body-hurt."

"Yeah, I got it. I ain't stupid."

The manticore stopped and nuzzled my shoulder like she was an overgrown cat. "I thought he returned your affection. Humans seem to care about happiness. I wished to gift some to you. In exchange for combing my mane."

I scowled. "You had me do it so you could eat him."

"Well, yes, that too."

I didn't say nothing.

"One does not negate the other," she added.

"Well, you just made things worse." Not exactly the wounding insult I'd hoped for, but I was too tired from everything to be clever.

"I know," she said.

And then she knelt down in the sand. "If you would like, I'll allow you to ride me."

I stared at her. "Is this a trick?"

She peered up at me through the frame of her fur. "No trick, girl-human. It is a great honor to ride a manticore."

"Are you gonna stab me with your tail once I get up there?"

"If I wished to poison you, I would shoot the spine into your heart from here."

That was probably true.

"Come along, girl-human. We are far from your rock-nest, and I will not kneel like this all day."

I looked at her, considering. My body ached and I was sick of walking. And it would be something to say I got to ride a manticore.

Besides, she still looked kinda guilty, and I realized I actually believed her: that she thought she had been helping – at least up until we cured the rest of the curse and she got to snack on him.

"Alright," I said.

I swung my leg over her shoulder and settled myself between her leathery wings. She straightened up, tall as a pony. I wrapped my arms around her neck, leaning into her soft mane-fur, which smelled clean, like the woods after a rainfall.

"Do not fall off," she said.

"Ain't planning on it."

And then she took off in a gallop, moving like liquid over the sand. A cold wind blew off the sea and pushed my hair back from my face. She let out this great trumpeting laugh that echoed through the woods, stirring up the birds, and after a minute I started laughing with her. The anger washed out of me, and the sadness and the fear and the humiliation. The wind coursed around us like we were flying, and it stripped Naji right out of my mind.

The manticore got me that gift of happiness after all.

Course, it didn't last. We had to arrive back at the cave eventually, and as the manticore slowed to a trot, I could see Naji pacing back and forth across the beach. He was wrapped up in his black Jadorr'a robe and he looked like a smear of ink against the impossibly wide sky.

"You must disembark," the manticore said, kneeling. I climbed off her and gave her a pat on the shoulder.

"Thanks for the ride," I said.

"It was my gift to you."

Naji had stopped pacing and he stared at me, his hair and cloak blowing off to the side. I trudged across the beach toward him, sand stinging me in the eyes.

"Why did you undo the protective spell?" The wind caught my voice and my question rose and fell like it belonged to a ghost. "The one that's supposed to keep me safe from the Mists?"

"Have you gone mad?" Naji stared at me. "Why would you think I'd do that?"

"Because Echo showed up. That's why I was *in danger*."

Naji's face went pale beneath his scars.

"I didn't hand you over," I said. "Obviously. But it was a pretty crap thing for you to just – expose me like that."

"I told you, I didn't undo the spell."

"Then why did Echo find me?" I shouted, the wind ripping my question to shreds.

A peculiar expression crossed over Naji's face. It almost looked like pain, like guilt or sorrow or even worry, but I knew better. "I would never do something to put you in danger."

"Yeah, just to save your own skin. I imagine you were willing to put up with a headache if it meant getting back at me."

"I had more than a headache." Naji's voice was low. "I would have come myself, but I didn't think you wanted my help. I would gladly offer–"

"You're right," I snapped. "I didn't want your help. I can take care of myself. You're the one with the problem here."

"I don't want you to think I put you in danger," Naji said. "It was... The magic must have weakened more than I thought– "

His words wounded me. "So you did weaken it, then."

"No." He shook his head. There was that peculiar expression again. "No, absolutely not. It was an... ah, emotional weakening." He took a deep breath. "Intense emotional reactions can sometimes interfere with magic. It will sort itself out, I swear to you. But to have you so upset with me, my magic wasn't as powerful..." His voice trailed off.

I focused my gaze on him, sharpening it. Anger built up in my chest again. "Upset with you?"

"Yes, when I, um, didn't reciprocate–"

"Kaol, stop talking!" My hands curled into fists and I thought about pulling my knife out and stabbing him in the thigh, the way I had the night I met him. "Guess I just ruin everything, don't I? Not like I fulfilled one of the tasks for you or anything."

"I told you I was grateful for that," Naji said quietly, but he didn't look at me.

I whirled away from him. I couldn't look at him another damn second. My whole body was shaking. This was why I hadn't kissed him for so long. Because I knew this would happen. My kiss was so repellant that it shut down all his damn spells.

"Maybe I'll just leave," I said, speaking to the sea, my back still turned to him. "Maybe that'll make things easier."

"Ananna–"

I didn't let him finish. I walked away from him, past the manticore and into the woods. He didn't follow.

I slept outside that night, in a nest of pine needles and fallen tree branches that the manticore had stacked up deep in a clearing in the woods, not far from the shack. I could smell the smoke from the hearth. Naji'd been tending the fire the last few days, making sure it smoked proper and didn't go out. I didn't know if he tended it tonight. I didn't care, neither.

I fell asleep early, after eating some berries and caribou, and curled up along the manticore's massive shaggy side. Her heart beat against the walls of her chest, slower and heavier than a human's heart. There was something comforting about it, like a drum beat setting time to a story.

I woke up in the middle of the night.

The manticore was still sleeping and the forest was quiet as death, which set my nerves on end. Forests ain't never quiet, not even in the middle of the night.

I peeled myself away from the manticore and scanned the darkness. I was still wearing Naji's charm even though I'd wanted to take it off – but the thing had kept Echo from touching me enough times that I figured that was the kind of stupid Mama would've slapped me for. And as I crouched there in the shadows, I was more grateful for it than I cared to admit.

"It really doesn't seem fair, don't you think?"

Echo.

My blood froze in my veins, and I leapt to my feet, all the muscles in my back and my arms tensing up. Her voice was coming from all over the place, like she'd melted in with the forest.

"It doesn't seem fair," she said, "that you can strike me in the face, and I can't even touch you."

"Seems plenty fair to me," I called out, managing to choke back the quiver in my words. Echo laughed. The trees rustled a response. I beat my hands up against the manticore's side, but she didn't move.

"I'm afraid that won't work, Ananna. We hold sway over the beasts of your world."

"The manticore ain't no beast."

More laughter. I shoved up against the manticore and kicked at her haunches. But she just slept on.

"This is growing tiresome," Echo said.

"I know," I told her. "Suggests you ought to just move on, don't it?"

Something flashed behind my eyes, and next thing I knew I was standing on the beach, in the cold open wind, next to the bonfire.

This was the closest I'd been to it since the day Naji set it to burning. It was bigger now, the figures writhing in its flames more defined. I could make out the features of their faces. Those faces weren't something I wanted to see.

"This is much better, don't you think?" Echo stepped into the hazy golden light. It shone straight through her so she glowed like a magic-cast lantern. "Easier to see each other."

I kept my eyes on her, even though the fire flickering off to the side made me want to turn my head. Both times we'd gotten rid of her involved hitting her unawares: Naji with his sword, me with my fist. So I did the first thing that came to my head. I lunged at her.

She glided out of the way, and I landed face-first in the sand behind her. I didn't waste no time feeling sorry for myself – a sucker punch don't work more than once that often – and twisted around so I could see her again. She floated there beside the fire, her arms crossed over her chest.

"What do you want?" I said. "You know I ain't gonna hand over Naji."

She sighed. "I really wish you would stop saying that."

She kept on sizing me up, and I knew there wasn't nothing she could do or else she would've done it already.

"We just gonna stand here till the sun comes up?" I asked. "You wanna place bets on what side of the island it'll be? I bet it's over that way." I tilted my head off to the left. "Ain't seen it rise over that half of the island in a while. Figure we're due."

"That wasn't my intention, no," Echo said. And she gave me this hard cruel smile that I didn't like one bit and gestured at the fire. "This is lovely. The assassin's handiwork, yes? I've seen this sort of magic before. It's rather unstable."

She glanced over at the fire. "You don't spend much time here, I've noticed, watching the flames. They're quite remarkable. I'm sure my lord could teach you to do this sort of thing, if you were so inclined. Our world is the world of magic, did you know? It's the place all your magic is born."

"I already know one way to build fires," I said. "I don't need another."

"This isn't a fire," she said. "It's far more dangerous."

That was when I looked. I tore my eyes away from her and looked at the fire. It'd been tickling there at the edges of my sight all that time, like an itch I wanted to scratch, and I finally turned my head and looked.

It swallowed me whole, all that golden light. Sparks and a warmth like the bright sun at home. The pale northern sun didn't even compare. And here: Naji'd brought a piece of that familiar sun here, he'd set it to burning on the sand.

The bodies in the flames swirled and danced and called me over.

Echo was up close to me, whispering in my ear, and the fire burned away the coldness of her breath. "You can create that yourself. He'll never teach you. But we can. I can. You can carry that light with you everywhere you go."

I stared at the fire, my hands tingling. I tried to tell her I couldn't do magic. But maybe I could, if I was part of the Mists.

"Who wants to be a pirate when you can be a witch? The most powerful witch the world has ever known. You won't just control the seas, you'll control the pulse of life. That pulse is what makes these flames burn. It is what gives power to that silly trinket around your neck-"

That brought me out of myself. She wasn't offering power, she wasn't even offering magic. She was after Naji. Always had been.

And the fire, for all its beauty, for all its magic, was still fire. It would only burn me if I got too close. Just as it had done Naji.

I dipped forward and yanked a stick out from under the fire. It was hot, but I didn't drop it; no, I spun around and flung the stick and the lick of flame at Echo, and her eyes went wide with surprise and then with anger, and then the stick sliced straight through her and she turned to mist and disappeared.

I collapsed on the sand. My hand stung. In the golden light I saw the place where the stick had touched my skin, saw the red line it left there.

The beach stayed empty. The wind howled and the waves crashed down below. I forced myself to stand up, legs wobbling, and began to pick my way across the beach. I didn't realize I was heading for the cave till I got there and found myself swaying outside its entrance, the dim, flickering light from the campfire casting long uneven shadows.

Inside the cave, Naji groaned.

"Naji?" I stepped in, leaning up against the damp stones for support. Naji was curled up in front of the fire, his hands pressing up against his forehead. He stirred when I said his name.

I shuffled forward and knelt beside him. Prodded him in the shoulder. He lifted his head.

"What did they do to you?" he rasped.

"Nothing." I leaned back, didn't look at him. I was too tired to be embarrassed. "Tried to get me to hand you over. I didn't, course, even though–" I decided not to finish that thought.

Naji stared at me. "What?" He pushed himself up. He was pale and ashen, his scars dark against his skin. His hair hung in sweaty clumps into his eyes. "Wait, you mean the Otherworld..." He collapsed back down on his back, looking up at the ceiling.

"Of course I mean the Otherworld. Who else would be chasing after me?"

"The flames," he said. "I felt them. The heat..."

I kept real quiet. My hand started stinging again, and I had to look at it. A thick red line cutting diagonal across my palm.

"We were by the fire," I said. "Echo took me there."

"Echo?" Naji sat up again. He didn't look so pale no more. "You know her name?"

"It ain't her name. It's what she told me to call her."

"Oh, of course." Naji closed his eyes. "She can't hurt you, you know."

"I know. The charm."

Naji looked at me, looked at the charm resting against my chest.

"So why in all the darkest of nights did you touch the flames?"

"What?" I slipped my hand behind my back. "The hell are you talking about?"

"The flames, Ananna. The *fire*. I know you touched it. It struck me down so hard I couldn't even come save you."

"I don't need you to save me." I stood up. "And it's not like you want to save me anyway." Naji didn't move, his eyes following me across the cave as I scooped up the cooking pot we'd filched out of the Wizard Eirnin's house. I set water to boiling on the fire.

"You still touched the flames."

"Do I look like I touched any flames?"

Naji got real quiet, and his eyes darkened, and he tilted his head so his hair fell over his scar. I felt suddenly sheepish.

"I didn't touch no flames," I said. "But I yanked out one of the sticks to send Echo back to the Mists."

Naji glared at me.

"Had to use something," I said. "Didn't have your sword." The water was boiling. I poured it into one of Eirnin's tin cups and dropped in the flat green leaves Naji used to make tea. Some herb that only grew in the north. I didn't know its name.

"That was very stupid," he said.

"It was just a stick!"

"It burned you."

He said this more gently than I expected, but I still shoved the tea at him, sloshing a little across his chest. He glanced down at it like he'd never seen a cup of tea before, but after a few seconds he wrapped his hand around the cup and drank.

"Not bad," I said.

"What?"

"It didn't burn me bad." And I showed him my hand.

"Would a stick pulled from any other fire have burned you at all?" he asked.

I scowled at him. "You only care cause the burn hurt you. But it ain't hurting no more, right? So could we just drop it?"

"It's not about the burn hurting me–"

"Oh, shut up."

"Ananna–"

"Shut up!" I was regretting coming back to the cave now. I should have just trudged back to the manticore. The damn beast probably slept through the whole thing, but at least she wouldn't nag me about getting burned by magical fires or look at me like I was this big disappointment cause I was the one in love with him and not some pretty little river witch.

Naji didn't try to say nothing else to me, which was a relief. I curled up on a pile of moss near the entrance to the cave, where I could hear the trees and the ocean, and pretended to fall asleep.

CHAPTER FOUR

I woke up the next morning to the manticore licking my face.

"Stop it!" I shouted, rolling away from her. "Feels like you're skinning me alive."

"Girl-human," she said. "The Jadorr'a asked me to fetch you."

"Again?" I twisted my head around and squinted up at her. Sunlight shone around her big glossy mane. "I ain't in no danger."

"He said it was urgent. I told him I wouldn't do it, that I am not his personal servant, but..." Her tail curled up into a tight little coil at the base of her spine.

"Urgent?" I asked. "Is it the Mists?"

"Oh, no. He said it wasn't a matter of danger."

"Then what is it a matter of?"

She blinked her big golden eyes at me. "I don't know."

Figures. Still, I roused myself up, taking my time cause it was the worst thing I could do to Naji, making him wait. Me and the manticore strode side by side down to the beach, where the smoke from the bonfire bloomed up against the sky, dark gray on light gray.

I crossed my arms over my chest. "Where the hell is he?"

"He said he would meet you here."

I sighed and scanned over the horizon. Nothing but emptiness. Except–

There were two people standing beside the fire.

I'd gotten so accustomed to the aloneness of the island that the sight of two human figures at once startled me. One of 'em was definitely Naji, cause he stood farther back from the flames, wearing some dark cloak I didn't recognize, one that wasn't tattered beyond repair. And the other–

I leaned forward, squinted.

"Marjani!" I shrieked

"What is that?" asked the manticore.

"Remember how I said a friend was coming to pick us up from the island? Well, she's here!"

"We can leave?"

"I hope so."

The manticore reared up on her hind legs and let out a string of trumpets and then raced toward the fire before I could stop her. I pounded along in the sun, the wind cold and biting, my breath coming out in puffs. Marjani stared at us. She was wearing a bright red fur-lined cloak that I gotta admit I wanted. It looked warmer than anything I'd nicked from the Wizard Eirnin's house.

"What the hell?" she said.

The manticore skittered to a stop a few feet away from her. I snuck a look at Naji – he had his arms crossed over his chest, his face dark with intensity. "Don't get too close to the flames," he said.

"I won't," I said. The sight of him twisted my stomach up into knots for a few seconds before I shoved it all away.

Marjani's voice interrupted my thoughts. "Is that a–"

"Oh! This is the manticore," I said, like I was making introductions.

The manticore lowered her head, all deferential and polite like she was meeting a lady. She must've wanted off the island more than I realized.

"My name is Ongraygeeomryn, and I am most grateful for your assistance."

"You never talked that nice to me," I said.

"You never had a water-nest."

Marjani stayed calm, although the longer she looked at the manticore the deeper her frown became. I ran up to her and threw my arms around her shoulders and she laughed and hugged me back.

"I am so glad to see you right now," I said. Now that I was across the beach I could just make out some big white sails way off in the distance. It was a bigger ship than the *Ayel's Revenge*, probably a warship, though I couldn't tell from that far off.

"They wouldn't come any closer," Marjani said.

"How'd you get on land?"

"I climbed." She jerked her head over to the place where the beach dropped off, and there was a hook wedged into the sand.

"That held?" I said.

"Barely." She smiled.

"You came back," I said, cause part of me still thought it was hard to believe. I knew it wasn't the easy thing to do. Hell, probably wasn't even the most honorable, what with Naji being a murderer and a mutineer and all. At least she didn't know about what I'd done to Tarrin of the *Hariri*, about how I'd had to kill him in self-defense. I didn't like thinking about it.

"Of course I did," she said. "I promised. Besides, I need your help. His too."

Naji glanced at her, his eyes all suspicious. "Help with what?"

"I'll explain once we're on the ship. I don't imagine the crew's gonna be too happy about sitting out this close to the Isles of the Sky for much longer." She turned to the manticore. "Naji told me about the, ah, arrangement you made with Ananna. I'll allow it, but you should know I'm not taking you aboard if you intend on eating any of the men on that ship."

"What?" The manticore bared her teeth and hissed.

"Sorry." And Marjani pulled out a pistol and pointed it at the manticore's heart. The manticore drew back, not quite into a cower. She kept her teeth out, though. "You'll stay in the brig for the entire trip. I'd muzzle you if I could."

"But you'll let her onboard?" I asked.

Marjani sighed. "I'm not about to double-cross a deal you made with a manticore."

I wondered if Naji'd told her about the three impossible tasks as well. Probably. But I doubted he'd tell her about the kiss. Hoped he wouldn't.

"Get your things," she said. She threw me a second pistol and a pouch of powder and shot. "And keep that damn manticore in line."

The manticore hissed, crouching low to the ground.

It didn't take long for me and Naji to gather up our clothes and Naji's weapons. I didn't talk to him, didn't even look at him, but as I walked out of the cave he put his hand on my arm and said, "We should take the caribou."

"Don't touch me."

Naji didn't say nothing for a few moments. Then: "It hasn't quite finished drying out yet, but perhaps we can find a place on the ship. Payment for bringing a manticore on board."

He was right and I knew it, even though the thought of spending another minute alone with him, remembering everything about what happened the last few nights, the good parts and the horrible parts both, made me want to throw up.

"Fine," I said, dumping my clothes on the ground.

We wrapped the meat in his old assassin's robe. There was so much we only took half the strips, leaving the other half there to rot or feed the noisy creatures of the island.

I hated every minute of it. I kept waiting for him to say something about the fire or even about the kiss, but he never did.

Marjani was waiting for us by the fire once we finished, sitting on a piece of driftwood with her pistol pointed at the manticore. The manticore was curled up on the sand, eyes full of hate.

"I didn't look at it once," Marjani said as Naji and me walked up. "But you're insane if you think I'm going to forsake a fire in all this coldness."

Naji scowled and didn't say nothing.

"I do not like this friend-girl-human," the manticore said.

"Well, she's the one with the boat." I stopped in front of Marjani. "We got dried caribou to give to the crew."

"They'll like that. Half of them are from the ice-islands."

I carried my stuff up to the beach's edge, next to the place where Marjani had thrown her rope. Something about the edge of the island made me dizzy, like it was the place where the world cut off.

I peered down. A rowboat bobbed in the water. I tied me and Naji's clothes up together and tossed them down, then tossed down the caribou meat too. Both landed right in the middle of the boat. A useful trick, Papa'd told me when he taught me. Never know when you'll need to toss something.

"Are we gonna climb down?" I asked.

"I can't climb," the manticore said.

"I'll take you." Naji cut across the beach. "All of you," he added, when the manticore opened her mouth.

I remembered the day we arrived on the island, how close he pressed me into his chest. And it was weird, cause the last thing I wanted in the world was for him to hold me – but at the same time, it was the only thing.

Instead, he asked me if my hand hurt.

"What?"

"Your hand. That you burnt last night."

Thinking about it made my skin tingle, but it didn't hurt none at all. "No, it doesn't. Told you it was fine."

Naji gave me a hard look. I stared back long as I could.

"I'll bring the manticore and Marjani down to the boat one at a time," he said. "Don't start rowing out to the ship yet."

"I know that."

Another dark look and then:

"Don't leave me on the island, either. You know what would happen if I stepped out of the shadows on that ship. The crew won't trust that sort of magic. I'd be tossed overboard."

"I ain't gonna leave you!" It took every ounce of willpower not to smack him hard across the face. "I ain't cruel, Naji. I ain't *you*."

He glowered at me. I glowered right back.

"Good," he said, and then he grabbed me by my uninjured hand and the darkness came in.

Marjani's ship was a big Qilari warship called *Goldlife*, and it didn't belong to Marjani but to a skinny, mean-looking captain named Chijal who had a jagged white scar dividing his face clean in half. Nobody so much as glanced at Naji's face when they hauled the rowboat up on deck – and though she didn't say nothing I had a feeling Chijal was the reason Marjani had bartered her way onto this particular ship.

The crew was rowdy and loud, drunker as a group than the crew on the *Revenge*, and even more lewd. The first day I had to hold my knife to some guy's throat to keep him from grabbing at me.

When night fell, and we'd cleared out of sight of the Isles of the Sky, Marjani took me and Naji down to the brig. Nobody was down there on account of the manticore, though she seemed more preoccupied with trying to lick every spot of brig-sludge off her coat.

"Girl-human!" she bellowed when I dropped off the ladder. "I demand my release at once!"

I pressed my hands against the bars. I felt sorry for her, I really did, but even I wasn't about to let her free on a ship full of men.

"If I let you out, you'll eat half the crew," I said. "And a ship this size, we need 'em to get you back to the Island of the Sun."

She pouted.

"Yes," said Marjani. "That's what I wanted to talk to you about."

I turned to look at her. Somebody'd strung up a trio of magic-cast lanterns that swayed with the rhythm of the boat, casting liquid shadows across Marjani and Naji.

"We're not going to the Island of the Sun," I said.

The manticore hissed. So did Naji.

"You realize that manticore wishes to eat me, correct?" he said, sounding like snakes.

"No, we definitely are dropping off the manticore," said Marjani.

The manticore hissed again, and I turned and shushed her.

"We're just not doing it with this boat."

Me and Naji both stared at Marjani, and she gave us this wry little smile.

"This is about that favor you want from us, isn't it?" Naji asked.

"It won't be difficult," she said. "Certainly not for you..." she looked at me when she said that bit. "The *Goldlife* crew are gonna help us steal a merchant ship, and then we're gonna sail her into Bone Island and get her a crew."

"And then you'll take me home?" the manticore asked. "Will you cure the Jadorr'a's curse first?"

Nobody answered her.

"Who's gonna captain?" I asked. "One of Chijal's men?" The thought of it turned my stomach. The officers were just as loutish as the crewmen.

"Oh, absolutely not," said Marjani. "We'll captain her. Me and you together."

Naji looked relieved, but I just stared at her.

"That'll never work," I said. "Ain't no man'll sail under a woman–"

Marjani held up one hand. "That's why I needed both of you."

"No," said Naji. "Absolutely not."

I looked from him to Marjani and back again, and in those sliding soft shadows I saw her plan taking shape: put Naji in some rotted old Empire nobility cloaks and he'd look the part of captain sure enough. A mean one, too, what with the scar.

"You won't actually captain anything," I said. "Right? We'll use him to book a crew."

"Exactly," said Marjani. "Captain Namir yi Nadir. I started spinning tales about him while I was looking for a ship to bring me out here."

"What!" Naji asked. "Why?"

"So men'll want to sail with you," I told him. "What kinda captain is he?" I grinned. "Brutal and unforgiving, always quick to settle a dispute with the sharp end of a blade? Knows how to whisper the sea into a fury anytime a man disobeys him? A real *monster* of a captain, right?"

Naji was glaring at me, his eyes full of fire. Seeing him angry like that soothed the hurt inside me. Not a whole lot, mind, but enough that some of the sting disappeared.

"Of course not," Marjani said. "I want men to sail with us, not fear us." She turned to Naji. "I put out stories about you sacking the Emperor's City with a single cannon and a pair of pistols and another one about you seducing a siren before she could sing you to your death."

The anger washed out of Naji's face. "And people believed that?"

"People'll believe anything, the story's good enough. I also put out word that you pay your men fair, you offer cuts of the bounty even to the injured, and you'll sail with women."

"I do all that?" Naji frowned. "I'm not even a pirate."

"No, you're an assassin," I said.

The anger came back again, just a flash across his eyes, but it was enough.

Marjani gave me a look that told me to cut it out.

"All of this is moot until we get a ship," she went on. "So Ananna, I'd like to see you arm yourself with more than a pistol and a knife. Naji..." She gave him a half smile. "Well, your Jadorr'a skills may be required."

Naji scowled.

"This is the only way we'll be able to complete the rest of the tasks," Marjani said, and my face went hot, cause I knew then that he'd told her everything, about the curse's cure and my kiss. "You'll never be able to convince Chijal to do it, that's for certain."

And then she walked out of the brig before Naji had a chance to answer.

We sailed for four days and didn't see another soul, just the gray expanse of sea and sky. It was colder on the boat than it had been on land, the wind sharp against the skin of my hands and face, like it could flay it from my bones. One of the crewmen, a boy from the ice-islands named Esjar who had white-yellow hair and looked about my age, gave me a pair of sheepskin gloves.

"For the *lady*," he said, with this weird flourish I realized was meant to be an Empire bow.

I took the gloves and stared at them. Papa'd always told me to treat the ropes with my bare hands. Ship gets pissy otherwise, he said. Rope'll slip clean away from you.

"They stop the cold." Esjar spoke Empire, but he had the same hissing accent as Eirnin. "We ain't in Empire seas anymore. Out here, you need them, same as you need that pretty red cloak."

I glanced down. Marjani'd let me have her cloak once we came on board – she had another one, dark blue, that she said she liked better – and I had to admit it kept me warmer than any clothes I'd ever owned. So I slipped on the gloves.

They helped. Yeah, the ropes slipped out of my hands more often, but at least my fingers could move.

Esjar and I became friends after that, chatting sometimes as we were working the ropes. He'd actually heard of the Mists – most of the ice-islanders had, in fact, which surprised me, seeing as how they ain't so well known in the south. Esjar explained to me that the boundaries between worlds are thinner up at the top of the world, and most ice-island children learn early on to look out for flat gray eyes and cold mist.

"Which is tricky," he said, looping the ropes into a sheet knot. "Cause mist is all over the place in the north, and gray eyes ain't too uncommon either. So you learn to pay attention to the differences."

"The differences?"

"Yeah." Esjar nodded, tugging the ropes tight. "Nothing from the Mists is human, and you can tell that, when they're creeping around. Something's off about them. Like they don't got a soul."

I nodded, remembering my encounters with Echo and the others back in Lisirra. "But you don't really notice until it's too late."

"That's the trouble with them." Esjar started knotting the next two ropes together. "The whole thing with them is that they want to get to our world, cause our world's more stable. Not so much magic."

I laughed at that. "There's magic all over the damn place."

"Sure, but not like in the Mists! Those floating islands we just picked you up from – that's what the Mists are like, only worse, much worse. They're built out of magic, see? And a little bit seeps through to our world and the magicians can make it work. But in the Mists magic is everywhere. So they want to come here and take over cause it's safer."

I shivered. Esjar hunched over his work, face scrunched up in concentration. I remembered the story Naji had told me, about how he'd stopped a lord of the Mists from crossing over permanently. That was why they were after him now, and it'd never made much sense to me, how persistent they were. But the Isles of the Sky, especially before Naji worked his spells to keep us safe, had been awful – not just cause of the cold and the rain, but cause everything was so uncertain.

And living in a world like that, only worse? I'd be trying to cross over too.

"What else do you know about them?" I asked. Esjar tied off the last of his knots and looked at me.

"Not much," he said. "Why you asking?"

"Just curious, is all." I grinned as if that would prove it. "It's creepy, you know, like the stories of the dead my old crew liked to tell."

Esjar grinned back. "In the south you fear the dead. In the north we fear the Mists." He squinted out at the horizon line. "Not much else to tell, truthfully. Their magic is dangerous, cause they're so seeped in it. My papa told me a story once about a cousin who faced down a man of the Mists, and his skin turned to tree bark and he rotted into the soil before anyone could save him. Supposedly he was alive for the whole thing – people could hear him screaming and begging for mercy and whatnot."

My whole body went cold.

Esjar looked at me and frowned. "But my papa was known for bullshitting," he said quickly. "So it probably wasn't that bad."

The sails snapped around us, the wind cold and biting, and I forced myself to believe him.

One evening the crew all gathered up on deck for drinking and singing and storytelling. I went too even though it meant having to listen to stupid jokes all night – I noticed Marjani made herself scarce.

I hadn't been out there an hour when Naji slunk up, sword hanging at his side, rubbing at his head like something must've kicked up his curse. Probably from some of the crew leering at me all night.

"I don't need your help," I hissed at him, dragging him over to the railing. The sea was a churn of black and stars.

"I'm not here for you," he said. "Though you really should be more careful. Those men aren't... they aren't honorable."

I crossed my arms over my chest and glared at him. "You think I've never been on a ship full of drunk pirates before?"

"They could still overpower you–"

"I thought you weren't out here for me."

He didn't say nothing, just turned his face toward the sea. I stalked away from him. Fine. Let him slash at any asshole who tried to grab at me. Get us tossed into the ocean, he would.

I huddled up near the fire some crewman had got going for warmth. Esjar was sitting over by the fore mast, playing a tune on this beat-up old Qilari guitar. I glanced over my shoulder at Naji – he was watching me, one hand on his sword hilt. Conspicuous as hell. But at least he'd see what I was about to do.

I walked over to the mast. "Hey, ice boy," I said.

He stopped playing and looked up at me. "Hey, sun girl."

I shifted my weight from one foot to the other. I ain't never been any good at flirting, but Esjar looked at me with these heavy-lidded eyes and said, "See you're still wearing my gloves."

"Oh." I held up my hand to show him, even though he'd obviously already noticed. "Yeah. You're right, I needed 'em."

He laughed and started plucking out a Confederation tune on his guitar. I didn't say nothing – I wasn't too keen on letting him know who I was, since the Hariri clan almost certainly still had a watch out for my head, despite all the time that had passed – but I did sit down beside him. His fingers moved deft and sure over the guitar strings.

Naji was still watching us.

I was sweating underneath my cloak and the cold sea air, nervous. Esjar finished up his song and set the guitar off to the side.

"So what's your story?" he asked me. I was surprised; for all our conversations, we'd never really talked about ourselves before.

"Ain't got one."

Esjar kinda smiled at that, but he didn't ask no more questions. We sat side by side for a few minutes, not talking. I scooted closer to him. He put his hand on my knee.

"I don't got much of a story, either," he said.

We sat in another few moments of awkward silence while I tried to figure out what my next move should be. I was aware of Naji standing at the railing, turned sideways to us, like he was watching us out of the corner of his eye. I was about to ask Esjar if he wanted to go down below, but then a couple of crewman struck up an old Empire song, bright and cheerful.

"Hey, sun girl, you know this one?" Esjar asked.

"Sure do. It's got a dance that goes with it. I can show you if you want." When Esjar nodded, I stood up and held out my hands. He laughed and grabbed both of them and I pulled him to his feet.

I looked over at Naji, trying to be casual about it. He was frowning at us.

Least your head ain't hurting no more, I thought bitterly.

I led Esjar to the center of the deck and showed him the basic steps. In truth, I didn't know the dance all that well – I'd watched people do it whenever I made port in Lisirra with Mama and Papa, and I'd followed along with the steps once or twice. But I knew enough to show Esjar: mirrored steps, back, right, forward, swinging your hips all the while. He took to it quickly enough, and we swung over the deck, laughing and whirling while the rest of the crew stomped out a beat.

When the song ended, the crew burst into applause, and Esjar pulled me into him and kissed me.

It surprised me, but I liked it, too, and I kissed back, tasting the sea salt on his lips. Part of me wanted to see how Naji was reacting, but part of me just wanted to kiss Esjar until the sun came up.

We pulled apart. I couldn't help myself this time, and I glanced over at Naji, who was watching us with his face shrouded in shadows.

Then the crew started another Empire song, and Esjar whooped and pulled me into the dance again, and for the first time in months, it was almost like Naji didn't exist.

The next morning, I got a couple of water rations from the galley and then headed down to the brig, where I found the manticore, curled up in the corner and mewling like a kitten.

"I brought you some water," I said.

"I want meat, girl-human!"

"You'll have meat tonight." I picked the lock with my knife and let myself in, skirting around the neat pile of crushed pig bones. The crew kept some livestock on board, and they gave her the bits nobody wanted to eat, plus fish, which she apparently ate despite claiming it wasn't food. "Once me and Marjani have our own boat I'll make sure you get real food."

"Manflesh?" Her head perked up. Her face was dirty, her mane matted even though I'd worked through the tangles a few days earlier. The sight of her twisted my stomach.

"I'll see what I can do. Here." I dumped the water in her bowl and she knelt down and lapped at it. I sat beside her, stroking her side, listening to the *drip drip* of seawater coming through the boards.

Footsteps on the stairs. I prayed to Kaol that it wasn't Naji.

Marjani's head appeared in the doorway. "Brought you something," she said. "Oh, Ananna, you're down here."

"Where else would I be?"

She shrugged, then grinned at me. She had a burlap sack with her, the bottom stained red. The manticore lifted up her head and sniffed.

"Animal meat," she grunted.

"Yeah, well, I keep hoping some of those barbarians'll hack each other to bits, but they just… don't." Marjani pushed open the cell and dumped out the contents of the burlap sack: fish heads and a pair of shriveled up old pig's feet, more than a little moldy.

"Best I could do," Marjani said.

The manticore returned to her water.

Marjani gestured for me to get out of the cell. I sighed, patted the manticore's shoulder, and stood up. I knew the manticore would eat the food Marjani brought her, but she'd only do it alone. Pride. And I couldn't much blame her.

"Heard you had a good time last night," Marjani said.

"Yeah? Who'd you hear that from?"

"Half the crew. And Naji," she added, giving me this disapproving look I didn't like one bit.

I wasn't gonna ask her what he said. I wasn't going to ask her if he seemed angry about it or annoyed or sad. Mostly cause if she told me he didn't care, I was pretty sure I might die.

"We just danced," I said.

Marjani laughed. "And kissed. A couple times." She paused. "Do you know how to make the moon tonic? The cook should have all the ingredients."

I blushed and nodded. Mama had shown me how to mix it up when I turned fifteen.

"I doubt he'll know what you're making," she added gently. "The cook isn't exactly well informed on the matters of women."

"I told you, I don't need it! We didn't do anything!"

"For the future, then." She smiled. "Anyway, that's not actually what I need to talk to you about." She peered out the brig doorway, and then turned back to me. "Those... people... who are after Naji. They're here."

My stomach turned to ice, but then I realized we were still sailing along, no magic erupting out behind us, no soldiers of the Mists crawling over the deck. But Marjani looked skittish, almost scared. I grabbed her by the hand and led her over to the bench built into the wall.

"What happened?" I said. "Tell me everything."

She took a deep breath. "I was in the navigation room last night, checking our progress. Alone. And then all of sudden this woman was in there with me. I didn't hear the door. She was just... *there*." Marjani shivered.

"Echo," I said.

"What?"

"That's her name. She was kind of smoky, right? Like she's not quite in this world?"

Marjani frowned. "Sort of. When I refused to take her Naji, she fought me."

"What! You mean she could touch you?"

"Yeah. Can she not touch you?" Marjani tilted her head, studying me, like she was trying to work out all the pieces.

"No, she can't–" And then I remembered the charm around my neck. "Oh," I said. "You don't have Naji's protection."

"Protection?"

I lifted my charm out from shirt collar and showed it to her. "I can't take it off," I said. "It'll flare up Naji's curse otherwise. But whenever I'm wearing it, she can't touch me." I slipped it back inside my shirt. "I'll tell him to make you one, once we get to land. We probably don't have the ingredients on the boat."

"I'd like that." Then Marjani gave me a quick, nervous smile. "Although I did beat her back easily enough last night. I don't think she was expecting me to be carrying a loaded pistol."

"You killed her?" I thought of the lone pistol shot I'd been given when the *Ayel's Revenge* captain marooned

me and Naji on the Isles of the Sky. I'd used it to start a
fire that went out in the rain. If only I'd saved it–

"No, she billowed out like dust and disappeared."
Marjani sighed. "Why the hell are they coming after
me? You've got the curse, so you're at least... *magically*
tied to him." She looked at me closely then. "And maybe
more than magically, right?"

I looked down at my lap. "That ain't important.
They're after you because you know him. They can't get
to him, see, because he's hidden himself with his magic–"

"So they go after the next best thing. I get it." Marjani
shook her head. "He just keeps bringing around trouble,
doesn't he? The magic onboard the *Ayel's Revenge*, and
now this." She laughed.

I couldn't disagree with her. "He's nothing but trouble,"
I said. "Although he was trying to save the ship, during
that mess with the *Ayel's Revenge*. He just did it in a...
Naji way."

Marjani laughed at that. But when her laughter faded
she took on a serious, intense expression.

"How dangerous do you think she is?" she asked.
"Without the protection charm."

It was a reasonable question, and I wanted more than
anything to give Marjani a reasonable answer. But I didn't
have one. I'd never fought Echo. She whispered pretty
words in my head and I had to remind myself where
my loyalties lay. Maybe they were misplaced, setting 'em
with Naji.

"She's dangerous when she talks," I finally said.
"Cause it ain't death she's dealing. If a pistol shot'll send

her away, that should be enough to keep you safe until landfall. But just – be careful if she tries to talk to you."

Marjani looked at me for a long time. "I understand," she said. Then: "I'll let you know if I see her again."

"Have you told Naji about this?"

Marjani shook her head. "I wanted to hear what you had to say about it. Naji's a little…" She waved her hand through the air like she could catch the right word. "A little intense. He reminds me of the academics I met at university. So focused. You can see the bigger picture."

I beamed at that.

"I should still mention it to him though, shouldn't I?" Marjani ran her hands over her hair. "It's got me spooked, I have to admit."

"I'll go with you," I said, even though I didn't particularly want to see him just yet. "We can ask him about the protection spell too." I stood up and turned to wave goodbye to the manticore. She'd fallen asleep. "And if you want me to go to the navigation room with you, next time, I can do that too."

"Thanks." She grinned at me, although I could see a bit of nervousness in her eyes.

We left the brig together.

CHAPTER FIVE

I was up in the rigging a week later when the alarm went up. Somebody'd spotted a ship.

I immediately slid down a nearby rope and scurried down below to grab my sword out from the little corner where I'd stashed it. The quartermaster had given it to me when we first boarded, but I never liked carrying a sword around when I was working the ropes.

Marjani was up at the helm, talking to the first mate, her arms crossed over her chest, her expression serious. The ship was a flurry of men and their swords and pistols as the crew scrambled for their battle stations. Somebody was pounding on the drum, and cannons were wheeling across deck. The ship was a bright smear of red and gold on the horizon. The colors of the Empire.

Naji appeared beside me, and put his hand on my arm. I jumped and yanked it away.

"What's going on?" he asked. "Are we under attack?"

Marjani called us over to the helm, waving her arm wide. "It's an Empire sloop," she shouted over the din of battle preparations. "We're gonna have to fight for her."

Naji gave me a sideways glance and set his face in stone.

"I don't need your protection," I told him.

Naji frowned and didn't say anything. Marjani jumped down from the stern deck and pulled out her own sword and her pistol and nodded at me. "Captain's lending us Tavin, Ajim, and Gorry," she said. "And his weapons. Otherwise, we got to take the ship ourselves."

It's best to take a ship without violence. You ride on board with your fiercest looking men, fire off a couple of shots, hold a knife to the captain's throat. But you don't kill nobody. Merchants' ships are the easiest for that. The crew don't value their cargo more than their lives.

But this wasn't a merchant ship, it was Empire standard, and I could bet they were loading up their cannons and singing their battle songs as we waited. I bet they had their blood-drop battle flags raised and at the ready. Empire soldiers ain't no merchants. They'll die for their ship.

And then I had an idea.

"I'll be back," I told Marjani. "I ain't running. Just... I'll be back."

"No!" she said. "They'll be here–"

"Give me five minutes," I said. "I'll be back."

And then I took off, scrambling down the ladder to get to the brig.

The manticore was pacing in her cell, tail curling and uncurling. She looked up at me when I came in, her face wan and pale.

"I got somebody you can eat," I said.

Her lips sneered back. "Don't lie to me, girl-human."

"I ain't lying," I said. "I got lots of somebodies, in fact. We're about to board an Empire sloop, to take her. There'll be fighting, but–"

She ran her tongue over her lips, though I could tell from the darkness in her eyes she still didn't believe me.

"I'm gonna let you out," I said. "But you gotta swear – swear on our friendship, and I know we got one – that you'll only go after a man in Empire uniform. You know what that looks like?"

She shook her head. Her teeth were like daggers.

"Red," I said. "They wear red with a gold snake on the chest. Tie up their hair in red scarves. You got that? A man's got on red and gold, you can eat him."

"If you are lying to me," she said. "I will fill you full of poison and drop you to the bottom of the sea."

"Fair enough." I yanked out my knife and picked the lock on her gate, swung it open. She bounded out, snarling and hissing, and then stopped right beside the doorway. She looked at me over her shoulder.

"Once I have eaten," she said, "You may ride me. For your battle."

"Fine." I pushed her toward the doorway. I didn't have the heart to tell her sea-battles don't work that way.

We ran side by side through the lower decks, men screeching and drawing swords as we passed. "She ain't gonna hurt you!" I shouted, waving my pistol around, afraid somebody was gonna shoot her before we got to battle. "She's got a taste for Empire men!"

As many ice-islanders were in that crew, I figured they'd like the sound of that, and it didn't take long before the crew was cheering us instead of shrinking from us, calling out they hoped she'd rip them Empire scummies to pieces and eat their intestines. I blamed the battle fever. Sends men into such a frothing rage they forget to be scared of a manticore.

Marjani glared at me when we got up on deck.

"I was really hoping that's not what you were going to do," she said.

"She's *starving*," I told her. "You expect me to keep her locked away while we're piling up dead men out here?"

Marjani crossed her arms in front of her chest.

"It's an Empire ship! They won't come peaceful and you know it."

She did know it. She nodded at me, and then turned to Naji, started telling him the protocol for boarding a ship. He stared at her, face blank.

I wondered if he was as scared as I was.

The manticore growled. "Where are the red-and-gold men?" she asked me, her breath hot against the side of my neck.

"There." I pointed out to sea with my sword. The Empire ship was coming closer, her red bow veering in for us. Dots of light flashed on her deck. Empire swords.

"We're gonna board her," I added, cause I figured the manticore was wondering.

And then Marjani's hand was on my arm. She pushed me toward the rowboats that hung off the side of the ship. "You want the manticore, you get to take her across the water."

"You got rope?" I asked.

"What?" said Naji. "You're going to send her out there... no. No, absolutely not. It'll completely incapacitate me–"

"Then go with her!" Marjani shoved Naji at me. "I'll take the *Goldlife* crewmen and swing across. You don't have much time before they start firing. *Go*."

For a second Naji and me stared at each other and I knew I couldn't let him get to me, not now. An Empire man'll die for his ship. I wasn't gonna die for my broken heart.

"Come on!" I climbed into one of the boats, the manticore at my side. She trumpeted – not the way she had when we were racing across the beach. This sounded like a damn battle horn.

The *Goldlife* crew let out a cheer, all throaty with bloodlust.

And then the Empire fired its first volley of cannons.

Naji let out a shout and jumped into the boat beside me. Marjani swung her sword through the rope and we crashed into the water, the air thick with black smoke and the scent of cannon fire. The manticore wasn't trumpeting no more, but flattened down in the center of the boat, one paw pressed over her head, whimpering. I grabbed hold of the oars and pushed off toward the Empire ship, trying to ignore the booms and thuds echoing overhead.

Naji flung himself on top of me, his weight pressing me into the manticore.

"What you doing?" I shouted. I could taste the gun-powder in the air.

"Protecting you," Naji snarled. He was already covered in sweat; it must be hurting him, us being out on the water.

"Then help me row!"

He grabbed one of the oars and we pushed off together, the Empire ship looming tall in front of our little rowboat, sunlight making the water sparkle. Debris showered down on top of us, bits of wood and sail and metal and probably blood and bone, though I couldn't think about that. Naji screamed, the muscles bunching up in his arms, and he kept shouting, "The shadow! The shadow!" and I didn't know what the hell he meant at first, cause all I could think about was getting us out of the water. And then I realized the Empire ship was casting a long dark shadow across the sea, and once we got there he could slip us on board so we wouldn't have to scamper up the side of the ship.

I rowed harder. Water splashed over the side of the boat, soaking me through. I could hear men screaming up on the ships, both of 'em, and pistols going off, and the cannons, booming and booming and booming like never-ending thunder.

And then we crossed the shadowline. Naji wrapped his arm around my shoulder and shoved his hand in the manticore's fur, and all the noise fell away.

It was nice in the shadow, quiet and cool, with Naji's body pressing up against me like maybe we were lovers after all. And I floated there in the darkness like I was underwater, and I didn't want to come out, I didn't–

We slammed onto the deck of the Empire ship.

The *Goldlife* hadn't fired on her yet, of course, cause we were looking to take her, not steal from her, but those Empire soldiers were firing off their cannons quick as they could, and the deck was thick with the residue from the powder. Nobody noticed us at first, not in the fury of the battle, but then the manticore reared up on her hind legs and roared so loud the wood vibrated.

Everything stopped.

I pulled out my sword and pistol. Naji lifted his sword over his head.

All those Empire men turned from the stations and stared at us, a Confederation pirate and a Jadorr'a and a hungry manticore.

I'd never boarded a ship during a battle before. I'd always stayed with Papa's boat and fought alongside Mama. But I heard the stories from the crewman who'd come back, bragging up their fighting, and all those Empire crewman were staring at me like they were expecting something.

"We're here to take your ship," I said, and I'm proud to say my voice didn't waver none at all.

The manticore roared again, and then she lunged forward, knocking down this poor Empire soldier with her great sharp claws, burying her face in his belly. Blood splattered across the deck.

I looked away, my stomach clenching.

And then all those Empire men started screaming – I didn't blame 'em one bit – and shooting at the manticore. She lifted her head out of her meal, blood smeared all over her face, teeth gleaming in the sun, and hissed.

Spines shot out of her tail, impaling soldiers in the heart, in the head, in the belly.

Naji yanked me down to the deck, slapping his hand over my head. "I think this is one battle where we're not needed," he said.

"They're gonna kill her!" I squirmed away from him, lifted my head up enough to see a soldier running up to the manticore with his sword outstretched. I shot him.

"Ananna!" Naji hissed my name like he did when he was angry. I ignored him, just jumped to my feet and launched into a crush of soldiers, slicing at them with my sword to keep them off the manticore. Her spines whizzed past my head but none of them ever hit me.

And then Naji was fighting alongside me, his sword spinning out in a flashing silver circle. He moved like a shadow, darting between soldiers, keeping them off me as I kept them off the manticore.

Where the hell is Marjani? I kept thinking, cause I'd no idea how to take a ship. I knew in theory, but here in practice all I cared about was keeping me and Naji and the manticore alive. So I poured all my concentration into fighting, and I didn't feel no pain or fear, just my heartbeat and my breath.

Dully, I was aware of the manticore taking down another soldier, his screams echoing out across the sea, the scatter of soldiers rippling backward across the deck as he fell.

I fought.

And then the fighting stopped.

I wanted to keep going, all that blood rushing through my veins, all that blood soaking into my skin, but Naji got me in a lock and pulled me still. The Empire peace horn was blowing, long and low. The Empire men had all thrown down their weapons.

Marjani was standing up at the helm, a knife pressing into the captain's neck, two *Goldlife* crewmen at her side.

The manticore was eating.

"It's over," Naji told me, his mouth close to my ear. "We have the ship."

I felt like I'd woken up from a fever dream, everything distorted and strange. The sunlight was too bright. The blood on the deck too red.

The peace horn died away.

Marjani dropped her knife from the captain's throat, and Gorry and Ajim took him by the arms, dragged him away from the helm. Marjani leaned forward.

"This ship is under the control of the Pirate Captain Namir yi Nadir." She jabbed her finger toward Naji, who tensed his arm. "Any man who wishes to join our crew may do so and no harm will come to him. Those of you who wish to die for the Empire…" She turned to the manticore, who was still hunched over the remains of the soldier. "You will have that chance as well."

Goldlife pirates were streaming on board, but nobody moved to stop them. Tavin hoisted up the boat's new colors, some flag Marjani had sewn before she picked us up at the Isles of the Sky: a black background and a dancing skeleton stitched in red silk. It snapped and fluttered in the sea wind and for a second the scent of blood and fear got wiped away, and the ship was almost silent.

Silent. Peaceful. And all I wanted to do was lie down and sleep.

I slept in the captain's quarters that night, after stripping away my bloody clothes and swimming in the cold ocean to wash the blood from my skin. There was a real bed in there, big enough that two people could share. Naji let me and Marjani sleep in the bed while he hung a hammock from the corner and slept there. I fell asleep easy enough. I woke up in the middle of the night, the cabin dark and shadowy and unfamiliar.

I listened to Marjani and Naji breathe for a while, their breaths soft and out of synch, and when I realized I wasn't gonna fall back asleep I rolled out of bed and pulled on one of the Empire captain's gold cloaks and went up on deck.

Nearly all of the Empire men had chosen service over capture – Empire don't train 'em as well as they think, I guess – but we were still headed for Bone Island, on account of Marjani not trusting a ship full of ex-soldiers. I didn't blame her. We'd dump 'em there and let 'em find their own way back to their lives, then pick up a crew of our own.

But for now, we had 'em running the night shift, and they all shrunk away from me when I came up, turning back to their ropes and riggings. I ignored 'em, just walked up to the bow and leaned over the edge to feel the cool salt air on my face.

"Girl-human."

I turned around. The manticore padded up to me, her face cleaned of blood, her mane brushed and shining –

some poor Empire sap had been assigned to tend to her grooming needs.

"What are you doing up here?"

"I do not like the underneath," she said. We hadn't locked her up in the brig, but I'd asked her to stay down below in the hold on account of her presence making the men jumpy.

I didn't say nothing and she added, "It stinks of human filth."

"Hard to take a bath on a ship," I told her.

"You're surrounded by water!"

I didn't have anything to say to that.

The manticore sat beside me, wings tucked into her sides, her tail curling up along her back. We didn't speak for a long time.

"Thank you for allowing me to eat." She sounded sincere, too, and kind of sad. "I had been very hungry before."

"I know." I stroked her mane and she nuzzled against my hand like a pet.

"I will not eat any men without your permission."

It still creeped me out a little, that she ate humans, but part of me knew it was just the way things were, like me having to eat fish and sheep and goat. It wasn't her fault that she ate people.

And I'd killed more men than she could eat that afternoon, all cause they were trying to kill her, but I tried to put it out of my mind the way Papa told me to, cause dwelling on it can turn you dark. But it was hard.

She gave me one of her sharp smiles and turned back to the sea. "It is strange, living with humans. But I am growing used to it."

"I thought you lived with humans on the Island of the Sun."

The manticore flicked her tail. "That's different. They are our servants, girl-human, our slaves. Here, we are equals." Another flick. "Or as equal as human and manticore can be."

"Oh, is that so?" I leaned over the railing and looked down at the black ocean water skimming up along the side of the boat. "So tell me, how was it a human managed to kidnap you?"

The manticore let out one of her low, quiet hisses. "He was treacherous and dishonest. Not like you, or even the Jadorr'a." She licked her lips and looked up at me. "You should not trust wizard-humans, as a rule."

"I'll keep that in mind."

"It was my parents' fault," she went on, like I hadn't spoken. "His water-nest crashed onto our beach. We were going to eat him, of course, but he had magic, and my parents were willing to strike a deal."

That caught my attention, since everybody'd been warning me about the dangers of striking a deal with a manticore. Looks like it got Eirnin killed.

"Did he double-cross them?" I asked. "Your parents?"

"Of course, he did, girl-human! We traded him his life for some of his spells and potions, but during the trade he cast a great smoke-cloud and paralyzed me. I do not know how he dragged me back to his water-nest, but I learned quickly that it hadn't been broken at all. It had been a ruse, designed to ensnare me."

"Why?" I said. "It's not like he tried to sell you or anything–"

"Sell me! If only he had tried. No, he planned to cut me open and use my heart for some foul wizardry or other. Every morning for those three life cycles he taunted me with his knife. The morning that I escaped was the morning he was to kill me."

I stared at her in the moonlit gloom. Her human-looking face was lovely in that silvery-white light, but she looked sad and lonely – or at least as sad and lonely as a manticore could. I draped my arm around her shoulder and leaned up against her mane, and she let out a little trill that sounded almost grateful.

"If I'd known you were there," I said, "I'd have cut you loose myself."

"I do not blame you for the not-knowing," she said. "He hid me behind a veil of magic."

"Well," I said, pulling away from her. "You don't have to worry about it anymore. We'll get you home soon."

"Yes," the manticore said, and she let out a sweet ringing chiming call. "I know."

The next morning, me and Naji and Marjani met up in the captain's quarters to talk about what we were gonna do after we got our crew sorted.

"Drop off the manticore," I said.

Marjani stood staring out the porthole, gazing, I suppose, at the sea. A beam of sunlight settled across the bridge of her nose. "I already told you, I'm not letting that manticore stay onboard my ship longer than I have to." She turned to Naji. "What were the two remaining tasks? Finding a princess–" Her voice trailed off, and she had a strange, troubled expression.

"Starstones," Naji said. "Find a princess's starstones and hold them against my skin."

Marjani stared at him. "Yes," she said softly, "I remember now."

"And the other was to create life out of an act of violence," I said. "Whatever the hell that means."

Marjani frowned. "Riddles."

"Of course." Naji said. "It's a northern curse."

"And what the hell's a starstone anyway?" I asked.

"Magic," Marjani said, and she turned back to the porthole, her face blank.

"They're rare," Naji said, although he sounded distracted and uncomfortable. "And honestly, I'm not too keen on chasing after them–"

"Why not?"

But Naji and Marjani both ignored me.

"Well?" I said, annoyed. "Why not?"

"It's dangerous," Naji said.

"Easy answer."

"Perhaps we could go to one of the universities," Marjani said. "The scholars might be able to help you." She was still staring out the porthole. "The university in Arkuz is excellent…" But her voice wavered a little, and I could tell that whatever had sent her off to a life of piracy in the first place still lingered back in Jokja. I had a feeling it was more than complicated than what Chari, the old pirate I'd befriended back on the *Ayel's Revenge*, had told me, about her not wanting to marry some nobleman – but I didn't much want to pry, either.

"Lisirra would be better," Naji said. "I have more ties there."

Marjani looked at him. "I suppose that makes sense." I could hear the relief in her voice.

"What do you think, Ananna?" Naji asked.

I glanced over at Marjani. She wasn't staring out the window no more, just leaning up against the wall with her arms crossed over her chest. It was clear to me she didn't want to go back to Jokja. I thought about Lisirra, the sunny streets and the water wells and the sweet-scented gardens. The exact opposite of the Isles of the Sky.

"Lisirra sounds good to me."

And so it was decided. The pirate ship *Nadir*, formally a nameless Empire sloop, would load up a new crew, drop off a manticore, and sail to the universities of Lisirra.

It only took a day to sail into Bone Island, faster than should've been possible. We had favorable winds, and the ship was quicker than any sloop in the Confederation, though Marjani said the Jokja navy had built some rumored to sail even faster. She sneered at a knot of Empire sailors as she told me, like they'd stolen the ship plans from Jokja themselves.

But I suspected Naji might've had something to do with the speediness of our trip – he stayed in the captain's quarters most of the time, the way Marjani told him to, and when I took him some food at Marjani's request I saw spots of blood on the writing desk.

The day we pulled into port was bright and sunny and shot through with the first warmth I'd felt in months. As the crew prepared to make port, I marched into the captain's quarters.

Naji was stretched out on the bed, staring up at the ceiling. He lifted his head when I came in. We'd hardly spoken since the battle.

"You look like an Empire commander," he told me. I was still wearing that gold cloak and had taken to knotting my hair back in the Empire style, cause it did do a better job of keeping my hair out of the way.

"You look like a Port Iskassaya drunk." I hadn't meant to sass him, but I couldn't help it, he was so bedraggled. "We're gonna have to clean you up before we take you in to sign up a crew."

"Marjani has already informed me."

We stood in silence for a minute longer. Then he lifted his head. "Did you need something, Ananna?"

I stared at him.

"Thank you for calling down the winds," I finally said. "To get us here faster."

His face was blank as always, but something glittered in his eyes, some flash of appreciation. I left the captain's quarters before he could say anything more.

Bone Island had always been my favorite outlaw port of call when I was a kid, cause it's big enough that it almost feels like a real city, and there are merchants selling clothes and silks and fancy Qilari desserts, instead of just whores and weapons, like at some of the other pirate islands. And it's always mild there, never cold and never too hot, and the water in the beaches is pure bright blue, the same color as the sky. Even the rains are warm.

Marjani put me in charge of prettying up Naji and making him look like a captain. I didn't want to do it – I wanted to stay on board the boat with the manticore. But when I said something about it Marjani didn't even glance up from her maps and notes.

"The manticore," she said, "will not get us a crew."

I knew she was right and I knew she was my captain now, too, not in name but in action. I didn't talk back.

Naji was waiting for me on the docks, his hair brushed out and combed over his scar – otherwise he was filthy. It almost hurt to look at him.

"I want a bath," he said. "I don't care if it won't make me a believable captain. *I want a bath*."

"Already planning on it."

I took him to the Night Porch, a whorehouse down near the beach that was attached to the nicest bathhouse on the whole island. Led him round back so I wouldn't have to see him staring at the whores all draped out in the main room in their silks and jewelry, all of 'em prettier than me.

The baths were nice as I remembered, clean and misty and smelling of aloe and basil. We stood in the entryway, steam curling up Naji's hair, and he said in this voice like a sigh, "Civilization."

"Not exactly," I said. "But close enough." I jutted my head toward the main room. Men's laughter boomed out with the steam. "You can go in there." I tried not to think about the women they kept on hand to slough men's backs and wash their hair. "I'll be in the secondary room there."

Naji frowned. "They separate men and women? In a pleasure house?"

"No," I said.

Naji opened his mouth, but I whirled away from before he asked me some question I didn't want to answer. The thought of him seeing me naked next to all those perfect whores made my skin crawl.

"It'll be difficult for me to relax if we aren't in the same room," Naji called out behind me. "The headaches–"

I stopped, one hand on the doorway. I could hear water splashing, the low hum of women's voices, and I wondered why he was bothering to mention that to me. I knew about his damned headaches, and I also knew there wasn't any danger here. Part of me wondered if maybe he just wanted my company – but no. I knew better.

"Too bad," I said.

The secondary room is the one where the whores go when they ain't working, and men don't usually venture in cause there ain't no one to wash 'em and flirt with 'em and make 'em feel wanted. I stripped over in the corner where no one would pay no attention to me, and then I slipped in the soft warm bathwater, bubbling up from some spring deep in the ground. It was my first proper bath in ages and I stayed in for longer than I normally did, dropping my head below the water and watching all the ladies' legs kicking through the murk. Nobody said anything to me, which was exactly how I wanted it.

I met Naji in the garden after my bath. He came out with his hair wet and shining in the sun, his dirty clothes out of place against his gleaming skin. I was sitting underneath a jacaranda tree that kept dropping purple blossoms in my hair.

He sat beside me.

His presence still gave me a little thrill. We sat in silence for a moment, and I enjoyed it, his closeness and the warm sun and my clean skin. Felt nice.

"Do I look like a pirate captain now?" he asked.

"No." I didn't look at him. "You need new clothes."

"Ah. Of course."

I leaned forward, resting my elbows on my knees. I didn't quite know how to go about doing this. It wouldn't do to have word spread around about some man going shopping, then turning up in those same clothes at the Starshot drinkhouse as the Pirate Namir yi Nadir. Cutthroats are a gossipy bunch. Gotta be; it's how you find out the best schemes and stratagems. Nobody wants to get caught unawares.

It was hard to think out there in the warm sun, all clean and bright, with Naji sitting beside me, but an idea came to me anyway, a big flash of an idea.

"I know what we can do," I said, straightening up.

"Shopping?" Naji asked. "Or stealing?"

"Neither." I stood up and led him out of the garden, away from the whorehouse and the fresh steam of the baths. Paid a carriage driver a couple pieces of pressed copper to take us out of town, down to the rows of little ramshackle shacks that sprouted up along the oceanline like barnacles. Naji didn't say a word the whole time. I figured he wanted out of those rotted clothes more than he was letting on.

The house looked the way I remembered it, a little wooden shack with banana trees out front, the backyard sloping down to the ocean. I jumped out of the carriage. Naji stared at me.

"What are we doing?" he asked.

"Getting you some clothes. Come on."

He stepped out of the carriage like I was setting him up for some kind of con. I stomped through the soft seagrass in front of the house and rapped my fist against the door.

"Where are we?" Naji asked.

"You got a headache?"

"No."

"Then you know I ain't in danger. Stop asking questions."

He frowned and I thought his eyes looked kinda wounded, but he didn't say nothing.

The door swung open, and Old Ceria, my old sea magic teacher, stuck her head out, squinting in the sunlight. She looked at me and then she looked at Naji.

"What happened to his face?" she asked. "Looks like what happens when you let Lady Starshine in charge of the roast at the dry season festival. Charred on the outside, bloody on the inside."

Naji turned to stone, his eyes burning with anger. Before the kiss, I might've warned him.

"He got hurt a long time ago," I said. "Ceria, we need to borrow some clothes, if it's not too much trouble."

"You mean *take some clothes*." But she held the door wider and let me and Naji step inside. It was dark in there, with heavy curtains pulled over the windows. Dried-out seaweed hung from the rafters, and all manner of sea creatures lay out on the cabinet – or the shells of 'em did, anyway. The smell was the same, too, stale and salty.

Old Ceria was a seawitch, like Mama, and Mama would always bring me to see her when I was a little girl, to try and extract magic out of me. Ceria lived on Bone Island cause she couldn't abide Empire rule, but she didn't have no love for the Confederation neither – for pirates in general. She barely tolerated Mama, truth be told, but she was willing to put aside differences far as magic was concerned.

I hadn't seen Ceria in years, but she looked the same as she did when I was younger, as dried out as her seaweed and her dead crabs.

"He the reason you ran off from the Hariri clan?" Ceria asked me, jutting her head toward Naji.

Shit. I didn't think she would've heard.

She gave me a narrow, sharp-toothed smile.

I didn't answer her, didn't even move my head to shake it yes or no. I could feel Naji staring at me, staring at her.

"Oh, don't worry," she said, grinning wider. "You think I care about Confederation politics? Just asking cause it ain't never wise to give your heart to a blood magician."

I went hot at that.

Old Ceria chuckled and even though she was an old woman and I knew that meant she deserved my respect, I kinda wanted to hit her.

"You two wait here," she said. "I take it you want the clothes for him? You're looking awful dapper in that Empire cloak." A little curl of her lip when she said *Empire.*

She disappeared into the back of the house. Naji and me stood in silence, and I listened to the waves rolling in to the beach behind us. Naji was still fuming over Ceria's comment about his face – I could see it in the way he kept balling up the rotted fabric of his shirt in one hand.

I tried to work up the nerve to apologize to him.

Naji said, "Captain Namir yi Nadir will cover his face."

"Marjani won't like that."

"Marjani can dress up as a man if she wants a captain so badly. I'm covering my face."

Old Ceria came into the room, a tattered brocade coat tossed over one arm, some trousers and shirts tossed over another.

"I should be getting you a scarf, then," she said.

Naji sneered at her and she threw the clothes at him.

"Ain't scared of you, blood magician. Got nothing but seawater in these veins." She nodded at me. "You best watch out, girl."

"He won't hurt me," I said.

"Seems to me he already has."

Naji stalked outside with his new captain's clothes, but I stayed in the house for a minute or two longer, staring at her, thinking back to those horrible afternoons as a kid, digging up sand on the beach for her spells.

"How'd you know?" I asked.

"I'm a witch, darling," she said. "I saw you coming two weeks back. I know his story too, the curse and all. The kiss." She winked at me.

I scowled at her, then jumped up and pushed out of the house before I said something I'd regret. With a jolt, I wondered if she would tell the Hariris that she saw me, but then I remembered she'd always hated the Hariris more than other pirates. Maybe she'd just tell Mama.

Still, it was a reminder that I wasn't in the north anymore – I was back in the parts of the world where the Hariri clan had plenty of eyes, and no doubt they'd still be looking for me, even if I'd mostly forgotten about them over the last few months, seeing as how I had bigger problems on my mind. I'd have to come up with some excuse for not dawdling in port. Threaten to feed some Empire man to the manticore. I felt sorry enough for her as it was, having to eat fish bones and sea birds again.

Naji stood at the side of the road, pulling his hair over his scar, the clothes lying in a pile at his feet.

"You're getting 'em all dusty!" I shouted.

"Who cares?" Naji asked. "They're just going to rot once we make sail."

I picked up the clothes and shoved them at him. He yanked them away from me, his hair hanging in curls across his face.

"Why did you bring me here?" he asked.

"To get you clothes."

"You knew she would–" His face twisted up with anger. "You knew she would say something. You wanted her to."

I looked away from him, cheeks burning.

"Why?" The question was sharp and painful as a knife. It cut into me and I knew I deserved it. "Why did you do it?"

"You should change," I muttered. "Before we go back into town."

He glared at me.

"I'm sorry. I didn't think... I didn't do it on purpose." I still couldn't look at him. "And your face doesn't look like a half-roasted pig anyway."

Silence. The wind blew in from the ocean, stirring up sand and dust.

"You have no idea what it's like," Naji said.

I kept my eyes on my feet and listened to his footsteps crunch over the road and then rustle into the grass. And when I glanced up he was over on the side of Old Ceria's house, half-hidden by the banana trees, pulling his new shirt over his head.

CHAPTER SIX

Marjani had already set up at the Starshot drinkhouse, claiming a table in the back, away from the singer warbling some old Confederation tunes. I threaded through the crowd, Naji behind me in his captain's outfit. It suited him, I thought, especially the brocade coat. Before he'd covered up his face – with a scarf I nicked for him off one of the carts outside – he'd been so handsome my chest hurt to look at him.

When she saw us, Marjani folded her arms over her chest.

"Take it off," she said.

"No," I told her, before Naji could say anything.

She flicked her eyes over to me.

"It makes him look more formidable," I said.

"I'm not leaving my face uncovered," Naji said.

Marjani sighed. "No one's going to say anything–"

"Yes," Naji said. "They will."

I stepped in between the two of them and said, "We should probably do this fast. Manticore's gonna get hungry out on that boat. Don't know how long she'll be able to avoid temptation."

Marjani sighed. "Yes, I'd thought of that myself. You stay here and get the drunks. I'll go out in the street and look for the desperates."

And then she was out the door.

It didn't take long for word to circulate that the Pirate Namir yi Nadir was in port and that he was signing up men for his new crew. Probably helped that an Empire warship flying pirate colors was waiting out in the docks, but mostly it was the fact that pirates can't keep their mouths shut for longer than five minutes. It occurred to me that leaving port early probably wasn't gonna be good enough – I needed to keep my face covered, too, before some Hariri ally or wannabe-ally or plain ol' asshole who wanted to kick up a fight spotted me and kidnapped me back to Lisirra.

All that time on the Isles of the Sky, with no company but Naji and the manticore, had left me soft. Not wary enough, like the Mist woman had said.

So I snuck out back and slipped down the street till I came to a shop selling scarves and jewelry. I bought a pair of scarves and covered my face the way Naji did and wrapped my hair up in the Empire style, though with a black scarf instead of a red one. The cloak hid my chest well enough. I figured I could pass for a man.

"And who the hell are you supposed to be?" Marjani asked when she came back in with some men she'd picked up off the streets.

"The rat who got Captain Namir yi Nadir the ship," I said.

She frowned. I could tell she didn't approve. Messed up his reputation, having a ship handed to him on account of subterfuge.

"A prisoner?" I said. "Who agreed to sail under his colors? And by allowing me my freedom we can see the extent of his mercy?"

"Better," Marjani said. "And the mask?"

"A show of solidarity."

She didn't push that none, neither. I don't know why I hadn't yet told her about the Hariri clan. Felt bad about lying in the first place, I guess. And she'd had this all planned out – it was the reason me and Naji weren't still stuck on that frozen floating slab of rock after all. I didn't want to be the one to throw a kink in her plans.

I'd just keep my face covered, and we'd be fine.

It was mostly Marjani who did the recruiting anyway. She'd done it before, I could tell. Even now that she was back in the drinkhouse, she didn't just sit down and wait for men to come to her – she wove through the place, Naji trailing behind her like a puppy, dodging whores and serving girls and the worthless outlaws who came out here not knowing one whit about sailing a ship. She had an eye for the ones that would know what they were doing, and she knew how to catch 'em at their drunkest, when they would slap an X on anything you stuck in front of 'em.

She left me in charge of the table, in case anyone came asking. I leaned back in my chair and sipped from my pint of beer and tried not to think about Naji.

"Excuse me? This where I sign up to sail with Captain Namir yi Nadir's crew?"

The voice was speaking Empire all posh and educated, and when I dropped down in my chair and looked up I saw one of the soldiers we'd cut free when we made port.

"What you want to sail with us for?"

"Are you the manticore's trainer?" The soldier reached over and plucked at the mask. I slapped his hand away.

"I ain't her trainer. And we ain't taking on mutineers."

"I'm not a mutineer." The soldier sat down at the table. "Where are you sailing?"

I crossed my arms over my chest.

"Well?"

Marjani had given me some story or another, but most of it had slipped out of my head due to drink. "Captain's sailing after treasure."

"All pirates sail after treasure," the soldier said. "What in particular is he looking for?"

I fixed him my steeliest glare. "Gotta ask him yourself."

The soldier looked me right in the eye. "I will. Once I'm onboard your ship. What about that manticore? She sailing with us, too?"

That, at least, I could answer. "At least as far as the Island of the Sun. She and I made a deal, and now I'm making good on it and taking her home."

The soldier arched his eyebrow. "You made a deal with a manticore?"

I shrugged.

"Well," he said. "That if nothing else has convinced me." He grabbed the name sheet and the quill Marjani had left with me. I tried to snatch it away from him – no luck. "There isn't an Empire general alive who could make a deal with a manticore and survive." He scrawled his name across the sheet. *Jeric yi Niru.* The *yi* gave him away as nobility, I knew, and I knew too his nobility was real, since no Empire soldier would lie about his status the way a pirate would – the way, for example, Marjani had lied about the status of the pirate Namir yi Nadir. I scowled at the sheet.

"I'll feed you to the manticore first sign of trouble," I told him.

He gave me a smile. He was older, with streaks of gray in his hair, although his skin wasn't as weatherworn as it would've been had he spent his whole life at sea.

"The Empire look suits you," he said before turning away and heading off toward one of the serving maids. I don't trust handsome people, and he wasn't handsome in the slightest. I decided to give him the benefit of the doubt.

"Hey!" I shouted. "Snakeheart!"

He looked over at me. "I'm not an Empire soldier anymore. I'm afraid the epithet no longer fits."

"We set sail at sunrise tomorrow. You're not there, we're leaving you."

He gave me a nod.

"And I ain't kidding about the manticore!"

He just laughed, which pissed me off. I wanted to shout something back to him, but he was talking to the serving girl again, leaning in close to her, and I figured he wasn't gonna pay me no mind.

Marjani and Captain Namir yi Nadir came back about thirty minutes later. I hadn't gotten anybody to sign up save for Jeric yi Niru, who seemed to have stashed himself in a corner with a pitcher of ale. Marjani handed me her logbook, folded open to the first page. There were names spelled out in her neat, tidy handwriting down one side, a row of mostly Xs cascading down the other, mixed in with the occasional signature.

She tucked my loose sheet of paper, with its one signature, back in the logbook. "Our crew, Captain."

"Stop calling me that," said Naji.

"Just getting you used to it," she said.

Naji turned to me, his eyes big and dark over the edge of his mask. "Are you my decoy?" he asked.

"What?"

He ran his fingers across my scarf. I could feel his touch through the fabric, on my lips, and my whole body shivered.

"No." I stood up, pulling myself away from him. "I need something to drink."

He didn't say nothing more, though Marjani watched us close, eyes flicking back and forth, until I turned and melted into the crowd.

The crew we signed up turned out decent. Not as good as Papa's crew, but better than the *Goldlife* bunch. A handful of 'em were Confederation drifters, men who got the tattoo but don't stick to one particular ship, but most were unaffiliated sailors from the Free Countries in the south. A crew like Papa's, which is bound to one particular ship and captain, aren't so keen to sail with outsiders. It's an honor thing, though Mama used to tell me it was really just plain ol' snobbery, the way Empire nobility looks down on the merchants. But the drifters aren't so particular, probably cause they're used to a crew like Papa's looking down on 'em for jumping from boat to boat, and our crew blended together without much trouble.

I kept my face covered the first few days, but got sick of it soon enough, the cloth half-smothering me in the humid ocean air.

"Finally," Marjani said. I'd taken my hair out of the Empire scarf, too. I was still wearing the cloak, though I kept it open at the neck on account of the heat. "I was starting to hear rumbling about how you and Captain Namir yi Nadir were the same man."

"What? That don't make no sense. They've seen us together before."

She waved her hand dismissively. "They thought he could copy himself, be in two places at once."

"They thought I was Naji? I don't look nothing like him!"

"I told you," Marjani said. "People will believe anything."

In truth, I could see how the crew might've gotten that idea about Naji. He kept to his captain's quarters most of the time and let Marjani do all the captaining. She got me to be her first mate – "Second mate," she called it – and at first I wasn't quite sure how to act. I'd seen Mama plenty, of course, so I tried to act like her. I kept my back straight and my head high and I carried a dagger and a pistol with me everywhere I went. Got real good at whipping out the dagger and holding it up to some back-talking crewman's neck, too.

Besides which, I didn't keep the manticore in the brig.

"They're scared of you," Marjani told me one morning, the sun warm and lemony, the wind pushing us toward the south, toward the Island of the Sun. We were up at the helm, the crew sitting in little clumps down on deck, not working so hard cause they didn't have to. The manticore was sunning herself over at the stern, her tail thwapping against the deck as she slept.

"They are?"

"Sure. It's a good thing, though." She leaned against the ship's wheel, squinted into the sun. "Because you're a woman. If they're scared of you, they'll listen to you."

"That's how it works with men too."

Marjani shook her head and laughed. "Not always. Men have the option of earning respect."

The wind picked up, billowing out the sails. The boat picked up speed. One of the crewmen hollered up in the ropes. Probably Naji's doing, that wind. There was something unnatural about it.

"I always wanted to captain a ship," I said after a while. "When I was a little kid." I didn't mention that I'd still wanted it when I was seventeen years old and about to be married off to Tarrin of the *Hariri*. "Used to fancy I could dress up like a boy and everyone would listen to me. I never thought about getting some man to stand in as a proxy."

Marjani squinted out at the horizon. "Dressing up as a man can get you in trouble."

"What do you mean? Always figured it'd be nice. I could never pull it off proper, cause of my chest."

Normally Marjani might've laughed at that, but today she just ran her hand over the wheel and said, "I used to dress as a man to visit someone I loved. It was a sort of game. I met her when my father sent me to university, since I split my time between my studies and court, like a half-proper lady." Marjani laughed. "When she came of age she'd complain about suitors constantly – this one was too skinny, this one was too old, this one talked too much about politics." Marjani kinda smiled, but mostly she just looked sad. "And so I decided to surprise her, and show up as a suitor."

"Did it work?"

"For a little while. I didn't fool *her*, of course, and she loved it, but I fooled her parents. One of the noblewomen figured it out, though, and I spent some time in prison for lying about my identity."

"Is that why you left Jokja?" I asked. "Why you took to piracy?"

All the emotion left Marjani's face. "Yes."

We stood in silence, the unnatural warm wind blowing us toward the Island of the Sun. I knew she'd told me something important, something secret. And I felt even worse about keeping the Hariri clan from her.

I tried to tell her. I did. I started forming the words in my head. But then one of the crew called up to her about trouble in the galley over some sugar-wine rations, and she leapt over the railing to deal with it, and the moment was lost.

A few days passed, and we got closer and closer to the Island of the Sun. One afternoon I went down to the galley to get some food for myself and some scraps of meat for the manticore. There wasn't a whole lot there, though. Fish parts and some dried sheep meat. I kept the sheep meat for myself, started dropping the fish into a rucksack.

"Still wearing my captain's old uniform, I see."

At the sound of Jeric yi Niru's voice I almost dropped the sack of fish. I whirled around. He lounged against the doorway, a trio of seabirds hanging on a rope from his belt.

"What do you want?" I narrowed my eyes at the seabirds. "And where the hell did you get those?"

"Shot 'em down." He slung the birds over the table. "I trained in archery before I was a sailor. We must be nearing land. The manticore's island, I hope?"

"You hope?" I shoved another fish head in the sack. "What do you care? She ain't bothering nobody on this boat."

"She's hungry."

I scowled. "You don't think I haven't noticed?"

"I appreciate you not feeding any of us to her."

I didn't say anything.

"Here." He slid one of the birds off the rope and handed it to me. I stared at it, at the black empty beads of its eyes, the orange triangle of its beak. "For the manticore," he said.

I lifted my head enough to meet his eye. He gave me another one of his easy smiles.

"Thanks," I said.

"Always willing to help the first mate."

I froze. "You mean navigator."

He winked at me. "No," he said. "I don't."

I yanked out my knife and lunged toward him, but he was faster, and he grabbed my arm and twisted me around so he had my back up against his chest. I struggled against him but couldn't break free, and my heart started pounding and I was scared, but I knew I couldn't let him know.

"I wouldn't do that," he whispered into my ear. He plucked the knife out of my hand. "You're going to need me."

"Need you?" He dropped my arm and I stumbled away from him. When I turned around, he was examining my knife. Hell and sea salt.

"Yes," he said. "To find the starstones. That is what we're looking for, isn't it? After we leave the Island of the Sun?"

My whole body went cold. I didn't even bother to lie. "How do you know that?"

Jeric tapped his ear. "I pay attention. Even when I'm held prisoner aboard a pirate ship, I pay attention. You do realize starstones aren't the sort of treasure the crew is expecting, don't you? Even the more educated among them has never heard of a starstone – they'll think you're chasing after magician's treasure." A slow grin. "Fool's treasure, is how you pirates would put it, yes?"

I did my best Mama impression. I kept my face blank and my eyes mean. It didn't seem to work.

"You'll have a difficult time keeping the crew," he said, "once you tell them what you're after." Jeric tilted his head. "And you'll have an even more difficult time if I were to let slip what I discovered about the captain and *her* first mate–"

I snarled and leapt forward and grabbed the knife from him. He let me have it without a fight.

"What's to stop me from killing you?" I said, shoving the knife up at his throat. "Got a hungry manticore and–" I almost said *Jadorr'a*, but stopped myself in time. "I could feed you to her right now."

Beneath the mask of his smirk, Jeric's face went pale.

"Or I could wait," I said. "And feed you to her on the Island of the Sun. Her whole family could feast on you." I smiled.

"You don't know what you're dealing with," Jeric said softly. "Chasing after starstones."

I shrugged. "Don't screw with me. Or my captain. And maybe you won't wake with a manticore's spine in your belly." I grabbed the seabird off the table. "Maybe."

I stalked out of the galley angry and shaking. I didn't know anything about starstones. I'd never even heard of them before the Wizard Eirnin had rattled them off as part of Naji's cure, and as far as I knew Marjani and Naji hadn't talked about them in detail. But I guess I was wrong, if Jeric yi Niru had managed to pick up on it. Ship walls leak secrets.

I went back up on deck. Marjani wasn't nowhere to be seen – some old Confederation pirate was handling the helm. She was probably in the captain's quarters. Maybe she could find some excuse to toss Jeric in the brig and I wouldn't have to worry about it no more.

The manticore was stretched out over on the starboard side, her head lying on top of her paws. I stopped by to drop off her food.

"Hello, girl-human," she said. "We are close to the Island of the Sun, yes? I can smell their sands on the air."

"Yeah, we're close." I dumped out the fish and the seabird. She sniffed at 'em, didn't say nothing. No surprise there.

"You'll get to eat all the humans you want soon," I said.

"Yes," she said, sounding glum. "I had hoped the Jadorr'a's curse would have been broken–"

"You want to stay on the boat?" I said. "You can stay. Munch him all you want once we've cured him."

The manticore looked at me with horror. "No more boat."

I smiled. "I figured."

She leaned forward and swallowed a fish head with one gulp. "You wouldn't bring him back to the island?" She looked at me, fish scales glittering on her lips. "Even after he soul-hurt you?"

"That's not a good reason to kill a man."

"You aren't killing him," she said. "You're feeding me. His energy would live on." Her eyes were clear and golden, like water filled with sunlight. "For us to eat a man, it is a great gift."

"Dead's dead," I told her. "Sorry."

She blinked like she didn't understand, and I ran my fingers through her mane and left her to her meal.

I walked over to the captain's quarters and banged on the door.

"Open up!" I shouted. "It's me."

Naji answered, his face still covered. I don't know why he bothered when he locked himself away in his quarters all the time.

"Hello, Ananna," he said, and the fact that he hadn't come down to the galley when Jeric was threatening me lingered on the air.

"Marjani in there?"

Naji held the door open wider and stepped back. Marjani was leaning over the navigation maps.

"Oh good," she said when she saw me. "My navigator."

"We need to talk," I said.

She thrust the sexton at me. "Check our course," she said. "You needed to do that this morning."

I looked down at the map. An emerald brooch was stuck in the Island of the Sun, a lady's hairpin stuck in the southern coast of Jokja. Shouldn't it be Lisirra? But I didn't say nothing about it; I had bigger concerns at the moment.

"You know that Empire soldier we signed up?" I said.

"Not Empire anymore," Marjani said.

"He threatened me."

That got her attention. She lifted her head, eyes concerned. "What?"

And so I told her what had happened in the galley, about him being onto our ruse with Naji, and knowing we were chasing after the starstones, all of it. Marjani listened to me and the lines in her brow grew deeper and deeper the longer I talked.

"We should be able to hold him off until we arrive at the manticore's island," she said when I finished. "We may have to leave him there." Though I could tell that didn't sit right with her at all.

Naji had slipped over beside us while I spoke, and he looked at her above his mask, and he said, "Don't."

"Don't what?"

"Leave him with the manticores." Naji hesitated. "We may need... he may prove useful."

There was this long stifling silence.

"Oh?" Marjani asked. "You've decided to play captain now?"

I'll give him credit; Naji didn't even flinch. "Marjani," he said. "Have you ever *seen* a starstone?"

Marjani glared at him.

"Neither have I," he said. "But when I asked the Order about them..." his voice trailed off. "If the man has knowledge, it may come in useful."

"Absolutely not. He'll stir up a mutiny if we leave him on board."

"She's right," I said. "An Empire soldier learns how to be a weasel from boyhood. He wants something from us–"

"Then give it to him."

Marjani and me both looked at Naji in surprise, but he didn't seem to notice. He pulled the mask away from his face, and even though I didn't want it to, my breath caught in my throat.

"I want rid of this curse, and I'm not taking any chances," he said. "Keep him alive, this Empire soldier. Keep an eye on him, and keep Ongraygeeomryn near you, but don't kill him."

He glanced at me out of the corner of his eye. "What's his name? This soldier? Do you know it?"

"Jeric." I hesitated. "Uh, yi Niru."

"Oh," said Naji, frowning. "He's a noble."

"Yeah, which means he's doubly untrustworthy."

"Just keep him alive," Naji said.

Marjani shot him another dark look, but he pulled the mask back over his face and turned away. I leaned back over the navigation map and set up the divider.

Then the warning bells rang.

Another ship was approaching.

CHAPTER SEVEN

We ran out on deck, swords and pistols drawn. The crew were lined up against the starboard side, their voices a low murmur.

"The hell are you doing!" Marjani screamed at them. "Get your asses to work!"

They turned around, and when they saw Naji with his sword and his mask, they took off scrambling across the deck. Something glinted out on the horizon. Smoke trickled into the air. Fear clenched in my belly.

Marjani grabbed the spyglass off the helmsman and peered through it.

"Holy hell," she said. "They're Confederation." She laughed.

Naji slunk up behind me and put a hand on my arm. I didn't try to shake him off.

"What clan?" I whispered.

"Dunno." She peered through the spyglass again. "Red background, black skull–"

"With a crown?" I could hardly breathe. "A skull wearing a crown?"

"Looks like it, yeah."

"The Hariris," I said.

Naji pulled me close to him. My heart jolted in my chest like lightning was running through my body. "Go down below," he said. "And stay there. Take the manticore with you."

"What?" Marjani looked from him back to me. "Why? They'll see us flying pirate colors and let us–"

"They're after me."

Marjani's face went dark.

"I'm sorry, I shoulda told you–"

"Why in hell is the Hariri clan after you?"

"Ananna," Naji said. "Please. Go."

"No," Marjani said. "Don't you dare move from that spot. What do the Hariris want with you?"

My voice shook when I spoke. "I was supposed to marry Tarrin – Captain Hariri's son – and I didn't want to… and then I killed him…"

This time, Marjani's face turned ashen.

"You killed a captain's son?"

I nodded.

"For Kaol's sake, Ananna, why?"

"He was gonna kill me–"

She shook her head. "No. Explain this to me later." She clanged the attack bells, deep and ominous and so loud they hurt my ears.

"Arm the cannons!" Marjani shouted. "Prepare for battle!"

"Please, Ananna," said Naji. "Please hide."

"No!" I jerked around to face him. "This is my fault. I ain't gonna go cower in the brig while you and Marjani and everybody fights for me."

Naji's eyes looked sad, and for a half-second I thought maybe he was worried about *me* and not about the pain of the curse.

I pulled away from him and raced across the deck toward the manticore, who had stood up, her tail curling and uncurling.

"This noise, girl-human," she said. "Are we close to land?"

"Fraid not." I stood face to face with her. "You see that speck of light out there..." I pointed to the horizon. "It's a ship full of men you can eat."

Her eyes lit up.

"In exchange for a meal," I said, "may I ride you? Into battle?"

"With the other ship?"

I nodded. "They're after me, and I bet they try to board." I took a deep breath. "I need you to protect me."

She scowled. "Do I look like the Jadorr'a?"

"Please, Ongraygeeomryn." I know I mangled her name cause it came out sounding like a blood-cough and not like bells at all, but she still smiled without showing her teeth. "It would do me great honor to ride you into battle."

She dipped her shoulder, and I climbed on. Her wings rose up around me like a shield.

"Where should I go?" she asked.

"The helm, the helm!" I pointed with my sword. Men were stopping their work to stare at us, but I ignored them as the manticore bounded across the deck, leaping up beside Marjani.

Naji didn't say nothing at all.

"Bring the ship around starboard!" Marjani shouted. The men scrambled up in the rigging, moving the sails. She grabbed the wheel and yanked it hand over hand. The manticore trumpeted and dug her claws into the wood as the ship tilted and turned.

Naji's eyes began to glow.

"I wouldn't–" Marjani said.

"You are not me." Naji crouched beside the manticore, his eyes fixed on the *Hariri* as she loomed larger and larger.

"Do they have another assas... another Jadorr'a on board?" I asked him.

"No." He pushed his coat sleeves up to his elbow and drew the knife over the swirl of one of his tattoos. Blood welled up in thick shining drops. He dropped it over the deck, and when it struck the wood it began to glow pale, pale blue.

The manticore licked her lips. I yanked on her mane. "You'll be eating soon enough."

Naji ignored both of us.

At the helm, Marjani screamed, "Keep working! Get those cannons lined up! Ral, I don't want to see you looking over here. The *Hariri*'s your concern now! Move! Go!"

My heart pounded up near my throat. Naji knelt down at the splatter of his blood and began to chant.

The *Hariri* got closer and closer.

I threaded my fingers through the manticore's fur.

The wind was warm and the air was clean and Naji's voice hummed with my heartbeat.

And then the *Hariri* fired her cannons.

The *Nadir* jolted, sending me and the manticore skittering backward. Naji slammed forward on the deck but didn't stop chanting. Marjani brought the ship around, side by side with the *Hariri*.

"Fire!" she screamed.

A chunk of the *Hariri*'s side blew out across the water. Smoke curled up in the air.

And then I saw it.

The machines the *Hariri*s had out in the desert, the ones that glinted metal and glass: they had them on the boat, too. That glint of light flashing off the surface of the sea – it'd been their machines.

"What in hell?" asked Marjani.

"Oh no," I said, my body shaking.

Naji glanced up, his eyes bright and empty-looking.

One of the machines unfolded itself from the deck of the *Hariri*, looking like some golden insect. With a long, whining shriek, it leapt up into the air, metal wings beating into a blur, heading straight for the deck of the *Nadir*. The men screamed and scattered.

Naji said something in his language.

The machine froze in mid-flight, its wings stilled. For a second, it hung there, shining like a piece of jewelry.

Then it crashed down into the sea, water sloshing in a great wave over the side of the boat.

Silence and smoke.

"Keep firing!" Marjani shouted.

The men listened to her. Cannon fire erupted across the side of the *Hariri*.

More machines lifted up off her deck. They were like wasps, like spiders, like stinging scorpions. Only all of them could fly, and all of them were big enough to hold a pair of grown men.

"What are those things?" Marjani yelled.

"Metallurgy." Naji's voice shook.

The machines buzzed through the air. Ten of them. Fifteen.

"We can't turn the cannons up," I said.

"Fire!" Marjani shouted out to the crew. "Use your pistols!"

Shot blasts erupted all over the deck. The machines moved forward.

Naji chanted. One of the machines sputtered and crashed into the water. Another. Another. But his voice was fading, turning scratchy and old-sounding. They were closer, closer – one of them began to spiral out, and it spun and spun and then slammed into the side of the *Nadir*. The whole boat tilted.

Naji collapsed across the deck.

I leapt off the manticore and knelt beside him. His breath came out raspy and weak. I yanked the mask away from his face and he sucked in air. His skin was pale, his brow lined with sweat. But he sat up.

"I couldn't breathe," he said softly.

"Don't wear your mask." And I flung it aside, just as the machines landed across our deck.

"Get on the manticore." He shoved me away and stood up, his movements shaking but strong. I clambered onto the manticore's back.

"I can't eat these creatures," she said to me, and for a minute I thought she sounded scared.

"You'll eat what's inside of 'em," I said.

The largest of the machines groaned and split open. Captain and Mistress Hariri sat beneath the shield, both of them dressed for battle and armed with a trio of pistols each.

"We're here for Ananna of the *Tanarau*," said Mistress Hariri, her voice like death. "She murdered our son. By the rules of the Confederation, you must hand her over."

The men lined up along the edge of the boat, pistols pointed at the *Hariri*s. Half of them were Confederation, and they knew better than to fire.

"We aren't flying Confederation colors," Marjani said. "We don't have to adhere to Confederation rules."

"Where's the captain?" asked Captain Hariri. "Captain Namir yi Nadir? Where is he?"

Marjani didn't answer. She just pulled out her pistol and cocked it back.

"Here." Naji stepped forward.

Captain Hariri looked at him for a long time.

"You're not a pirate," he said. "You're a–"

Then Naji spoke in his language, and light erupted out from the lines of his tattoos and the splatters of his blood on the ship's wood, and it arced across the ship and slammed into Captain Hariri's machine. The machine shot across the deck.

Both of the Hariris jumped out of the way, nimble as cats, and everything started again.

The rest of the machines roared open. *Hariri* crewmen poured out. That knocked our own crew out of their stun, and they launched forward in melee, pistols blasting and swords ringing.

"Ongraygeeomryn!" I shouted, pulling out my sword. "Now!"

"Ananna, no!"

But I wasn't listening to Naji. We flew off the stern deck, the manticore trumpeting loud and perfect. She landed square on the chest of some poor Hariri clansman and his blood spilled across the deck. I caught sight of Captain Hariri in the blur of pistol-smoke and fighting and got off one shot and missed. He disappeared behind one of the machines.

"Manticore, this way!"

She lifted her head and hissed. Nobody was coming anywhere close to us, which probably made Naji happy – if it weren't for the occasional bullet whizzing past my head, anyway. But I needed to get to Captain Hariri. It was the only way to end this.

"Come on!" I shouted. "Time to eat later!"

She leapt to her feet and then galloped across the deck. I swung my sword out against a *Hariri* crewman and tried to find Captain Hariri in all the confusion.

"The machines!" I shouted, pointing with my sword. The manticore hissed again, but she slunk up to them, her ears pressed flat against her head. I felt like I was in the chiming forest again, all that sunlight bouncing off the spindly metal legs.

We crept slowly, cautiously.

A shot fired off and zipped past my head. I crouched down and buried my face in the manticore's mane while she reared around and sent a pair of spines zinging through the air. I heard a man scream.

The manticore skulked forward, the muscles in her back and shoulders tensed and hard. She sniffed at the ground.

For a moment, the smoke cleared, and there was Captain Hariri, reloading his pistol.

I yanked out my second pistol, took aim–

A blast of Naji's magic echoed across the boat, bright blue and smelling of spider mint. Everything tilted. My head spun. The manticore snarled and leapt out of the way of the falling machines; Captain Hariri disappeared, knocked out by the force of Naji's blow.

Magic showered over the side of the boat, staining the water that icy Naji-blue. The *Hariri* smoked and glowed – she had moved closer to us, her cannons firing.

Another blast of magic.

This one knocked me off the manticore, and I slid across the deck, my body smearing with salt water and blood. All over the ship, men were fighting best they could in the daze of magic, swords swinging sloppy and wide. I caught sight of Jeric yi Niru drawing his blade across the stomach of a *Hariri* crewman. When the crewman fell, Jeric dragged me to my feet.

"First mate," he said. "Your captain is dying."

"What?" I took him to mean Marjani, but when I turned to the stern deck she was still spinning the wheel one-handed, her pistol cocked and ready in the other. Not dying at all.

"No," he said. "The fake captain."

"Naji!" I pulled away from him and raced across the deck. I could hear the manticore behind me, the soft snapping squelch of her jaws on some crewman's neck. Men's screams. I didn't look back.

Naji was sprawled out on the bow, his arms soaked with blood, his face drawn, his skin almost blue. I knelt beside him, and he turned toward me. Pressed one hand against my face. His blood was hot and sticky against my skin.

"I can't do it anymore," he said, his voice like broken glass. "I'm sorry."

"Did someone hurt you?" I felt around for a wound. "Where are you hurt? I can fix it–"

"Ananna, you don't understand... I need blood..."

The magic. Nobody had cut him or shot him, it was the magic.

"Mine," I said. "You can have mine."

He shook his head, but I didn't listen to him earlier and I wasn't listening to him now. I drew the tip of my sword down my arm. The sting of it took my breath away.

"Here," I said, and there were tears in my eyes and I hoped he'd think it was from the cannon smoke. "What should I do with it?"

"No..." He closed his eyes. "I don't want... Not from you... It'll connect us... It's invasive..."

"What are you talking about? We're connected already! We need to kill Captain Hariri. His wife too. I can't find 'em in all this! Can you do it?"

He didn't answer.

"Can you track 'em? Naji! You have to pull 'em out! I'll kill 'em, alright? But it's the only way they'll stop."

The boat lurched. Marjani screamed orders from the helm, but my head was spinning from the blood seeping out of my arm. "Naji!" I said.

He took hold of my bleeding arm. I braced myself against the deck as the boat tilted farther. Men were scrambling up in the riggings, trying to get her righted.

"Hurry!"

He ran his hand up my arm, blood oozing between his fingers. I ground my teeth together so I wouldn't scream at the pain of it. He began to chant, and his words rolled over me and then I didn't feel the pain no more.

His voice strengthened. He gripped tight on my wrist. My blood rolled in rivers down the length of my arm. He sat up. The shadows underneath the machines started to wriggle and squirm, and men were screaming and moaning.

He leaned close to me, and put his mouth on my ear. "I won't make you kill them," he whispered. "I know it hurts you."

It stunned me, that sudden burst of kindness, that suggestion that he might care for me, might care for my well-being.

The fact that he knew it hurt me, when I hurt people.

"Thank you," I murmured.

He stood up. The glow in his eyes brightened, and for a second I felt this weird tingle in the arm I'd cut for him, this hum of magic rippling across my skin. And then the tingle was everywhere, sparking up the air, the way it gets before a lightning storm in the desert. Naji was close to me, his body and his mind both, and I felt a surge of warmth from him. A feeling of things being *right*. And then I got the sense of all these hearts beating, every heart on that boat, the blood and the life of every crewman who hadn't gotten tossed down to the deep.

I wondered if this was how Naji felt all the time.

He spoke. His voice echoed inside my head, that secret rose-petal language, like I was hearing his thoughts and his words both. A connection.

The shadows billowed up like smoke, thick enough to rip the Hariri machines into shreds, into long glinting metal ribbons. Men flung themselves against the side of the boat. The *Hariri* fired off another volley of cannons.

And then in all that confusion, all those glints of metal, all that smoke, all that splintered wood, I knew where Captain and Mistress Hariri were.

I didn't see them.

I just knew.

They were on the bow of the ship, cutting their way through *Nadir* crewman.

I jumped to my feet. Naji grabbed my arm, turned his glowing eyes toward me.

"I know where they are," I said.

"I know." He blinked and I felt a surge of worry. "Ananna, I can protect you."

"You don't have to protect me!" And I wrenched my arm free, despite the strength of his magic – the strength my blood had given him. I leapt off the helm and followed the trail of the shadows, listening to the beating of those two hearts that wanted me dead.

"Girl-human!" The manticore galloped up behind me. I glanced at her over my shoulder. Her entire face was covered in blood. Her teeth shone like knives.

"You smell like Jadorr'a," she said. "But I will not eat you." She dipped her shoulder down. With Naji's magic inside me, I swung myself onto her back.

"To the bow!" I wound my fingers in her mane and pressed myself low against her back. We pressed on together, the shadows sliding over us like water.

I still couldn't see the Hariris, but they were there, I *knew* it, I could feel the proximity–

Off in the distance, a *pop*.

Warmth spread across my belly. Pain. Warmth and pain. I looked down.

Blood.

The smell of smoke and metal.

Someone was laughing. A woman. Shrill and mean. I recognized it–

"Girl-human! You are body-hurt!"

"She shot me," I said, cause I couldn't believe it.

"Yes, Ananna of the *Tanarau*," said Captain Hariri. He lifted up his pistol, pointed it at me. The barrel loomed huge and dark. "She shot you."

Lightning arced across the boat.

The Hariris both crumpled like rag dolls.

I blinked.

"Lightning doesn't move sideways," I said. The world was spinning round and round. The pain in my stomach was dazzling.

I wasn't gonna scream. I wasn't gonna cry.

And then I heard a voice like roses and darkness, and I smelled mint and medicine, and strong sure hands wrapped round my chest, and I was tumbling, tumbling, tumbling into the warm soft sea, but I was safe. That I knew.

I was safe. I was protected.

CHAPTER EIGHT

I woke up in a room made of light.

I blinked and rubbed at my eyes and slowly things started moving into focus: a big open window lined with gauzy fluttering curtains, the kind you use to keep bugs out. A table with a water pitcher. A bed, which I was in.

Otherwise, the room was empty.

When I tried to sit up pain exploded through the lower part of my stomach, and I fell back, gasping. I put my hands on my stomach. I wasn't wearing my Empire robe no more, but some kind of thin dress, and through the fabric I could feel the thick weight of a bandage.

I remembered the *pop* of Mistress Hariri's pistol, the swell of pain. Had the Hariris captured me? No, they were dead. Lightning had cut them down... No, that wasn't right, either–

"Hello?" I nudged myself up on one shoulder. That didn't hurt too bad. "Anybody around?"

No answer but the wind rustling the curtains. It smelled of the desert.

I lay back down. Stared up at the ceiling. It looked kinda like the clay they used in Lisirran houses, only it was red-orange, like a sunset.

Footsteps bounced off the walls.

"Hello?" I tried to sit up again, grinding my teeth against the pain.

"Ananna? What are you...? No, lie back down." Naji darted up next to the bed and pressed me gently against the soft downy pillows. "You shouldn't move yet."

He wasn't covering his face, and in the room's bright sunlight the twists of his scars made him look concerned.

"Where am I?"

"The Island of the Sun." Naji straightened up and walked over to the table, covered with scraps of parchment with brownish-red writing and vials of dried plants. He set something on it – another vial. "You woke up earlier than I was expecting. That's good."

"Did I die?" I asked. I couldn't remember nothing about what happened after the battle. How far had we been from the island when the Hariris struck? Not far: Jeric yi Niru had shot down seabirds...

"No." Naji sprinkled some of the plants onto one of the scraps of parchment and folded it into a package, the ends tucked inside themselves. "You came close, very close, but... I pulled you back."

He slipped the paper package underneath my pillows.

"With magic?" I hesitated. "Blood magic?"

"Yes." He sat down on the bed beside me, leaned up against the wall. "Medicine wouldn't have saved you."

"Oh." I paused. "Did it... did it hurt you bad? When I... when she shot me?"

Naji turned to me. "Yes," he said, but his eyes were soft, like he hadn't minded. "And I worked to save you, and that made the pain go away."

"I'm sorry."

He looked at me long and hard. "Don't apologize."

Then he brushed his hand over my forehead, pushing the hair out of my eyes. His touch startled me, the cool dry skin of his palm.

"Rest," he said. "I'll be back to check on you."

"Wait," I said. He stopped. "How long we been here?"

"We sailed in yesterday evening." His face hardened. "It seems your manticore is the daughter of the island's pride leader, so our plan for a quick getaway would be distressingly rude. They want to give us a feast when you're better."

My expression must have told him something, cause he said, "They swore they will not force us to engage in cannibalism. Still, most of the crew have opted to sleep on the boat."

I kinda smiled at that. No wonder the manticore had been so demanding of me. Wasn't a manticore thing, it was a *royalty* thing. Well.

"When you sleep," Naji said, "the dreaming will help you heal faster."

"Oh." I frowned. "I didn't think blood magic could save people–"

"Blood magic can do whatever I will it to do."

I didn't say anything to that, and Naji gave me a nod. I expected him to leave, but instead he walked over next to the window and pushed the curtains aside and looked out. I watched him for a little while, as the curtains fluttered around him like butterflies. The wind blowing in was hot and dry and smelled of clay. It made me sleepy. Or maybe it was the spells he cast, the little packet of dried herbs under my pillow.

It didn't take long before my eyes refused to stay open, and I curled up on top of the blankets and the dreams came in like the wind.

They were dark and strange, those dreams, and I was back in that black-glass desert, only this time I wasn't scared. Nobody was searching for me. I just wandered across the desert, the glass smooth and strangely cool beneath my bare feet. I wore that same dress I'd had on when Naji and me crossed the desert together after I saved him, on our way to the canyon that was supposed to hold a cure to his curse. Sometimes I thought I saw creatures made out of ink and shadow. I'd turn to look at 'em and they'd dart out of my line of sight, but they left dark streaky trails in their wake, and when I touched them my fingers came back sticky with blood.

When I woke up again it was dark outside and my stomach didn't hurt no more. Torches flickered pale gold against the walls. Naji was gone.

This time I was able to sit up, but it exhausted me, and I leaned against the wall and took deep gulping breaths while my heart pounded against my chest. The bedside table was still littered with Naji's parchments. I picked one up. It was in his language, and I didn't recognize the alphabet, couldn't match the letters to the sounds.

And yet I could hear his voice inside my head, gruff and throaty, chanting the song that had saved me. I couldn't read the parchments, but I could understand it.

Weird.

"Ananna?"

It wasn't him, it was Marjani. I dropped the scraps of parchment, and they fluttered across the top of my bed like flower petals.

"Naji said you had woken up–"

"Yeah." I gathered up the parchment, my movements slow and heavy like I was underwater. "He told me there's gonna be a feast."

"Don't remind me." Marjani rolled her eyes. "They've already begun preparations. I've had to reassure them about fifty times that we don't mind eating 'servant food'."

I grinned.

We sat in silence for a little while, the shadows sliding across the floor. I thought about the shadows in my dream, the shadows that had led me to the Hariris.

"How's the boat?" I asked.

"Got us here." Marjani sighed. "Still working on repairs, although it shouldn't be much longer. A day or so." She paused. "Jig's up on Captain Namir yi Nadir, by the way. Crew figured it out during the battle. Good news is they don't seem to mind."

"So Jeric yi Niru doesn't have nothing on us no more."

"I suppose that's true. He's still an eavesdropper. Untrustworthy." She sighed. "Only lost about ten men, all told. A few more were injured. I'm going to give them a higher cut for it. Next time we do some honest pirating, anyway."

"So you're the captain now?"

"That's what they've been calling me." She smiled at me, a real smile. "Naji makes them nervous now that they know about his magic, although I think they'll tolerate him being onboard on account of him blasting those damned metal bugs out of the sky."

She looked at me, then, and I knew she was looking for the story, about the Hariris and who I really was. Marjani knew subtlety. I'd warrant she'd won the crewmen over long before the battle – why else would they've listened to her when the Hariris attacked?

She'd won me over a long time ago, too.

So I finally told her everything. I told her about running away from Tarrin of the *Hariri*, and I told her how Naji was supposed to kill me, and that I saved his life and that in turn saved me – she already knew most of that already, just none of the details. And I told her about how I killed Tarrin in the desert.

And the whole time she kept her eyes on me, not moving or speaking, just watching me and listening.

When I finished, I expected her to do something, to yell at me for putting the *Nadir* in danger, or for not trusting her enough with the truth. But all she did was nod.

"I'm glad you told me." She stood up. "You still want to be my first mate?"

"You ain't pissed?"

"Don't be ridiculous. We all have secrets. Mine probably won't attack us with a swarm of flying machines, but..." She shrugged. "It's over now, right?"

"It's over." I pressed my head back against the wall and closed my eyes. "The Hariri clan'll disband now. Anybody comes after us for the captain's death, I got the right to go after him for revenge, or to send someone after him – doubt anyone'll bother."

Marjani looked amused. "I never understood the Confederation rules for revenge."

"Trust me, ain't no one in the Confederation understands 'em neither."

She laughed. Folded her arms over her chest. "I should go. Naji said sleep would help you get better – so, please, sleep for as long as it takes. I don't want to stay on this island much longer."

"Sure thing." I smiled. "Captain."

The manticores scheduled the feast for two days after I got up and walked around the manticores' palace garden. Naji took me down there, one hand pressed against my back as he led me out of the bare servants' quarters and across the island's dry red sands. As we walked, I kept thinking I heard him talking to me. But when I asked him what he wanted, he only shook his head and told me he hadn't said nothing.

"You're still in the process of recovering," he said stiffly. "Things will clear up for you soon enough."

As it turned out, the manticores' palace wasn't really a palace; it was big pile of red and yellow rocks surrounded on all sides by flowering vines and fruit trees and soft pale grasses. The human servants took care of the garden – I saw 'em working as I stumbled over the paths. My sunlit room was actually in the servants' quarters, which were a series of little clay shacks lining the edge of the garden. The manticore had explained to her father that sleeping inside was a human preference, and then he explained to me that these shacks were the best they had. I didn't mind. Better than sleeping in the grass.

Naji led me into the shade of a lemon tree and helped me sit down. The palace of rocks loomed up huge and tall against the cloudless blue sky.

"That ain't a palace," I said.

"Manticores don't live inside." Naji sat down beside me. "They think it's barbaric."

"How do you know that?"

"I found myself trapped in conversation with Ongraygeeomryn's father after we landed."

I looked out over the garden. The plants swayed in the hot desert wind. One of the servant girls walked alongside a row of ginger flowers, spilling water over each one from a bucket that came up almost to her knees.

I didn't see any servant boys.

"Do they all want to eat you as badly as she does?"

"Oh yes." He blinked. "For the first time, I find myself *grateful* for the curse."

I didn't know if it was alright to laugh, so I just kinda squinted at him and nodded. He had covered his face to walk me out to the gardens. I wanted to tell him he didn't need to do that, that he was handsome even with the scars, that the scars made him more beautiful than any untrustworthy pretty boy lurking in some Empire palace.

I didn't, though, cause I knew if I did he would leave. And he only saved my life cause of his curse, but out there in the garden, the scent of jasmine heavy on the air, it was easy to pretend otherwise.

For those two days before the feast, Naji wouldn't let me go any farther than the gardens – he said I still wasn't strong enough – and every day at sunrise and sunset he came into my room and slipped another packet of blood-spells and dried herbs underneath my pillow. Sometimes he sang this song in his dead-rose language and I'd fall asleep and dream of the black-glass desert and a dry wind full of starlight that would blow me across the landscape and cradle me gentle as a lover.

Sometimes, even when I was alone, I'd hear him singing. I'd hear him *thinking*. I figured it must be leftover from the magic.

The manticore came to visit me too. The first time she came trotting up to us while Naji led me through a maze of thorny red flowers in the garden.

"You lead her well, *Jadorr'a*," she said. "You've only taken one wrong turn so far. You'll arrive at the maze's center soon."

Naji gave her this annoyed stare, and I knew, suddenly and without explanation, that his magic showed him the way through the maze, and he hadn't taken a wrong turn at all.

"Girl-human," she said to me. "I am glad to see you have not died."

"Yeah, me too."

The manticore looked different now that she was home. Her mane shone like copper, and her coat was smooth and silky. Her eyes were ringed in red powder that made her look feral and haunted all at the same time.

"The servant-humans have promised you many delicious items for the feast," she said. "Fruit and fish and honey." She wrinkled her nose when she spoke.

"My father is most grateful that you have returned me," she went on. "Even though you could not bring us the Jadorr'a uncursed–"

Naji sighed.

"Still, he would like to meet with you, to thank you personally, and to offer you a boon."

"She isn't well enough," Naji said.

The manticore looked at me with concern. "But you are walking through our gardens!"

"A walk through the gardens isn't quite the same thing as a meeting with the pride leader." Naji stepped in front of me like he was protecting me, even though I wasn't in danger from the manticore.

She didn't seem to notice, though, just tossed back her mane and pawed at the ground. "At the feast, then. He is anxious to meet with you."

"At the feast." I nodded. "Looking forward to it." I pushed Naji aside. He stayed close, though. He'd been staying close a lot lately. Closer even than when we'd been stranded on the Isles of the Sky and had to stay close cause we were the only two humans around other than Eirnin.

"The feast!" the manticore cried, chiming with delight.

••••

The night of the feast, Marjani and Naji and me all walked from the servants' quarters to the garden together, along with the braver crewmen – including Jeric yi Niru, who Marjani didn't want leaving on the newly repaired boat alone. The manticores' servants brought us clean clothes, soft cotton robes dyed the color of pomegranates and saffron, and they gave us steam-baths and lined our eyes with red powder, the way the manticores did.

Naji had his face wrapped up in a scarf.

I wondered if he really thought the manticores cared about his scars.

The feast was in the garden, with long low tables set up beneath the fruit trees. We sat down in the grass, lining up on one side of the table, and waited.

"The pride will join you soon," said one of the servants, who tilted her head when she spoke and never looked any of us in the eye.

The sun was just starting to set, and the light in the garden was purple and gold and turned everything into shadow. A trio of servants began to strum harps and sing in a language I didn't recognize, and soft pale magic-cast lanterns blinked on one by one up among the trees.

"Why're they making us wait?" I asked Marjani.

Marjani shook her head. "I don't trust manticores."

"They won't do anything," Naji said. He leaned forward on the table, drumming his fingers against the wood. "As many deals as Ananna has made with Ongraygeeomryn, there's no way they'd risk killing her now."

"What? Why?"

"Their elaborate system of boons and favors." Naji looked at me. "You're lucky," he said.

I knew he wanted to say more, but a loud, reverberating trumpet cut through the thick air.

All the servants scrambled to line up behind us.

The music twinkled on in the background.

The manticores marched into the garden.

It was the entire pride, I guess, cause there were about fifteen manticores in all. They walked one after another in a long procession. Ongraygeeomryn came in toward the end, flanked by an older lady-manticore and man-manticore. They sat at the center of the table, right across from me.

The man-manticore reared back his head and trumpeted, and this was the loudest trumpet I'd ever heard. It seemed to echo out for miles.

The music stopped playing.

"Girl-human," he said, turning his golden eyes to me. "Do you have a name?"

The silence in the garden was so thick I thought I might choke on it. All the manticores stared at me expectantly.

"Yes," I said. "Your Grace."

"Don't call me that. I am not a human king." He leaned forward, sniffed the air. "What is your name?"

I glanced at Naji. Should you tell a manticore your name or not? He must've known what I was thinking, cause he kinda nodded at me like it was alright.

"Ananna of the *Nadir*."

Ongraygeeomryn smiled at me.

"Ananna," the manticore leader said. "I will gift you

a boon in exchange for rescuing my daughter from the foul Wizard Eirnin."

The other manticores trumpeted and flapped their wings and furled and unfurled their tails. I saw Marjani shrink down out of the corner of my eye, but nobody let loose any spines.

"You will receive the boon tonight, after the feast." He nodded at me. "It is rude to divulge the nature of the boon in public, but Ongraygeeomryn told me what you would like most in the world, and I am confident in her judgment."

That got my suspicions up a bit, cause much as I liked the manticore I wasn't convinced she knew what I wanted most in the world. Mostly cause I didn't know what I wanted most in the world. I used to think it was being a pirate captain, but I wasn't so sure of that anymore.

Still, I knew better than to say something. When it comes to dealing with people who think of themselves as important, it's usually best to keep your mouth shut.

"You will find the boon most satisfying," she told me. "I am certain of it."

I nodded and plastered on a smile that I hoped came across as polite.

"Servant-humans!" bellowed the manticore leader. "Bring us food!"

The servants disappeared into the gardens and then reappeared with heavy stone platters laden with fruits and little savory pies and bottles of Empire wine. They set them down first, and I could see all the manticores trying to act like it didn't turn their stomachs.

Then the servants brought out more stone platters covered with slabs of raw meat, pink and glistening in the candlelight. I knew it wasn't sheep.

"We thought this would be more comfortable for you," Ongraygeeomryn said to me, nodding her head at the piles of meat.

"Yes," said her father. "Normally we catch them alive." Marjani and I glanced at each other.

"We appreciate your thoughtfulness," Marjani said, though her mouth twisted up when she spoke.

Naji didn't say nothing, just slipped his mask into his lap and picked up a lemon-salt fish.

I'd never been to a proper feast before, just the big drunken parties that pirates call feasts. Nobody got up and danced on the table, or groped any of the servant girls – even the crewmen we had with us seemed too terrified to do anything but pick at their food. The music playing in the background was soft and fancy. The conversation was polite and didn't say nothing of any substance. The only thing that made me realize I wasn't up in the palace with the Emperor was the way the manticores ate: they leaned forward and tore chunks of meat off with their teeth, and red juices streamed down their faces and tangled up in the manes.

After dinner, the servants came around with cloths and wiped the manticores' faces clean. One of 'em came at me with a cloth but I declined polite as I could. So did Marjani, though she sounded like a right proper lady – "I don't require your services tonight, thank you." The servant kind of smiled at her. Then she turned to Naji, his scars shadowed and deep in the dim light. He scowled at her until she shuffled away.

When all the platters of food had been cleared, all us human stared at the manticores like we expected something bad to happen. I didn't think they were going to eat us or nothing, but I was still a little concerned about the boon.

"We would be most honored if you would share a dessert wine with us," said the manticore leader. "Ahiial. It is a delicacy from the northern part of our island, and a very precious nectar indeed."

"What's it made of?" I asked. Somebody had to say it.

"It's derived from the pollen of the ahiiala flower," said Ongraygeeomryn. "The only plant we consume."

"The stories say it has magical properties," said a lady-manticore with pale white dappling on her coat.

Marjani and me both looked at Naji.

"It's fine," he said.

"Of course it's fine!" boomed the manticore leader. "Servant-humans, bring us the wine!" He smiled, and he only showed the points of his teeth. "You will not be able to drink any of that human swill after tasting ahiial."

Naji shrugged, and I got the sense that he'd had it before.

The servants trotted up to the table, half of 'em holding shallow porcelain bowls and the other half holding rough-hewn stone goblets. They lined 'em up on the table. Then another row of servants marched out, this time carting huge carved pitchers. They made their way around the table, slowly pouring a bit of ahiial for each guest.

The ahiial was pale gold, the color of morning sunlight and a manticore's fur. It smelled sweet, like honey, like a man's perfume.

We all waited till everybody's cup or bowl had been filled. Then the manticore leader lifted one paw.

"To Ananna of the *Nadir*," he said. "Who saved my eldest daughter, the heir to my pride. I am indebted to you."

Naji squirmed beside me. I remembered what he'd said to me back on the Isles of the Sky – you made a deal with a manticore? And the way he said it, too, like I'd just confessed to killing my own mother. I could just about see him remembering it himself.

Well, too late now.

The manticore leader bowed his head and lapped at his wine. Even Marjani, who knew as well as I did how rude it was, hesitated.

But I also knew poison wasn't how a manticore killed – not poison in a glass of wine. If they wanted us dead they would have shot us full of spines or launched across their table with their mouths wide open, showing us all three rows of teeth. So I picked up my glass and drank.

It was sweet, sweeter than honey, and the taste of it filled my mouth up with flowers.

When I didn't keel over dead, or jump up, bewitched, and start clearing away the table like a servant, the rest of the crew followed suit. Jeric yi Niru knocked it back like a shot of rum. Marjani sipped it like a lady in a palace. Naji finished his off in a trio of gulps.

"What do you think?" the manticore leader asked me.

"Delicious," I said. And stronger than a barrel of sailor's rotgut. The whole garden was filled with light. All the flowers were glowing. Overhead, the stars left bright trails across the black sky. I laughed, suddenly full up with mirth, the way it happens when I get drunk under good circumstances, with a boat full of friends and the ocean stretching out empty and vast before us.

"Wonderful," the manticore leader said. He nodded his head and the music struck up, some bawdy song I recognized from whenever Papa's crew made port. "Servant-humans!" he called out. "Bring us more ahiial!"

They did, and we drank.

CHAPTER NINE

I sprawled out on my bed, music still drifting in from the garden through my open window. The manticores had proceeded back into their palace of rocks, and the rest of the crew had come crawling off the boat to flirt with the servants and drink ahiial and rum, which was when I decided to slink back to my room. My injury left me too tired to deal with a true pirates' feast.

Every now and then laughter exploded into the nighttime, drowning out the music. Men's laughter, women's laughter. The ahiial left me so happy I didn't even feel left out.

Somebody knocked on my door.

"Who is it?" But I felt a wriggle in the back of my brain, and I knew–

"Naji."

I sat up. "Ain't locked or nothing."

Naji pushed the door open. He had his mask on but his hair was all tousled from the wind. He hadn't been dancing after the feast, I remembered. Just sat on the sides and watched.

"You need to change the... the spell that was making me better?"

He shook his head and stepped inside. Came up right close to me, close enough that I could smell him: honey and medicine. He kept his eyes on me.

It was weird, and it confused me, but my heart pounded loud and fast from the way he looked at me.

Like I was Leila. The river witch. His old lover.

"Can I ask you a question?" he said.

I was too nervous to speak. I shrugged.

He took off his mask, yanking it hard away from his face. He let it drop to the floor.

"Do you remember when you told me I wasn't ugly?"

I stared at him. I couldn't get past the light in his eyes.

"You don't, do you?"

"Of course I do," I said, and my voice came out real small.

"Did you mean it?"

"That I don't think you're ugly?"

He nodded.

I couldn't think straight. All I knew was my heart slamming against my chest and his eyes drinking me up like ahiial. How many times had I thought about the answer to this question? How many nights had I spent trying to figure out the exact way to tell him what I thought of him, what I thought of his face and his hair and his body?

Too many to count.

"Of course," I said, voice hardly a whisper again. I swallowed. "I think... I think you're beautiful."

His face didn't move. "I thought you don't trust beautiful people."

"Not beautiful like that. I mean... I don't ever want to stop looking at you."

The funny thing is that I couldn't actually look at his face while I said that cause I was so embarrassed, and so I looked at his throat instead, at the little triangle of skin poking up out of his shirt. He'd taken off the pirate coat.

For a minute I wondered why the hell he was asking me this anyway.

And then he was kissing me.

I ain't kissed many boys before, but Naji knew what he was doing better than any of 'em. He put his hands on the side of my face and pressed himself close to me and the whole time it was like he and I were the only people in the world. My hands kept crawling over his chest and shoulders, trying to memorize the lines of his body, and I was dizzy, but in a good way, the way you get when you swing through the ropes on a clear sunny day. That was what kissing Naji was like: the best day at sea, warm sunlight and cool breeze. Happiness.

Kissing Naji was happiness.

When he pulled away from me he smoothed my hair off of my forehead. I was too stunned to do anything but stare at him.

"Is this alright?" he asked.

"Uh. Yeah." I frowned. He kissed me again, and I worked up the nerve to press my hands against his hips.

He wrapped his arms around my waist and pulled me close, and the smell of him was everywhere, and I swear I could feel his blood pulsing through his veins. The closeness of his body was so distracting, so wonderful, that I forgot to be nervous.

He lay me down on the bed, still kissing me, and my thoughts were a jumble of confusion and excitement and desire – his desire and my desire both, like two pieces of silk braiding together. I couldn't believe this was happening, couldn't believe he was gazing at me like he wanted me.

"Why are you doing this?" It came out wrong, kinda accusatory. He stopped.

"You said it was alright," he said.

Oh, now you've gone and messed everything up, I thought.

"It is." I reached out, tentative, and cupped the scarred side of his face in my hand. He jerked at my touch, but didn't pull away, and for a moment he looked as vulnerable as I felt. "I mean, I just don't understand... why now..."

He traced the line of my profile, one finger running over my forehead and my nose and finally my lips.

"I should have done it sooner," he said. "I should have done it on the Isles of the Sky." And he kissed me before I could say anything more. I got lost in it, the kissing. It went on for a long time. My lips thrummed, and my body was hot and distracted.

After a while, he pulled away, just a little, and we lay in silence, looking at each other.

I touched his scar, the skin rough and slick at the same time. He flinched away. I dropped my hand.

"I'm sorry," I said.

"No," he said. "No, I just... no one's ever... before."

"Oh."

Another long silence, and then I lifted my hand and touched him again. This time he only blinked.

"I like it," I said.

He didn't answer. His face was so serious, like always. Except for his eyes, which were gentle right now. Almost kind.

"Why don't you ever smile?"

"What?"

I traced a line from the unscarred skin of his brow down across the folds in his flesh to his chin. "I've never seen you smile."

"You don't want to."

"You don't know that."

"Yes, I do."

He pushed away from me. A coldness settled over me: he was going to leave.

"Wait," I said. "I'm sorry. I just... Ain't you happy right now?"

"You don't want to see me smile."

"But I do. Ever since..." There was no point. His eyes had gone cold and stony again. I'd ruined everything.

And then something dislodged itself in my brain.

I thought about him showing up at my room for no reason.

I thought about the kissing.

And a realization lit up bright and blazing as the sun.

"Oh," I said. "Oh, Kaol. You ain't happy at all."

He looked at me, pained, like he wanted to protest. But he didn't.

"This isn't you," I said, and the words turned to panic in my throat. "This isn't... you wouldn't on your... the boon."

Naji looked stricken. Confused. He didn't deny anything.

I felt like I was spitting out poison. I shoved myself off the bed. Heat rose up hot and angry in my chest. "It's the boon!" I shouted. "From the manticores!"

Kaol, why hadn't I stopped him when he first came in? Why hadn't I *known*?

"Ananna, no, you don't understand." His words shook. "The magic, it's–"

"Shut up!" I drew my robe tight over my body – it had slipped off my shoulders before. "I can't believe... I'm so sorry... I actually thought you wanted me–"

"I do." Naji rubbed his head. He still looked confused. "I do want you–"

"Get out!" Part of me didn't mean it. Part of me looked at Naji and thought about how he'd cared for me after I was shot, how he walked me around the gardens and stayed close to me even though I wasn't in any danger. But I couldn't run the risk of letting him hurt me. Not again.

"Get out of my room!" I shouted.

Naji stumbled out of the bed. He seemed drunk. The ahiial, I thought. They stuck something in his wine.

What you want most in the world. The manticore must've thought it was Naji.

"This isn't how I wanted things to happen," Naji said, still watching me with that pained, befuddled expression.

"It ain't how I wanted 'em to happen neither!" I yanked my sword out from its hiding place under the bed and brandished it at him. I couldn't decide if I was angry at him or at the manticores or at myself. "So get out now."

He stared at the sword and looked sad. "I do want you," he said.

Blood rushed in my ears. I remembered us standing in the sunlight of the garden, his hand on my arm, the scent of flowers heavy on the wind. I remember him looking at me, flush with happiness.

Naji turned and walked out the door.

I couldn't sleep. The bed smelled like Naji.

I left my room and followed the hallway through the servants' quarters, one hand trailing along the powdery walls, dust kicking up behind my feet. The quarters were silent and still, but the air was stuffy out in the hallways. No windows. So I went outside and sat down underneath a palm tree, leaning up against the trunk.

The desert swirled around me, cold and sad with the night-time.

I wasn't going to cry, and I wasn't going to remember.

"What are you doing awake?"

It was Marjani. She came walking from the direction of the desert, her robes stained with dirt at the hem.

"Where the hell were you?"

"Thinking." She folded her arms in front of her chest. "You look like you had too much ahiial."

"I left when you did," I muttered.

"I know." She sat down beside me. "What's wrong?"

"Nothing."

She folded her legs up against her chest and tucked her chin on her knees. "You got that boon yet?"

Kaol, she had to ask that, didn't she? I spat in the dirt.

"I'll take that as a no."

"Take it as a yes." I glared off into the darkness. "And I don't want to talk about it so don't ask."

Marjani blinked at me and then lay her cheek against the top of her knees. We sat in the dusty quiet until I couldn't stand the sound of silence no more.

"When we leaving?" I asked.

Marjani lifted her head. "Tomorrow, I imagine. Later, though. After the crew've all slept off their hangovers."

"We got a course laid out yet?"

Marjani hesitated. I peered at her, wondering what she was keeping from me. The mystery kept my mind off other things.

"We aren't going to Lisirra," she finally said.

"What? Why?" I dropped my head against the palm tree. "Another damn delay? Marjani, you've no idea how much I want to get rid of Naj... of the curse."

Marjani gave me a weird look, but all she said was, "We're going to Jokja. I know of starstones there."

"You didn't think that might've been important to mention *before*?" But then I remembered seeing that brooch stuck in the map at Arkuz. It hadn't registered at the time, but– "Kaol, how long have you been planning this?"

"Since Bone Island." Marjani's expression didn't change. "I shouldn't have kept it from you, but – I had my reasons."

I glared at her.

"I wasn't sure I wanted to... go back."

Something about her voice softened me. "Is it dangerous for you?"

"Probably not," she said softly. "The king died three weeks ago. I received word when we were on Bone Island."

"The king? You got banished on orders of the *king*?"

"The king had a... personal connection to the affair."

It took me a few minutes to realize what she was saying. "You tried to court the Jokja *princess*?"

Marjani blinked at me a few times, eyelashes fluttering against her cheek. Then she laughed. "I never thought about it that way before."

"But it's what you did! Merciful sea, Marjani, that's a hell of–" I stopped. "Wait, so she's the queen now? Your, ah, your friend? That's how it works in Jokja, yeah?"

"Yes."

"She ever pick a suitor?"

Marjani shook her head.

"That's the real reason you want to go back, ain't it?"

Marjani looked away, out toward the desert. "Saida's

family has owned a pair of starstones for several generations. I remember hearing about them from the court storyteller. And the condition of the curse required a princess, if you recall..." She laughed, shook her head. "It's really quite perfect."

Almost as perfect as me falling in love with him cause of helping him find his cure.

I was back in that bedroom, Naji kissing me and touching me and *looking* at me all cause of some manticore sorcery–

"Ananna? Are you sure you're alright?"

I scowled.

Marjani tilted her head in a way that reminded me of Mama, bending over to lay cool rags on my forehead whenever I had a fever. "It's about the boon, isn't it?"

"I told you I don't want to talk about it!"

"It might help you, though." Marjani eyes were wide and clear. "It helped me. Talking."

I stared at her and didn't say nothing.

"What did they give you, Ananna?" And her voice was soft like she was speaking to a child.

I hesitated.

"Ananna–"

"Naji!" I shouted. "They gave me Naji."

That was met with silence, like I figured it would. Then Marjani said, "Not as a meal, I hope–"

"No." The palm tree was leaking sap, sticky and cool against the skin of my back.

"Then wha... Oh."

I didn't say nothing.

"How'd they–"

"I don't know!" I slammed my fist into the ground. "Poisoned him or something. Magic. I don't know."

"Manticores with love spells," Marjani said. "Well, that's awfully terrifying."

"It ain't funny."

"No," she said. "It's not." She leaned forward, put one hand on my knee. "Sweetness, how do you *know* it was the boon?"

"Because there ain't no way he could want me on his own!"

Marjani frowned.

"And I asked him to smile and he wouldn't do it, and then he acted all confused, like he was coming out of a fever. Plus I can just *tell*, after spending every damn day with him."

"It might've been the boon," Marjani said. "But that sort of magic always builds upon latent desires–"

"Don't try to make me feel better!"

"I'm not." Her hand dropped off my knee. I thought about the way he held me close as he kissed me. All that manticore trickery. "I knew someone back in Jokja who studied magic. She explained how those kind of spells work, and she said you can't make anything happen if it's not there to start with it."

I'd heard that too, but this was manticore magic, and it was probably different.

Marjani and I sat in silence for a few moments longer, and then she said, "Was he at least any good?"

I looked up at her. Then I burst into laughter, relieved that she was here, that I could talk to her about this.

"Why would you ask me that?" I asked, still laughing.

"I'm just curious." She grinned. "A Jadorr'a... I always thought they sublimated their desires. You know. Abstinence so that their magic can work. Closeness to death and all that."

"He had desires," I said carefully. "And his magic still works."

She laughed, her voice breaking against the wind.

"And we didn't... didn't do everything," I finally said. "I figured out what happened before... before we could..."

At that, Marjani stopped laughing. She made this sympathetic clucking sound and stuck her arm around my shoulder, pulled me in close for a hug.

"I mean I've done it before. But it was never a big deal. It was always just... *weird*. And with Naji I thought... thought it might be special."

"Oh, sweetness."

"The others were just... boys I met. You know. And I was kind of hoping that I'd get to see what the big deal was."

"The big deal?"

"You know." I didn't know how to put it into words. "How it's supposed to feel really good, and you just... fall away..."

"Oh, that." Marjani laughed again. "You know you don't need Naji for that. Or anyone."

I frowned.

"Did you really never... Alright, listen." And then she leaned close to me and told me about my body, stuff nobody'd never told me before, like I was supposed to just *know*. I felt like some stupid little kid, listening to her, my eyes getting big and wide, but she didn't sound like she thought any less of me for not knowing.

"That's what I mean," she said when she had finished. "I know you think you're in love with him—"

"I don't just think!" I said. "The curse—"

"Oh, never mind the curse. You can't let that dictate your life." She paused. "You don't need Naji to give you pleasure, and you don't need Naji to make you happy."

Right now, it didn't feel like that, but I knew better than to say something to her.

"You killed the son of Captain Hariri," Marjani said, "one of the richest pirates in the Confederation, before he could kill you. You helped win a *sea battle* against the Hariri clan. You struck a deal with a manticore and lived. Why do you care what Naji thinks of you?"

I didn't have an answer to that.

She stood up and dusted the sand off her robes. "When we set sail for Jokja tomorrow, I don't want to see a single misty-eyed glance his way, do you understand? You have a ship to navigate and a crew to help command, and I have neither the patience nor the inclination to put up with a heartsick child."

"I ain't a child."

"Then act like it." She held out one hand and I took it and she pulled me to my feet. "Do you want me to command it? Cause I will, if that'll get you to stop mooning over him."

That got a grin out of me. "No, Captain."

"Captain." She laughed. "We'll see how long they call me that." She put her hand on my back. "Come on," she said. "I'll walk you inside."

I let her. And for a minute, forgetting Naji didn't seem totally impossible no more.

CHAPTER TEN

The manticore came to see me before we set sail the next day. I was up on the boat, screwing around with the rigging cause half the crew was too hungover to be of much use. One of the manticore's servants crept across the deck, and I damn near tossed a pile of ropes on her.

"Mistress," she whispered, keeping her eyes downcast. "Ongraygeeomryn would like to speak with you."

I'd kinda been hoping I wouldn't have to see the manticore before we left, cause I was still sore on account of what happened with Naji, even though I was trying real hard not to moon over him.

But I figured this was my chance to prove that I was strong and that I didn't need him, the way I'd proved it last night, underneath the thin rough blankets of my bed.

"Tell her she can come talk to me when she's ready," I said.

The servant trembled. "Mistress," she said. "The manticore doesn't wish to come aboard…"

"Oh, hell." Figures. "She on the beach, at least?"

"Yes, mistress." The servant pointed a trembling finger off to the side. "My rowboat is in the water. She doesn't wish to be kept waiting–"

"Of course she doesn't."

I rowed me and the servant back in to the beach, and sure enough, the manticore was stretched out on a quilted silk blanket on the sand, another servant standing beside her with a palm leaf.

"Girl-human!" she cried. "Did you enjoy your boon last night?"

"You mean Naji?"

"Of course! Such an easy one to enchant. Almost no convincing necessary at all." She looked closer at me. "You did want him still, yes? He is your true love."

Never mind the curse, I thought. But I didn't say nothing. The manticore looked so damned pleased with herself.

"He was very…" I glanced off in the direction of the palace, hoping he wouldn't show up while I was talking. "Skillful."

The manticore looked puzzled for a moment. "Is that a good thing?"

"Uh, yeah."

She beamed at me. "That is excellent news! We do not describe our matings as skillful; I shall remember that."

Part of me wanted to ask her how she did it, if it really had been the ahiial, or some other manticore spell, maybe drawn out of the red desert sand. The sandcharmers in Lisirra could do that; I remembered from my trips to the night market. But what would be the point? It had happened, and not cause he wanted it.

Something else was bothering me, though.

"So he isn't... he isn't gonna keep bugging me after this?" I asked. "I've heard about love spells, and they always... persist, if you know what I mean."

"Persist?" The manticore frowned. "No, girl-human. Love does not persist! It is allotted to us once a life-cycle."

Oh. Like cats.

"The boon was only for one love-period," the manticore said. Her eyes dimmed. "I could ask my father to recast it in perpetuity–"

"No!" I held out my hands. "No, it's fine. Once was... once was enough."

"Spoken like a manticore!" She smiled big and bright at me. "I knew you were of a superior mind to the servants."

"I'm gonna miss you, Ongraygeeomryn," I said, stumbling over the last syllable.

And even with the boon, I still meant it.

"When the Jadorr'a is free of his curse, you are always welcome to return him to us. Remember, it would do him a great honor."

I just looked at her, although I thought about how easy it would be to cart him back here.

Easy, but not *fair* and wrong to boot. Dishonorable. Even if he had soul-hurt me a million and one ways.

No. I promised Marjani I wasn't gonna moon over him.

So I threw my arms around the manticore's neck and gave her a big hug. She nuzzled me back, her mane tickling my nose.

"You are always welcome on the Island of the Sun as a guest," she said. Her tongue swiped across my cheek and left my skin stinging. "With or without the Jadorr'a. You are always a friend."

Jokja was two weeks' sail from the Island of the Sun, through water bright and green as glass. It was an easy voyage. Once Naji found out where we were headed and why, he called down favorable winds every morning, and we had plenty of food. The best bit of all was that the crew listened to Marjani and called her captain. They didn't even grumble about chasing after starstones, since our chase was taking us into Jokja. Plenty of treasure there if you know where to look.

Some afternoons I'd sit up in the riggings, whenever there wasn't nothing else to do, and remember how I used to dream about captaining my own ship, knowing all along it was as impossible a dream as marrying into the Emperor's family or becoming as powerful a witch as Mama. But Marjani had managed it easy enough. Maybe I could too.

The only trouble with the voyage was Naji. I did my best to avoid him after what happened. He and Marjani slept in the captain's quarters, same as before, but I couldn't stand the thought of sharing the cabin with him. So I dragged a hammock down to the crew's quarters and cleared out a spot of my own in the corner. It was as awful as you'd expect, but better than having to spend my nights so close to Naji. Sometimes when I was close to him I felt like his thoughts were trying to crowd into mine. I hated it.

Daytime, it was easier to avoid him. He rarely came out on deck, despite everyone knowing he wasn't really Captain Nadir, and so I just made sure not to go to the captain's quarters. Marjani didn't like it, but she put up with it, sending word through one of the crew to come meet her at the helm whenever she needed me.

One afternoon I was sitting up in the rigging, watching the waves break up against the side of the boat. Wasn't much work to be done that day; the breeze was just enough to glide us along. The ropes cradled me as I leaned back and blinked up at the bright blue sky.

Everything was beautiful enough for me to forget my troubles.

And then I felt a tension in the ropes. A tug.

"Who is it?" I called out. My shift wasn't over till sunset, but it could've been one of Marjani's messengers. The ropes tugged again, and then I knew who it was. I couldn't say how. I just *knew*.

Naji climbed up onto the yard, his dark hair appearing first, and then his mask, and then his dark clothes. My heart started pounding, but I didn't say anything, just watched him climb. When he finished, he tottered back and forth, one hand clinging to the mast, watching me.

We sat in silence for a long time, the wind whistling around us.

I could hardly stand it. Everything up here in the rigging was bright – the white sails, the sunlight. And then Naji had to show up, a dark imperfection.

"You sure you should be out of your cabin?" I asked, hoping if I said something he'd go away. "Not really Captain Nadir's style, you know."

Naji shifted his weight, looking uneasy. "I'm not Captain Nadir." He took a deep breath. "Ananna, I'd like to speak with you."

I shrugged.

"About–" He edged forward on the mast, moving closer to me. I pulled myself in like I could disappear.

He stopped.

"We still have two more tasks to complete," he said. "And you clearly can't stand the thought of my company."

I looked away from him, out to sea.

"If this is what you want," he said, "to sleep down below, and to spend your days in the rigging – then it's fine, for our time on the ship." His voice wobbled when he said *fine*, like he didn't mean it. I looked at him, not sure what I expected to see. What I found was an intensity in his expression. A hopelessness, maybe.

Love spells build on existing desires.

"But when the time comes for us to disembark, we're going to have to be in close proximity again. You know I can't leave you alone in the city, especially not with the Mists still a factor." He leaned up against the mast and looked exhausted. "You're going to have to speak to me eventually. I'm sorry... sorry about what happened, and I want you to know that it isn't how it seemed–"

"Yeah," I snapped. "That was the whole problem."

"That isn't what I meant." Naji scowled. "If you don't want to make amends, fine. But I need to know you aren't going to run off the moment we make port. That will kill me. Do you understand? It will kill me."

My skin felt hot. Of course I knew it would kill him. That was the whole reason I'd agreed to help him in the first place, that night in Lisirra.

"I ain't gonna run off," I said. "And if you need me to travel with you, then I guess I'll have to do it. But we're on the boat right now, so it ain't much of a problem, is it?"

He stared at me with that same intensity as before, and I could feel him burning through me. I shook my head. "Is that all you want?"

He didn't move. The wind blew his hair across his forehead and dislodged his mask enough that a bit of scar peeked through, brownish-red in the sunlight.

"Well?" I asked.

"Yes." He turned away from me. "Yes, that's all I wanted."

The day we arrived in Arkuz was hot and bright, the sun an unblinking eye overhead. The docks were busy and close to full, but Marjani sweet-talked our way into a slot near the marketplace. I'd been to Jokja before, but always on Papa's boat, and we always sailed along the coasts to plunder, cause Jokja's got a lot of wealth, like all the Free Countries do. They have access to the mines in the jungle, which everyone from outside the Free Countries is afraid to travel through cause of all the magic there, plus some of the fastest and best-equipped ships on the seas. Jokja's navy is the one navy a pirate,

Confederate or otherwise, doesn't want to cross. The Empire navy might be bigger, but Jokja's got technology on their side. Fast ships and quick cannons. Papa was brave to sack the Jokja coast, all things considered.

Anyway, I'd never much had a chance to just wander around Arkuz the way I did in Lisirra, and I was looking forward to it, to seeing the acacia trees and tasting the chili-spiced fruit Marjani was always going on about.

After we'd docked, Marjani ordered the crew to take shifts watching the ship. As she was sorting 'em out, Jeric yi Niru slipped out from down below and grabbed me by the wrist. I had my knife out before he could say anything. Naji wasn't nowhere to be seen. I wondered if it hurt him and he was just respecting my wishes not to see him, or if Jeric yi Niru had no intention of harming me.

"Still chasing after fool's treasure?" he whispered.

"Let go." I wrenched my arm free of his grip, though I kept my knife leveled at his throat. "What do you want?"

"You really think you'll find the starstones here? Jokja's a land of science, not magic."

"Magic's everywhere, snakeheart. And what do you care anyway? You'll still get paid."

"With what? Starstones?" He laughed again. "Do you even know what they are, first mate?" He leered at me and I pressed the knife up against his skin, not enough to hurt him but enough to draw blood. He didn't even move. "Have you ever seen a starstone before?"

I didn't answer. Off in the distance, I could hear Marjani shouting at the crew, but I didn't dare take my eyes off Jeric yi Niru's face.

"I'll take that as a no." He laughed. "I have. They're awfully pretty. Like the stars fell from the sky. That's where the name comes from, did you know that? There's a story, an old Empire story. The nobles like to tell it. A man was pursuing a woman, the most beautiful woman in the Empire. She told him she would marry him, but only if he fit a starstone into a ring for her to wear. He spent years seeking one out, and when he finally found it, do you know what happened?"

I pressed my lips tight together and kept my knife at his throat and didn't say a word.

"He scooped it up in his bare hand and all the life fell out of him. The starstone sucked it right up."

"He died?" I hadn't meant to act like I cared, but it came out anyway.

"Yes, first mate. He died. His life flowed into the stone. That's what makes them so beautiful, you know. All that human life trapped in such a small space."

Find the princess's starstones, the Wizard Eirnin had said, and hold them, skin against stone.

Skin against stone.

I scowled, though I eased up on my knife a bit. I'd be damned if I let Jeric yi Niru know what I was thinking. "Sounds like Empire trash to me. Let me guess: the woman in the story was above his station and the man had to be punished for chasing after her? Half the Empire stories I've heard end like that."

"No," Jeric yi Niru said, "that isn't it at all."

"Jeric!" Marjani's voice cut across the ship. "Ananna! What the hell are you two doing?"

"We were talking, Captain," Jeric yi Niru said.

Marjani gave him the iciest glare I'd ever seen her take on. "Nothing's ever just talking with you, Jeric. If I hear one word of trouble from you, you can stay behind in Arkuz in your Empire robes when we make sail."

That shut him up. The people of the Free Countries don't take too kindly to Empire soldiers milling around their cities, even a turncoat like Jeric.

Once the boat was secure enough for Marjani's liking, she led me and Naji off the docks and through the hot bright streets of Arkuz. I kept a big space between me and Naji cause it seemed easier that way, but the whole time I was thinking about that stupid story Jeric yi Niru had told me. The task was impossible not because starstones are rare, but because touching 'em killed you.

I glanced at Naji out of the corner of my eye, but he stared straight ahead, his face covered with a desert-mask that drew more looks from the Jokjana than his scar would've. It marked him as Empire, since there are no deserts in the Jokja. I wondered if he'd ever heard that story. Probably. He'd been pretty quiet on the subject of the starstones. It was mostly Marjani plotting everything out, bringing us here to Jokja. And I knew that didn't have nothing to do with Naji's curse or rocks that can destroy you at the touch.

My thoughts churned around inside me like a sickness.

We walked on and on, far enough that I lost the scent of the ocean and caught instead the rainy damp scent of the jungle. Arkuz reminded me of Lisirra, cause it was big and sprawling and crowded with street vendors selling spiced fruit and charred meat wrapped up in banana leaves, and shops full of spices and jewels and fabric dyes and precious metals. And everybody looked like nobility, the women in these long fluttering dresses, their shoulders bare and their wrists heavy with bangles, and the men in tailored slim-cut cotton shirts.

I speak a bit of Jokjani, enough to understand the vendors trying to entice me to come buy something from them, but not enough to have any idea what Marjani said to the guard at the entrance to Azende Palace once we finally arrived. He used a different dialect than I was used to, and Marjani matched it. For a while it didn't look like he was gonna let us pass – he was courteous enough to Marjani but kept glancing at me like I was some street rat trying to make off with his palace-issued bronze dagger, and he was obviously trying his best to not even look at Naji.

Marjani was getting more and more annoyed, I could tell, her hands clenching into fists. The guard kept shaking his head and saying something in Jokjani that I knew wasn't *no* but sounded close. Then Marjani took a deep breath, closed her eyes, and told him her name. Her full name, her old name, not Marjani of the *Nadir* but Marjani Anaja-tu. A noble's name. I'd never heard her say it.

The guard's eyes widened.

"Do you recognize that name?" Marjani asked. Her voice trembled a little, and I tensed up my arm, ready to grab my sword if anyone made a grab for her.

The guard answered with something that sounded like another name, and this time it was Marjani's eyes that got wide.

"Really?" she asked. Then she straightened her shoulders and said something I couldn't catch. The guard responded. I got *you* and *palace* and something about time and nothing else. Marjani didn't look upset though, which was a good sign. Then she said, "Take us to her."

The guard scowled and gave her this insolent little bow.

Naji frowned. "Was that true?" he asked Marjani in Empire.

"Every word," she answered in Jokjani. "Don't speak Empire here."

Naji glared at her. I wondered how much of that courtship story got related to the guard.

The guard led us through the palace gate and then through a garden laden with flowers and vines and palm fronds, like the royal family thought they could corral the Jokja jungle for their own use. The air smelled sweet and damp, and women in thin silky dresses looked up from their books and paintings as we walked past. All of 'em were pretty the way nobility always is – it's a prettiness that's painted on, not in-born, but it still made me nervous, the way they watched us with their polite, silent smiles.

The palace was open-air, the scent of the garden drifting into the room where the soldier left us waiting. "I'll alert the queen to your presence," he said to Marjani before he turned on his heel, footsteps echoing in his wake. Naji and me both sat down on the big brocade-covered chairs set up next to the windows. Marjani stayed standing.

"Are they going to arrest you?" I asked.

"What?" Naji asked.

Marjani didn't answer.

"That is what you told him, right?" I asked. "That story about what you told me–"

"No," Marjani said. "I didn't tell him the story I told you." Her fingers twisted around the hem of her shirt.

"Then what–"

"If you spoke better Jokjani," Marjani said, "you'd know."

That stung.

"Arrest her?" Naji asked. Marjani ignored him, and he turned to me, which made my heart pound for a few annoying seconds. "What do you mean?"

"Nothing," I snapped. "My Jokjani ain't good enough for me to know anything."

Worry lines appeared on Naji's brow.

The door banged open, and the sound of it echoed across the huge, empty room. A pair of guards came in – these had different uniforms from the one at the gate, and they carried swords instead of spears. Marjani straightened up. She didn't say nothing to me or Naji, just stood there smoothing her hands over the fabric of her shirt, all wrinkled up from where she'd been clutching it.

The guards walked across the room and stopped and turned to the door. And then two more guards walked in, and then a trio of pretty young attendants and then this graceful woman with dark brown skin and a halo of black hair. Figures she'd be beautiful.

"Saida," said Marjani, her voice husky.

The woman stopped. She lifted one hand to her mouth. "Jani?" she asked. "No, it can't–"

Marjani nodded. I realized her hands were shaking. The woman – Saida, the woman from the story, the princess, the *queen* – rushed forward, the soles of her shoes clicking across the floor.

The guards didn't even move.

"I thought you were dead!" She threw her arms around Marjani's neck and buried her face in Marjani's hair. Marjani scooped her arms around Queen Saida's waist and her eyes shimmered. When she blinked a tear fell down her cheek.

Naji looked back and forth between the two of them and then over at me.

Queen Saida kissed Marjani, and they stayed that way for a long time, like they'd forgotten what kissing was like. When they pulled apart, their hands stayed touching.

"You're queen," Marjani said, her voice full of wonder. They were speaking Jokjani, a dialect I had an easier time understanding.

"I am." Queen Saida gave this little bow like it was the other way around, like Marjani was the queen and not her. "Were you so far away that you couldn't hear news from Jokja?" She smiled. It made her light up like she was filled with stars.

"No, I heard. That's why I came. But I just... I couldn't quite *believe* it."

"You knew I'd inherit."

"I know, but it's one thing to hear about, another to actually see–" She shook her head. "And I've been in the Empire so long, I'd forgotten–"

"The Empire!" Queen Saida exclaimed. "What's that like? Have they invaded the ice-islands yet?"

Marjani rolled her eyes. "Surely the Queen of Jokja would know if the Empire had made a move for the ice-islands."

"I know they've been trying." Saida tilted her head. "Are you sure you were in the Empire? Because you look like a pirate."

"Well, I was doing that, too."

Queen Saida burst into laughter, though she covered her mouth up like a lady. Which I guess she was.

Marjani gave her a smile, small and sad.

And then Queen Saida turned to me and Naji. He pulled the mask away from his face, rose up from his chair, and gave her this handsome bow. Then he hauled me up by the arm.

"Saida, I would like you to meet Ananna of the *Nadir* and… Naji."

"Just Naji?" asked Saida.

"I am Jadorr'a."

Queen Saida's polite smile didn't waver once. "It is a pleasure to meet you," she said to Naji. She pressed her hand to her heart. Naji did the same and bowed again. Then she turned to me. "And you, Pirate Ananna." I gave her a bow cause I liked that she treated me and Naji like we were visiting nobility. Wouldn't expect that from somebody so beautiful.

"I'll arrange for rooms in the guest quarters," Queen Saida said. She looked at Marjani. "Would two suffice? One for each of your companions?"

The air was heavy with the scent of flowers. Marjani nodded slowly. Nobody said nothing about Marjani's room.

"Wonderful. I'm afraid I have business to attend to... I wasn't expecting you–"

"I'm sorry," Marjani said.

"Don't apologize. I'll let the cooks know you're here. You can join me for dinner."

She dipped her head again and then turned on her heel, skirts swirling around her legs. When she left the room, a scent like spice and flower petals lingered in the air.

One of the guards stayed behind.

"I can see you to the atrium while your rooms are being prepared," he said, in that stiff formal way soldiers get sometimes.

Marjani looked dazed. She didn't answer him, just stared at the door where Saida had disappeared.

"That would be fine," said Naji.

The guard glanced at him real quick and then averted his eyes.

The atrium turned out to be an enormous room filled with sunlight that overlooked the jungle. There was a guy there telling a story to some little kids, half of 'em looking like nobles and the other half looking like servants, and a table laid out with food, fresh fruit and sugared flowers and spicy herbed cheese, plus a sweet sugar-wine that reminded me a little of rum.

There were some guards, too, near the door, keeping their eye on everything. I was in half a mind to try and steal something just to see if I could.

Marjani collapsed on a pile of cushions near one of the windows. Sunlight sparkled across her face. She pressed her hand to her forehead and looked out at the jungle, green and undulating like the sea.

"You didn't ask her about the starstones," Naji said.

My stomach clenched up. I should tell him what Jeric had said. But not here, surrounded by stories and sunlight, even though I knew I'd have to tell him eventually: I didn't want him to die, no matter how bad he hurt me.

"The starstones aren't going anywhere," Marjani said. "I'll ask her tonight."

Naji frowned, and for the first time since I met her, I felt a sudden flash of irritation at Marjani.

The storyteller finished up, and the kids all burst into applause and started begging for another one. I slumped down next to Marjani.

"I didn't think I'd ever come back here," she said out of nowhere. "It's funny. This room – we used to listen to stories together right over there." She jerked her head to the corner with the storyteller. "And she'd bring in musicians sometimes and teach me how to dance. I'd never learned at home, cause Father was so keen on me becoming a scholar." She smiled again, and this time she looked wistful, which I guess was better than bitter. "I used to think about it sometimes, watching you dance on the deck of the *Ayel's Revenge*."

I blushed. "I don't dance like a queen."

"Neither did she."

We sat in silence for a few minutes longer. Naji seemed real intent on the surface of his wine.

Marjani turned her head back toward the jungle, and I wondered how best to tell Naji that the thing that could cure his curse would kill him in the process.

CHAPTER ELEVEN

My room was beautiful, with a soft canopied bed and windows that faced the jungle, and a huge porcelain washtub that the servants filled with cool, jasmine-scented water when they brought me into the room. First thing I did was take a bath. Sea baths will keep you clean enough, but nothing beats fresh water to slough all the salt off your skin.

The servants brought clothes, too, a thin cotton dress and a narrow gold belt that I cinched around my waist. I combed my hair out and sat on the window ledge and looked down at the wash of green roiling up against the city's walls. Papa'd told me once that he knew a man who had crossed the Jokja jungle and came out the most powerful sorcerer either the Empire or the Free Countries had ever seen. I'd never decided if I believed him or not.

For a minute, I wondered what Papa was doing. Had the Hariris gone after him first, back when I was crossing the desert with Naji? That wasn't usually the way of things, but you never knew with a clan so enamored of the land. Or had Papa and Mama even heard about what I did, to Tarrin, to his parents? Mama hadn't used her magic to track me, at least not that I could tell, although I might have been too far away from them for it work. Or maybe they just didn't care.

The wind blowing in through the windows changed. I noticed it as a prickle on my skin. The hairs raised up on my arms. A chill crept into the room.

I fumbled around on the bed, trying to find the knife I'd tossed there while I was taking my bath. The wind blew harder, and then a mist crept in – a northern mist, nothing I should have seen in Jokja.

I touched the charm around my neck.

"Ananna," Echo said.

I whirled around, knife out, heart racing. She stood beside the window, and she was dressed like a Jokja lady. But she had the same mean starry eyes and the same cold voice and the same swirl of mist where her feet should have been.

"Get out of here," I said.

"Still protecting him?" Echo drifted forward, bringing the cold damp in with her. "You've come up in the world since last we spoke."

I readied my knife.

She floated over to my bed and sank into it.

"But your affection for the assassin appears to be waning."

I glared at her, tensed my fingers against my knife.

She smiled hard and cold at me. "The offer still stands," she said. "Take us to him, and we'll grant you a thousand boons."

"Why?" I said. "Why do you want him so bad? Just cause he bested your lord?"

She looked at me, calm and implacable. "That's exactly why. My lord was humiliated by that particular defeat. We don't like being defeated, particularly by humans." She narrowed her eyes and wrinkled her nose in disgust. "And we don't like being humiliated either."

"Yeah? So you're just gonna let Naji keep defeating you every time you show up?" I jabbed my hand at the door. I didn't think this was about defeat at all. It was about wanting a place in our world, like Esjar had told me. "You just floated in here like there wasn't a door or walls. Go find him yourself. Or *make* me do it, you want him that bad."

"But I can't touch you," she said. "Because of that *thing* around your neck." She tilted her head. "Even after all the hurt he's caused you, you still wear it?"

"Apparently."

"So coy." She smiled again. "And as point of fact, the assassin has not defeated me. He's merely hidden himself with some silly human charm. It took three years by your reckoning to find him before – without anyone having to betray him, even. So don't think your refusal will actually save him. It only delays the inevitable." She laughed. "And rest assured that when I find him without your help – and I will – you will not be granted a thousand boons. And not even his pathetic human magic will protect you."

I waited for her to laugh again, or give me that infuriating mocking smile of hers, but she didn't. She just stared at me with a calm, placid expression and I thought about how he'd refused to smile for me like kissing me was the worst thing that could happen. I thought about how I didn't let myself think his wanting me was the result of a spell, *how it didn't even cross my mind* when it should've.

I thought about how he made me stupid.

"You're considering it," she said. "I can see it in your eyes."

"I ain't considering nothing." No, I'd been thinking about the manticore, and how dangerous everyone said that was, making a deal with her, and yet I'd managed to get away with my life intact.

I didn't want to hand the world over to the Mists, but maybe I could still hand over Naji, and save the world myself.

The door to my room slammed open, and there stood Naji with his sword and pirate's coat. He gave me a look so full of dismay it was like he could read my mind.

I jumped to my feet, heat rushing to my face.

Echo stiffened. She sniffed at the air, jerked her head around the room.

"I can smell him," she hissed. She didn't sound like nothing human. "He's here."

"No, he ain't," I said.

"Don't lie to me!" She slid forward, growling and spitting. "I told you, Ananna, I've found him before and I'll find him again."

Naji streaked forward and sliced her clean in half with the sword. She dispersed into mist. The room was so cold my teeth chattered.

Naji sat on the edge of my bed, his eyes staring at the space where she had been. I wrapped my arms around my chest. Slowly, the cold leaked out, the warmth came back in.

"You were going to betray me," Naji said.

"What!" My face got hot. "No, I wasn't." But the lie turned to ash in my mouth and I didn't try to deny it again.

Naji looked up at me. I expected anger but his expression was flat and empty. "Yes, you were. I could... tell."

"You could tell? How the hell could you tell?" I shook all over, staring at him. And then his voice was in my head.

Because we're connected.

I shrieked and jumped back, slamming my hands over my ears. Naji's mouth hadn't moved. He hadn't spoken. But I heard him.

I'd been hearing him, on and off, speaking when he wasn't speaking. I'd caught glimpses of his feelings. Not all the time. Just little enough that I thought it was my imagination, that I thought I was feeling my own emotions.

"Do you understand what happened during the sea battle?" Naji asked.

"I got shot through the belly." My voice trembled.

"Before that."

I closed my eyes. My arms tingled where I'd sliced open my skin.

"Yes," Naji said. "You gave me your blood. I tried to tell you..." His voice dropped, and I remembered. He was dying on the deck, choking out that my giving him blood would connect us. And I hadn't understood, because we were already connected, because of the curse, because I loved him.

"When you gave me your blood," he said. "That magic... it drew us together. It's ack'mora, not northern magic like the curse." He took a deep breath. "You wanting to betray me is like me wanting to betray myself. I had to fight... to fight from–"

"Stop," I said, because I could hear the rest of that sentence echoing in my head. Fight from handing myself over to the Mists.

Naji leaned up against the bedpost like he was trying to catch his breath. He peered up at me through the tangle of his hair. I could hardly breathe: I kept thinking about the moments I felt warmth from him when he was with me. Happiness. Comfort.

"When you shared your blood, it created intimacy," he said. "And the magic joined us together. It was like sex–"

His voice trailed off.

I glared at him, humiliated. "Wouldn't know," I snapped. "I figured the boon out before we let it get that far, remember?"

He stared at me, his mouth open like he wanted to say something. I could feel his thoughts, his emotions, crowding at the gates of my mind, but now that I knew what they were I shoved them away. I didn't need him inside my head.

"That wasn't my fault," Naji said.

I turned away from him, still flush with embarrassment. He was right, of course, but I wasn't gonna let him know that.

"Maybe you should leave." I glanced at him over my shoulder. "I'm not sure I want to talk to you right now."

"The boon wasn't my fault," Naji said. "But you were going to turn me over to the Otherworld. That was your choice." He looked sad, even though his words slashed at me like they were full of rage. I wasn't going to let him know I felt guilty about that, either.

"I was only thinking about it," I said. "She raises some good points."

His mouth hardened.

"I asked you to leave and you're still here."

He stood up. Grabbed his sword. But he didn't leave. He came and stood real close to me. The exact opposite of leaving.

"They lie," he said. "When they try to strike deals. You'll be in thrall to them, if you help them, if you–"

"I ain't gonna help 'em!" I shoved him away. "Get out of my room. And stay out of my head!"

"I'm not in your head," he said. "You've blocked me."

"Seems fair, given how I can't get in your head."

Naji gave me a long look. "Yes, you can," he said. I knew he was right. "You've been doing it all this time. You just don't seem to want to control it."

Anger flashed white-hot behind my eyes. "Don't tell me what I don't want to do!" I swung my fist at him, sloppy with rage. He caught my arm, and at his touch I saw a flash of that night after the manticore's feast, only it wasn't me looking up Naji, it was Naji looking down at me, his thoughts flushed with desire and... and affection.

I yanked away from him.

"There," he said. "You went inside my head."

I turned away from him, sucking in deep breaths. That desire, that affection – that wasn't from the boon. I felt it. It was from *him*.

"I know about the starstones," Naji said. "I know about your conversation with Jeric yi Niru." A pause. "I know you... worried."

"Oh, shut up!" I jerked away from him. "I did not."

Naji watched me.

"I have to try," he went on. "With the starstones. I've been communicating with the Order. I have to try–"

"Of course you have to try," I said. "It's the only way I'm going to get rid of you."

He recoiled, and something flashed across his face that I couldn't identify. I didn't bother peeking to see what it was; it might have been hurt. But then his eyes narrowed and he said, "You're never going to get rid of me. Not as long as your blood flows through my veins."

I scowled. "Get out of my room."

"I'm only warning you."

"Get out!"

"If you try to call down the Otherworld," he said, his voice low and dangerous. "I'll know. Don't ever forget that."

"For Kaol's sake, Naji, I ain't gonna call down the Otherworld. I just want you to leave me alone!" I whipped my knife at him without thinking. He slid away in a blink. The knife thrummed into the wall.

"That was unnecessary," he said.

"Get *out*."

He gave me one last hard cold look before melting into the shadows. I leaned up against the wall and dug the heels of my hand into my eyes, trying to stop the tears from flowing over my cheeks, and failing. I concentrated, trying to see if I could feel him hiding in the room, if I could slip into his thoughts the way I did earlier. But there was only emptiness, a blank space where he'd been.

I let out a deep breath, and I realized I was shaking.

The sun room was filled with the orange and pink light of the sunset by the time I dragged myself up there for dinner. The windows were all open-air and gauzed with fine white netting. Flowering vines traced along the walls, growing out of carved stone pots. There was a table in the center of the room stacked high with food: charred meats and fresh fruits and crusty fried breads, along with more bottles of that sweet sugar wine.

Marjani and Naji were waiting for me when we walked in, but there was no Queen Saida yet. Naji sat up straight in his chair and didn't look at me. Marjani seemed distracted.

I sat down at the table and poured a glass of wine.

"You shouldn't start yet," Naji said. I glared at him.

"This isn't a formal feast," Marjani said. "It's dinner. She can have a glass of wine if she wants."

Naji gave her one of his looks, but she didn't notice, just kept staring at the door. I drank my wine down, poured another glass.

We hadn't been waiting long when a pair of guards marched into the room, and then another pair, and then

Queen Saida, fluttering behind them like a flower. Her attendants weren't anywhere to be seen, but I guess she couldn't ditch her guards that easily. She smiled at each of us in turn and then sat down at the head of the table and plucked a mango slice off a nearby platter.

"Eat," she said cheerfully. "The cooks have been slaving away since this morning, I'm sure. I'd hate to tell them their efforts were wasted."

Didn't have to tell me twice. I scooped up a big pile of carrot salad and a lamb chop and took to eating. It wasn't quite like carrot salad in the Empire – they used some different sort of spice I didn't recognize – but it was still delicious.

For the first part of dinner, Queen Saida asked me and Naji a bunch of polite questions about our "journey", like we'd been onboard some passenger liner and not a pirate ship. She asked about the manticores like they were Empire nobility. When I told her about the Isle of the Sky, she sat there with her pretty head leaning to the side, her eyes on me the whole time I was speaking. I was halfway through talking about drying out the caribou meat when I realized I'd just spilled half my life story to this beautiful woman.

I took a big bite of lamb to shut myself up.

"And you, Naji of the Jadorr'a," said Queen Saida. "How did you come to know so much about... what was it called, caribou? Caribou preservation?"

Naji took a drink of wine. "I had a different life before I joined the Order."

"Of course." Another polite smile. I frowned. She was just so easy to trust.

I snuck a glance at Marjani. She'd stuck a lamb chop on her plate and pulled some of the meat away from the bone, but I could tell she hadn't eaten hardly any of it. She kept her eyes on Queen Saida the whole time, following the movement of the queen's graceful hand as she lifted spoonfuls of cream pudding to her mouth.

I wondered if Marjani was ever gonna ask about the starstones. Probably not. Probably Queen Saida didn't even *have* them, Marjani just wanted to come see her now that she had a ship and a crew that'd listen to her–

Queen Saida set her spoon down beside her plate.

"Alright," she said. "What is it?"

"What is what?" asked Marjani, though she flinched.

Queen Saida smiled. "You've been coy all day, dearest. You want to ask me something."

Naji took a long drink of wine. His face had turned stony.

"I don't know how you do that," Marjani said. Her expression was serious and concerned, but her eyes lit up like she thought it was funny.

"Intuition. Now spill it."

Marjani sighed. She tugged on the end of her locks.

"We need to borrow your starstones," I blurted out. "Naji has to touch them."

Naji let out a long sigh.

"My starstones?" Queen Saida laughed. "Is that why you sailed halfway across the world to see me?" She rested her chin in her hand and gazed at Marjani, who looked down at her lap like she was embarrassed.

"Don't be absurd," she said.

"It's for Naji," I said. "He has a curse."

"Are starstones a cure for curses?" Queen Saida turned to Naji. "I'm afraid I don't know much about magic."

"They are for this one," Naji said.

"I thought starstones were dangerous, though? The court wizard never let me near them."

"Your court wizard was correct." Naji glowered, his scar turning him menacing.

"Oh." Queen Saida frowned, and Kaol help me if it didn't make her look even lovelier than when she smiled. "Well, I would be glad to help you, but I'm afraid I don't have them anymore."

The room got so quiet and so still I swore I could hear everybody's hearts beating.

"You don't have them?" Marjani said. "But they're priceless–"

"They were stolen!" Queen Saida threw up her hands. "By members of your lot, in fact. Pirates."

"They are *not* my lot–"

"Oh, I was teasing, dearest." She looked back at Naji. "I'm truly sorry. Father kept them in the armory and during the last sacking... Well, that's always the first place pirates go."

"How could they take them?" Naji's voice had gone quiet and angry. "What pirate would possibly possess the knowledge–"

"Why were they in the armory?" I asked, cause I didn't feel like listening to Naji rant about the idiocy and unworldliness of pirates.

"Because Father thought of them as weapons." Queen Saida looked at me and I felt myself blushing under her gaze. "Not that he or anyone else could ever figure out how to *use* them as such. Not even the wizards would touch them without special gloves."

"Oh yes," said Marjani. "The gloves. I remember now... What was that lord's name, the one who always paraded around with them...?"

Queen Saida laughed. "The Lord of Juma. That was his title, anyway. I don't remember his proper name. But he was always showing off." She laughed again, and Marjani glowed. If the two of them were gonna be like that the whole time, we'd never get anything done.

"What pirates stole 'em?" I asked. "Were they Confederation?"

"Confederation?" Queen Saida furrowed her brow. "I'm not certain. They were pirates."

I frowned. "You didn't see their colors?"

"She means the flag," said Marjani.

Queen Saida shrugged. "I didn't see them. I get whisked away at the slightest hint of danger – you can ask the captain of the guard." She smiled at me. "Are you going to track them down, like in a story? I've heard some of the Empire stories about the starstones. You ought to be careful."

"Naji needs those stones," I said.

Naji looked up at me from across the table. I turned away.

"Gero!" Queen Saida called out. A man in bronzed armor detached himself from the wall and bowed. "I know you heard the question. No need to pretend in front of me. What do you remember about the ships that stole the starstones?"

Gero nodded again before he started speaking. "They were Confederation, my Light," he said.

"I still don't know what that means."

"Confederation pirates sail under common laws, although individual ships and fleets remain independently captained," Gero said, which wasn't quite true, but I didn't feel like correcting him. "I don't remember the flag, however. I'm sorry. It wasn't one I recognized."

"Who would you recognize?" I asked.

Gero turned to me. "The Lao clan," he said. "And the Shujares. The Hariris. The Liras."

The clans most prone to attacking the Free Countries.

"That at least narrows it down," I said. "Thanks."

The guard kinda squinted at me then, like he wanted to say something about me recognizing all those pirate clans. But he didn't. He just turned to Queen Saida and bowed and then pressed back against the wall.

"Well," said Queen Saida. "I'm truly sorry that wasn't more helpful." She looked at Naji while she spoke. "I'll see if I can find out more information for you, and when you make sail, I'll lend you some ships and crew from my own fleet."

"Saida, you don't have to–" Marjani leaned forward over the table and pressed her hand against Queen Saida's arm.

Queen Saida held up her own hand. "Of course I don't have to," she said. "It's not a matter of what I *have* to do; it's a matter of what I want to do."

"Thank you, my Light," murmured Naji. He dipped his head, and emotion flickered through me – despair, creeping in like the cold northern sea, and anger like the fury of the Empire sun. Not my emotions at all.

He was in my head or I was in his: it didn't matter. I saw past his blank assassin's face, and I knew his hopelessness.

And for a moment, my own anger relented.

CHAPTER TWELVE

For the next few days, I hardly saw Marjani at all; she spent all her time with the queen, or shunted off in the queen's apartments on the edge of the garden, doing Kaol knows what. I realized pretty quick that I was the one who was gonna have to check on the boat.

Naji went with me, dressed like a Jokja nobleman save for the scarf wrapped around his face. I hadn't told him I was planning on going; he just showed up at my room and said, "You know how much it hurts me for you to wander off on your own."

"Only if I'm in danger."

He didn't have anything to say to that, but there was no point in fighting with him. I didn't say a word to him as we walked through the city.

The *Nadir* was still docked at port, Kaol be praised, and she didn't look too worse for wear, neither. A handful of men were sitting around on the deck playing dice when me and Naji came on board. Fewer than I would've liked.

"Where's the rest of you?" I asked.

"Whoring," one of the men said. It was Jeric yi Niru. He squinted up at me. "Have you found the starstones yet? Given both of your life's light is intact, I would assume no."

I scowled at him. "She don't got 'em. Got nicked by some Confederation pirates a while back. We'll be setting after the stones once we know more."

"Ah," said Jeric yi Niru, giving me that smug nobleman's smile of his. "What is it with pirates? Does the threat of death engender an item with more value?"

"You're the one that joined up with the Empire navy. You tell me about threat of death."

The rest of the men laughed. Jeric frowned at me and then nodded at Naji. "The captain's look never suited you," he said. "I like this better."

"So do I." Naji's voice was cold and mean, an assassin's voice, and it shut up Jeric yi Niru fast. The other men stopped smirking, too.

I made a quick check of the boat and her stores – some of the rum was missing, and half the bottles of ahiial had been drained and piled up in a corner of the galley. The crew worked fast. But all the weapons were in the hold, and the chest of pressed copper and silver that'd been on board when we took the ship was locked away in the captain's quarters, protected not just with steel chains but with a bit of Naji's magic as well.

I slumped down on the captain's bed so I could listen to the waves slapping up against the ship's side. There's something about a boat that ain't moving. It feels empty. Hollow. Almost better to be on land.

Naji appeared in the doorway. He slid the mask away from his face but didn't bother to come any closer.

I got flashes of things in my head as he stared at me – worry about the starstones, some dull ache I now understood was part of the curse – and I rubbed at my eyes until they went away.

"Cut it out," I said.

"Cut what out?"

"Letting me see your thoughts."

"I'm not *letting* you. You just can. I explained this–"

"Well, stop it!" I scowled. "Is it gonna be like this for the rest of my life?"

"I told you it would. Don't you ever listen?"

He sounded like Mama for a minute there, scolding me for not being able to work magic proper.

"Apparently not," I said, which is what I always told Mama when she asked me. Then: "You're scared about the starstones."

I wanted to see if it would bother him, me knowing what he was thinking. The way it bothered me. But he just gazed at me across the captain's quarters and said, "Yes. The task's impossible for a reason."

There was this silence after he spoke, a place where I should've said, "The other one wasn't." But I kept my mouth shut.

"It has occurred to me," Naji said, "and to the members of the Order I've spoken to, that the only way to escape the curse may be to die." He shrugged. "And if that's what I have to do–"

A coldness struck me in my heart, a hand come out to squeeze the life away from me. Naji felt it too. I could see it in on his face, the way his expression softened as he looked at me. It pissed me off. I didn't want to care if he lived or died.

"We should get back," I muttered, and I pushed past him and made my way back on deck.

We stayed in Arkuz for near a month, waiting for Queen Saida's messengers to bring word of the starstones. One day I finally went to see her in her sun room, surrounded by guards and nobles and Marjani.

"Not yet," she said, courteous and smiling. Marjani gazed at me apologetically. She looked different in a noblewoman's clothes, her hair woven with ribbons and shells, her eyes lined with pale green powder. Like a right princess.

"You'll be the first to know as soon as I hear something," Queen Saida said. She took one of my hands in her own. Her skin was soft as silk. "I have twenty of my best men out looking for those stones."

"You know I can captain the ship myself," I said. "And leave Marjani here."

Marjani jerked her head up toward me but didn't say nothing. Queen Saida gave me a long, appraising look.

"I don't lie," she said. "My best men are looking for the stones."

That made me blush. She didn't even sound angry or nothing. Just a little disappointed in me, like I'd reminded her I wasn't a noble after all. And it actually made me feel kinda bad.

Afterward, I wandered around the gardens, sneaking past the guards and servants and ladies sitting in the sun. I could hear birds singing to one another out in the jungle. You wouldn't think you were in the city, there in the palace gardens.

I found a shady spot beneath some flowering bushes to sit and think. I was tired of hanging around Arkuz, waiting for something to happen. We were losing crewmen, too. You stay in a place long enough, they start thinking they like that place better. Especially a place like Arkuz. I couldn't much blame them.

The thing was, I didn't know if I wanted to find the starstones, not if it meant Naji would die. And the third task, the one about life coming out of violence – that didn't even make any sense. Knowing magicians, it was probably just some roundabout way of saying he had to kill himself on the starstones.

Ananna, you think too much about things that don't concern you.

I yelped and scrambled out from under the bushes, my knees and hands covered in dirt. Nobody was about but a sleepy-looking guard leaning up against his spear.

Stop worrying about me.

It was Naji's voice, and it was coming from inside my head.

"Naji!" I whispered. "I told you to stay out of my head!"

He didn't answer. I clenched my eyes shut and concentrated real hard, and I saw a window looking out over the jungle, and a bed draped with sheer curtains. He was in his room.

I stalked out of the garden and into the palace and right up to his room and pounded on his door until he answered.

"Ananna," he said. "Always nice to see you in person."

"Stay out of my head!" I shouted. I launched myself at him, aiming both of my hands for his chest, figuring I could at least topple him over. He grabbed me by the waist and swung me off to the side.

"You're such an ass," I told him.

He laughed. "Why? Because you couldn't knock me down?"

"Cause you tossed me around like a rag doll. Good thing I didn't have my pistol on me."

"Yes," he said. "Good for us all."

"Oh, shut up."

"I did want to tell you," he said, his voice serious and eyes bright, which made me want to punch him, "that I do appreciate your concern for me—"

"What concern?" Even though I knew he knew.

"Thinking you could set sail on your own and find the starstones for me – I'm sure there'd be a great sea battle involved, lots of cannon fire and swords and whatnot."

"Isn't that what you want?"

"Don't be absurd. You couldn't even imagine the headache it would give me—" He stopped. "Actually maybe you could now. You haven't been in sufficient danger for us to find out."

"That ain't what I meant. You want the starstones. So you can touch 'em and kill yourself and not have to deal with *me* no more."

Naji blinked at me. "No," he said. "That isn't what I want at all."

I could tell he meant it, his sincerity hanging over me like a storm cloud, but whatever it was he did want I couldn't see.

Off in the corner of the room, I heard this soft thumping noise, like a rug being beaten. And when I tore my gaze away from Naji I actually screamed, Kaol help me, cause standing next to the open window was the biggest damn bird I'd ever seen.

It let out a big screeching *caw*.

"The hell is it?" I shouted, going for my knife. Naji didn't move.

"An albatross."

"A what?" But I knew it was a seabird, one of the big white ones Qilari sailors think signal luck – good or bad, I can never remember.

"There's something tied to its foot." Naji leaned forward and snatched something from the side of the bird's leg. It was a little mother-of-pearl tube with a glass stopper. Naji pulled out the stopper and then drew out a second tube, this one made of paper. The bird cawed again and flapped its wings, stirring up the hot humid air.

"You think it's for the queen?" I asked.

"The Jokja don't communicate via albatross," Naji said.

The bird cawed again. Then it pecked at Naji's hand, the one holding the paper. Naji frowned.

Another caw.

"It wants you to read it," I said.

The bird lifted up its wings and hopped on the bed.

"See!"

Naji gave me a dark look, but he unrolled the paper, smoothing it out along his thigh. The writing on it was curved and ornamental, decorated with drawings of seashells and ocean waves. I leaned over his shoulder to read.

We hope this message reaches you with ease, Naji of the Jadorr'a. I am the Scrivener of the Court of the Waves and am writing to you at the behest of the King of Salt and Foam. The King would like to speak to you personally as soon as possible. He extends an invitation for you to visit the Court of the Waves. Regards, Jolin I.

"What?" I said. "The Court of the Waves? The hell is that?"

"I don't know." Naji slid the map out of the mother-of-pearl tube and unfurled it. The bird cawed – the sound of it made me jump – and then flapped its wings and lifted up into the air and out the window. I watched the bird fly away for a moment before turning back to the map. It showed the western stretch of the Green Glass Sea between the Island of the Sun, where the manticores live, and the Empire continent. There was a place marked in the middle of the water.

The mark was labeled: "We shall post sentries to help you find your way."

"This is very strange," Naji said.

"I don't trust it."

Naji frowned. "I don't either. I shall ask the Order about it. Perhaps that will give us some insight."

I didn't think the Order had much of value to say on anything, given its track record, but I knew Naji was gonna do it regardless. Still, I studied the map, tracing my finger across its width. I thought about staring at the maps onboard the *Nadir*, navigating our path to the Island of the Sun–

"This mark is where we fought the Hariri clan." A coldness gripped my blood, and the scar on my stomach ached.

"How can you possibly tell?"

"Cause I'm the damned navigator. And I know–"

"Ananna," Naji said gently. "The Hariris are dead. I killed them."

I pushed the map away. My hands were shaking. "We shoulda checked that bird," I said. "I bet it was metal, like those machines they've got…" And the more I thought about it the more convinced I was that the feathers had glittered in the sun, and it had left a streak of smoke as it flew off into the air.

Naji set the map and note on the bed and pressed his hand against my shoulder. I barely felt it. "You know I'm not going to put you in danger," he whispered.

But this wasn't danger; it was fear. It was the memory of a bullet tearing into my gut. It was Mistress Hariri laughing in the moments before I almost died – before I would've died, if Naji hadn't been around. If he hadn't decided I was worth saving.

When we finally made sail, a week later, it wasn't to chase after starstones or to return to the place where I'd nearly died. It was to visit the Aja Shore, down on the southern tip of Jokja. Queen Saida's idea.

She and Marjani sailed out on this lovely schooner, the wood painted orange and marigold and pink, the sails dyed the color of grass. It looked like a floating garden. Queen Saida, always gracious, offered me and Naji a spot on board, but I wasn't skipping town without the *Nadir*.

"Good," Marjani said when I told her, though she seemed distracted. We were ambling around the perimeter of the palace, next to the fence that kept the jungle from pushing in on the royal lands. "I really didn't want to leave her here." She crossed her arms over her chest, and all the bangles on her wrists tinkled like bits of glass. "You can captain her, if you'd like."

"What?" I stopped. "She's your boat!"

"We captured her with your manticore," Marjani said. "She's as much yours as she is mine."

"I can't captain a boat."

Marjani glanced at me over the top of one bare shoulder. "Of course you can," she said. "If I can do it, you can do it."

"You're smarter than me."

"Smarter doesn't necessarily make a good captain." She shrugged. "Clever does. And you're plenty clever."

I didn't know what to say. All my life I'd wanted to captain a ship, but lately it hadn't seemed that important to me anymore. I was distracted by that bird and its map and its weird note, afraid the Hariris weren't really dead. And I was afraid Naji would be, if we ever found the starstones.

"Besides," said Marjani. "It's just along the coast. A day and a half's journey. Think of it as practice."

Practice. Ha! Well, maybe I'd take off with her boat and her crew, see how she liked it then. Not that I knew where I'd go.

I ain't no mutineer. But I toyed with the thought for a few seconds anyway, the way I toyed with handing Naji over to the Mists. And I felt just as guilty about it afterward.

"We're leaving at dawn tomorrow morning," she said. "Saida really does want you to come. Naji too. She likes talking to him."

Naji and Saida had swapped magic stories at dinner, spells gone wrong and so on – she said she didn't know much about magic if you asked, though that was a right lie from hearing the way she talked. Naji stuck to discussing earth-magic. I wondered what Queen Saida would think if he told her about me spilling my blood on the deck of the *Nadir* so we could win the fight against the Hariri clan. Probably wrinkle her nose and reach for a piece of flatbread.

So that was how I came to captain the *Nadir* for a day and a half. Wasn't much to it, of course, cause we just followed behind Queen Saida's queen ship, the colors bright against the blue sky and the blue water. Crew was lazy on account of the smooth waves and the favorable winds. I wandered up and down the deck shouting every insult and curse word I knew, the way Papa always did, trying to get 'em off their asses.

"First mate!" Jeric yi Niru called out while I was making one of my rounds. I stopped and glared at him. He was up in the rigging.

"What do you want?" I shouted. "If you say the word *starstone* to me, I swear on Kaol and her watery birthbed that I will shoot you in the heart." And I pulled out my pistol like I meant to use it.

Jeric yi Niru laughed and came dropping down to deck on a line of rope. "You sound like an Empire captain," he said. "They like to threaten the lives of their crew too."

I shoved my gun back into the waistband of my pants. "What is it?" I asked.

"The crew," he said. "I want to apologize for them. You dragged them away from one of the wealthiest cities in the world. The dice houses here—" He shook his head in fake disbelief. I wanted to hit him. "And the women."

I rolled my eyes. "I'm taking 'em to the Aja Shore," I said. "There'll be whores and gambling aplenty there, too."

"Tell them that," said Jeric yi Niru. "I realize to a pirate captain's daughter the life of a captain is nothing but orders given and orders followed, but in truth it's an exchange."

I hate to admit it, but he had my attention. "An exchange?"

"Yes. Like your relationship with that manticore. It was built on favors, yes?"

I didn't say nothing. I wished to the deep blue sea I knew how he got his information.

"You tell the crew we're sailing to the Aja Shore at the lovely Queen Saida's request, but what do they care of Queen Saida? What do they care of *you*? All they care about—"

"Is pissing their money away at the dice houses. I get it."

Jeric yi Niru gave me one of his insolent Empire smiles. But he was right. I'd played the manticore and the manticore had played me and we'd wound up friends. Even if her boon hadn't turned out how she intended.

So I climbed up on the helm and rang the warning bell till I got the crew's attention.

"What is it, Lady Navigator?" one of 'em called out.

"I wanted to let you know!" I said. "That we'll be spending close to a week along the Aja Shore."

The crew all stared at me like I'd just turned into a kitten.

"I know the lot of you have already lost half your earnings to the gambling houses in Arkuz."

"Most of us more'n that!" somebody called out, and some of the crew laughed and some of them grumbled under their breaths.

"That's cause you were gambling in Arkuz," I said. "They take one look at your clothes and see an Empire scummy who don't know how to hold on to his money." I paused, looking out over them. "They *cheat*, is what I'm saying."

The crew clapped and stomped and hollered in agreement.

"But on the Aja Coast," I said, "they play nice and fair. You boys want to earn your pressed gold back? Now's your chance."

I had no idea how accurate any of this was, but the crew was hollering again.

"And the *whores*," I added, not knowing the slightest how to build on that. Apparently it was enough, though, cause the crew hooted and stomped and nudged one another. I guess just saying the word *whores* is enough to get them excited.

"So I want you boys to think about those Aja women and those Aja dice houses," I shouted. "While you're climbing up in the rigging and steering us forward. I ain't sailing on Queen Saida's command, I'm sailing to give the lot of you a little taste of paradise."

They actually cheered me. Not like a crowd cheering a champion in the fighting ring, mind, just some yelling and hollering and whatnot. Still felt good.

"Now!" I shouted. "Get back to work!"

And no one was as surprised as me when they did.

The Aja Shore reminded me of Bone Island, only cleaner and full of nobles and rich merchants instead of cutthroats and pirates. Queen Saida kept a private island set a ways off from the shore, with a big house filled with servants, who, far as I could see, got to live there all year and only had to work when Queen Saida decided she wanted a vacation.

We didn't bother making port at the dock, just dropped anchor out in the open sea off behind Queen Saida's island, the *Nadir* looking big and hulking and monstrous next to her pretty little garden-ship. I let the crew row in to the mainland to go chasing after the gambling I promised them. Then Naji and me made our way to Queen Saida's house. It was like being in the palace. Her private guards hung around trying to look inconspicuous, and the servants gave me weird looks before leading us up to our rooms. They seemed to give Naji a pass, probably cause every time he opened his mouth he sounded like a noble.

"We're preparing your midday meal now," the servant told us as she wandered around my room, pulling down sheets and drawing the curtains away from the open windows. The sea glittered in the sunlight. "The house bell will chime when it's prepared." She nodded at me and slipped off into the hallway.

I sank down on the bed and sighed. The warm wind blowing in through the windows made me sleepy, though at least it smelled like the sea, like home, instead of the jungle. It didn't take long before I drifted off to some breezy dream. Marjani was there, and Queen Saida and the manticore. No Naji. It was nice.

In the dream, Marjani knocked on wood, looking at me expectantly. She knocked so loud it woke me up, and I realized someone was knocking on my door. The little whisper in my head told me it was Naji.

"What do you want?" I called out.

He pushed the door open and stood there staring at me.

"Well?" I asked. "Ain't no Mist lady in here."

"I can see that," he said.

I had half a mind to go sifting through his head, but I didn't much feel like putting forth the energy.

"Seriously," I said, "did you need something?"

Naji shook his head silently and just kept staring at me. I sighed and rolled over onto my back, looked up at the ceiling.

"I spoke to the Order about this Court of the Waves," Naji said. "There's no record of such a place in any of our histories. Saida's librarian had never heard of it either."

I sighed. "Well then. I *really* don't trust it."

Bells started ringing.

"Well, that's proper timing, isn't it?" I sat up. "Food's always better than magical killing rocks."

"Wait," Naji said.

"What? They said they'd ring the bells for lunch."

Naji shook his head. "They aren't coming from the house."

I froze, listening. He was right. The bells were caught on the wind, blowing in from the sea–

And then I heard the faint boom of cannon fire.

That got me to my feet. I rolled off the bed and darted over to the window. I couldn't see nothing but the sparking sea, but the smell of cannon fire smoke, acrid and burning, was on the air.

Naji grabbed me by the arm, yanked me back. "My room," he said.

He dragged me down the hallway. His room looked the same as mine, but the thud of cannons was louder. I ran over to his window, which faced land.

The Aja Shore was burning in patches. A Confederation ship sidled up along it sideways. Another volley of cannon fire. I leaned out the window, ignoring the sudden pain in my temple, straining to see what colors she was flying – but the smoke was too thick.

The city bells clanged against my skull. Naji tried to pull me out of the window.

"No!" I shouted. "I gotta see which ship. If it's some Hariri allies–"

"Ananna, you're hurting me."

The pain in his voice startled me enough that I loosened my grip on the windowsill and went tumbling backward. He caught me before I could hit the floor. My headache evaporated.

"They aren't here for you," he said. "They're sacking the town."

"Yeah, looking for me!" I wrenched away from him and was halfway to the door when he had one hand on my shoulder, one arm wrapping around my chest, drawing me into an embrace that startled me into stillness.

"Please," he whispered into the top of my head. "Please. It hurts me even more now. Now that I–"

I pulled away from him. Whatever he almost said, I didn't care. And besides, I didn't have any other choice. I needed to get out to sea. It wouldn't take long before they made it to Queen Saida's island, before they saw our boat floating out in the water – if they hadn't already. We didn't have the colors up – I ain't stupid – but any pirate worth his salt would see that the *Nadir* was a gussied-up

Empire boat. And if these were Hariri allies, they would
know what that meant.

"I ain't safe here, neither," I finally told him, pulling
out one of my pistols. "And if we lose our ship, then we
lose everything."

And then I bounded out of the room.

CHAPTER THIRTEEN

Marjani caught me in the hallway. She had her sword in one hand and her pistol in the other, though she was still dressed like a princess.

"Do you know who it is?" I asked.

The smell of smoke was everywhere.

"Not any of the Hariri allies that I know about."

I slumped with relief, dropping my sword to my side.

"They're here because of Saida," she said. "The Aja merchants always bring out the best jewelry and silks when she comes to visit." Marjani took a deep breath. "Her guards have taken the queen's ship. I told her we'd take the *Nadir*."

"As privateers?" I frowned. "Are we gonna have to swear allegiance to Jokja and all that?"

Marjani scowled. "Does it matter? And not officially, no." She jerked her head in direction of the shore. "Those pirates are going to try and take the *Nadir* once they've finished sacking the shore anyway."

That was probably true.

We didn't have much crew on the *Nadir* – most of 'em were on shore, and so we just had the few scoundrels who got stuck with the second shift. Jeric yi Niru was one of them, though, and lo and behold he'd gotten them to ready the boat for battle. When me and Marjani came on board and saw the crew packing the cannons and readying the sails, he gave us both a bow and a tip of his Qilari hat.

"Captain," he said. "I imagine we'll need to fetch the rest of our soldiers for the battle."

"They're my crew, not soldiers," Marjani said. "But yes, you're right." She took the helm. I stood beside her, my heart pounding in my chest. The sky was black with smoke, and I could hear screaming and pistol blasts coming from the mainland. The queen ship was ahead of us, her green sails bright against the haze. My head ached some, from being separated from Naji, but it wasn't too bad. If I concentrated I could make it disappear completely.

"Ananna!"

It was Naji. He stepped out of the shadow of the mast, clutching a sword and a knife, his eyes glowing.

"I have to protect you," he said.

I didn't say anything.

Marjani glanced at him. "Oh, good, you're here. We're going to need all the help we can get."

Naji frowned at her, and then put his hand on my arm. His skin was warm through the fabric of my shirt. "Please," he said to me. "It's not your fight."

"It's my boat!" I said. "Marjani said so. The *Nadir*'s as much mine as she is hers. I ain't gonna let some Confederation scummies steal off with her."

The skin crinkled around Naji's eyes. He pulled out his sword.

"Hold steady!" Marjani shouted, leaning against the helm. We were close to the Confederation ship, close enough that they had to have spotted us–

They had. Their cannons were rotating.

"Fire!" Marjani screamed, and the whole boat rocked backward as the cannons fired, adding more smoke to the thick air. I braced myself against Naji. The Confederation ship shuddered, but we'd managed to knock half their cannons off the line of sight.

The men cheered. Marjani didn't; she just set her jaw straight and hard. "We haven't won yet."

I jumped down to the deck, figuring they'd need as much help in the reloading as possible. I ignored Naji following me as I worked on one of the cannons, the gunpowder making my eyes water.

The Confederation ship fired on us. I skittered backward, limbs flailing. Naji caught me even though I knew I'd slid past him in the explosion – his lightning-quick assassin dance again. He looked relieved.

I pushed up to my feet.

A wind blew in from the open sea, sweet and clean, and for a few quick seconds it cleared away the smoke.

I saw the other ship's colors.

A blue field. A gray skeleton, dancing the dance of the dead.

The *Tanarau*.

Mama. Papa.

"Stop!" I screamed. "Stop firing!" I was half-talking to the crew and half-talking to the *Tanarau*, even though I knew it was madness to think they could hear me across the water. "Stop! It's me! It's *me*!"

"What in the darkest of nights are you doing?" Naji grabbed at me but I wrenched free. I raced up to the flagpole and yanked on the rope. Our colors dropped.

"What in the holy hell!" Marjani leapt over the helm. "What do you think you're doing?"

"We have to surrender!" I shouted.

"What?"

I didn't answer, just pulled hard on the rope and caught the colors in my arms. One of the crewmen was on me with his sword, and I swung around and caught him, blade to blade, before he could cut me.

"I know that ship!" I shouted, but he didn't care. He just wanted to fight. The sound of our swords rang out across the deck. I tossed the colors aside, lunged at him. More cannon fire from the *Tanarau*, and the boat lifted up and slammed back down. I managed to stay on my feet.

Then Jeric yi Niru stepped in, nimble as a dancer, wedging himself between me and the crewman so that the crewman hit his sword instead of mine.

"Go on, first mate," he called out over his shoulder. "Hoist up the surrender flag."

Where the hell is Naji? I thought, and then I saw – Marjani'd gotten a couple of the bigger fellows to hold him down. And she was coming after me herself.

"It's my parents!" I screamed.

She froze in place. "Are you sure?"

"Course I'm sure. I sailed under those colors for close to two decades." I fumbled around on the deck for a scrap of sail. Yellow-white, but it would do. "Once we get them to stop firing I can go over and have them let us be."

"And how do you know that will work?" Her voice was quiet and cold, but she'd dropped her sword to her side.

"How'd you know it'd be safe for you to come back to Jokja?"

Her jaw moved up and down like she was trying out responses. Nothing came out. She gave me a curt nod, and I tied the scrap of sail to the flag rope and hoisted it up. Jeric yi Niru had knocked the crewman out and nobody else tried to stop me. The *Tanarau* stopped firing on us once the sail was halfway up, the way I figured she would. Papa always heeds calls to surrender.

Naji shrugged away from his captors.

"Let me do the parley," I said to Marjani.

"You bet your ass I will."

"No," said Naji. "If they harbor ill will because of the Hariri affair—"

"They won't." I was already readying the rowboat. I had my sword and my pistol and my heart was beating faster than it did before any battle. I called over Jeric yi Niru.

"Drop me down," I told him. I know it's crazy, but I trusted him more in that moment than I did anyone else, on account of him helping me call surrender.

"Aye aye," he said, eyes glinting like he was making fun of me.

"Wait!" Naji flashed across the deck and reappeared beside me in the boat. I didn't have time to protest before Jeric yi Niru cut the line and we crashed into the water.

I rowed us over to the *Tanarau*. The closer we got the slower I rowed. What if Naji was right? What if they were still sore about me running off on my wedding day? What if they pledged some sort of allegiance to the Hariris, and this was all a Hariri trap after all?

"You're right to worry," Naji said, staring straight ahead, looking grim.

"Shut up!" I said. "It's my family. They ain't gonna hurt me."

"You don't know that," Naji said, and he tapped his finger to my forehead. "Can you see what I'm thinking right now?"

"I don't got to. I know you think this is a bad idea." We were almost to the *Tanarau*. I pulled the oars in and let the waves knock us up against her side. A few seconds later, the ropes dropped down.

Two *Tanarau* men hauled us up. One of 'em I didn't recognize, but the other was Big Fawzi, and when he saw me he squinted and then widened his eyes.

"Hey," I said.

"Ananna? What the hell? We thought you were dead."

"Not yet."

And then I heard Mama's voice, sweet as a song, asking the men what the hell was going on. I jumped out of the rowboat, the feel of the *Tanarau* firm and familiar beneath my feet. The sails flapped and snapped in the wind, and the sound was different from the sails on the *Nadir* and the *Ayel's Revenge* and the *Goldlife*. The rigging hung different. It was like I never left.

"Ananna!" Mama pushed through the crew. She was decked out for battle in men's clothes, her belt lined with pistols, but when I saw her all I could think about was the way she'd looked when she wore her worn silk robe as she rocked me to sleep back when I was a little kid.

"Mama!" I raced forward. She caught me up in her embrace. The pirate in me thought back to Tarrin of the *Hariri*, reaching for his knife as he lay dying. But the daughter in me just wanted to be hugged.

"I never thought I'd see you again." She pulled away and I saw the smudges in her kohl where she'd started crying. Mama never lets you see her cry; she can stop a tear before it falls down her face. But if you know how to look for the signs, you can still spot it. "I'd heard the Hariris sent an assassin after you."

"They did."

Mama frowned, and before she could say anything, Papa's voice boomed across the ship.

"And what the hell kinda parley is thi–"

He stopped when he saw me. For a moment nobody moved. We all just stood there in the smoke and the sea breeze.

"Nana," he said. He threw off his sword belt and his pistols and then rushed toward me, scooping me up like I was a kid again. "You were dead," he said to me, leaning close. "You were dead. The assassin–"

"He's here," I said without thinking.

Everybody on the damn boat pulled out a weapon. Swords and pistols and daggers all threw off glints of light in the sun.

Naji slumped against the railing and sighed.

"No!" I said. "You don't understand. He didn't... he can't kill me, alright?"

"That him?" Papa jerked his chin toward Naji.

Naji looked back at him warily. "I won't allow any harm to come to your daughter."

"That right?" Papa stared at him for a long time. Naji hadn't pulled his sword, and his tattoos were all covered up, and he was still dressed like a pirate. Nothing about him, except maybe the scar, suggested that he was an assassin.

"I've protected her this long," Naji said.

Another long pause, and then Papa roared with laughter. He turned to me. "You've turned into a right princess, you need some shield-for-hire following you around. Like those foppy Empire nobles." He laughed again.

"I didn't hire him!"

Mama scooped her arm around me and pulled me close. "Throw up the peace flag!" she shouted. "And make sail for the open sea before the Jokja authorities show up."

That set the crew to scrambling. The queen's boat wasn't attacking no more, but it wouldn't be long before the queen's navy arrived. And I doubted Queen Saida would give amnesty to anybody who'd just burned half the Aja Shore, even if they were my parents.

When the *Tanarau* took to the water, the *Nadir* was right behind her. But not the queen's ship. Mama must've had somebody send word to Marjani. I wondered if she still thought we were in parley.

A pirate ship is outfitted to go faster than even the Empire's little sloops, but Papa had us sail out past sunset, to be sure. They stuck me and Naji up in the captain's quarters, like I was still five years old and liable to get underfoot. Though in truth I was grateful for it, cause I was tired, even though it hadn't been much of a battle.

Naji and me sat side by side on the little trundle bed. We didn't say much. I didn't even feel him inside my head. I think it was more under his control than he'd let me believe. Or maybe he'd just put it under his control.

Once we seemed clear of an attack, Mama and Papa came back into the cabin.

"I think you got a story to tell us, girl," Papa said. He pulled a jar of sugar-wine out of his cabinet and slid down in his big brass chair. Mama leaned against the wall. Both of them looked worn out.

The boat tipped back and forth from the winds and the speed on the water.

"I guess I do," I said.

Papa drank the sugar-wine straight from the bottle and slammed it down on the navigation table.

"Why'd you run off?" Mama asked.

"I didn't want to get married."

She frowned at me, but I could see Papa get a hint of a smile.

"Heard you killed the Hariri boy," he said.

"He was gonna kill me." But that wasn't the part of the story I wanted to tell, and I wrapped my arms around my stomach and took a deep breath. Naji glanced at me and frowned.

"She was saving her own life and mine," he told Papa. "They attacked us with… machines… out in the desert–"

"Sandships," Papa said. "Heard about 'em. Never seen 'em." He took another swig of wine and handed the bottle to Naji, who shook his head. I grabbed it instead, which made Papa laugh.

"So why didn't you kill her?" Mama asked Naji. She pulled her pipe out of her jacket pocket and a pouch of grayweed and took to packing it in tight.

Naji blinked.

"You're an assassin, yeah? That's what she said up on deck." She snapped her fingers and flames danced on top of her fingertips, and she lit her pipe. Another snap and they were gone. The sort of thing she used to call "courtier's tricks" back when I was trying to learn magic.

The scent of her smoke made me dizzy with homesickness, even though I was home.

"I am a member of the Jadorr'a," Naji said. "And yes, Captain Hariri hired me to…" His voice trailed off, and I almost took his hand in mine. Stopped myself just as my fingers grazed across his knuckles.

Mama must've seen cause she arched an eyebrow and said, "Didn't think you had it in you, Nana."

"What are you talking about?" I asked, scowling. And then before she could answer I blurted out the whole story about the snake and the curse and the Wizard Eirnin and the Isles of the Sky and the *Nadir* and the starstones. The whole time Mama and Papa listened, and the only time either of them moved was when Mama puffed on her pipe.

"Starstones," Mama said when I'd finished.

"Yeah," I said. "We gotta go find the sons of whores who stole 'em, but Marjani doesn't want to leave Jokja."

Papa squinted. "Well. That is a conundrum."

"You ought to just take her boat," Mama said.

"I ain't no mutineer."

They both laughed at that.

"It ain't funny!" I said.

"Well, she promised you starstones and then didn't deliver," Mama said. "I think that's reason enough to take her boat."

I could feel myself getting hot with anger, and I balled my hand up into a fist and thought about hitting somebody. The truth was my distaste with mutiny had nothing to do with it. I owed Marjani my loyalty for the rest of my life. After all, she came back to the Isles of the Sky for me.

Papa drained the last of the sugar-wine.

"Or we could stop screwing around with you," he said.

"What?" The anger flared up. Maybe it was mine, maybe it was Naji's. The blood-connection made my emotions confusing.

Papa chuckled and stood up. "Come down to the holding bay, I'll show you."

Mama smiled at me through the cloud of smoke.

And I got this thought in my head, like maybe they'd aligned themselves with the Hariris after all, and this was all a trap.

"Naji, come with me."

"Of course." When I stood up, he stood up. Mama shook her head.

"Never seen a pirate with a bodyguard," she said. "Thought I taught you to do your own fighting."

"He ain't my bodyguard!"

"Enough." Papa's voice boomed out in full-on captain's mode. "Sela, I know you're still sore about the marriage, but it's over with now. Ananna." He turned to me. "I ain't gonna hurt you. Blood ties are stronger than any Confederation law."

Mama huffed in the corner.

"I'm just a daughter," I said.

"You're my daughter, sure. Ain't no *just* about it."

I looked at him, unsure of what to say.

He clapped me on the back. "I'll let you follow, if it'll make you and your assassin feel better. Sela! Up here."

"Don't boss me," she said, but she joined him, and together we wound through the belly of the *Tanarau* to the holding bay. Some idiot part of me wanted to press close to Naji, but instead I clutched the hilt of my sword and kept my eyes out for an attack.

When we got to the holding bay, Papa undid the lock and kicked the door open. "Have a look," he said.

I could smell Empire spices and the faint briny seaweed scent of the charm Mama used to stop bugs from eating holes in the silks. It reminded me of sleeping down here, pretending I was a child of the desert and not the water.

I stepped inside.

"What am I looking for?" I asked, folding my hands over my chest. "It's just treas–"

Naji's sword clattered to the floorboards.

"Ah," Papa said. "He knows."

"The starstones," Naji said.

I felt like all the air'd been let out of me. Naji rushed forward, pushing me aside. He knelt down in front of a pile of Jokja cotton – and a trio of smooth white pebbles. I hadn't paid them any mind. I figured they were there to keep the cotton from sliding around. I was more concerned with the box sitting beside them, carved and jeweled in the Jokja style.

Naji reached out one hand. Stopped. He was trembling.

"I wouldn't touch 'em," Mama said.

"I know that." It came out in a hiss. I knelt beside him. The stones didn't look like nothing special. Just river rocks that'd been worn smooth by the water.

"You sure this is them?" I asked.

Mama snorted. "You shoulda seen 'em when Kel took 'em out of their box. Lit up all of down below, they did." There was something in her voice that sounded sad, and I knew Kel, whoever he was, was gone. I wondered if Mama and Papa had known what the starstones were when they brought them aboard.

"Can't you feel it?" Naji's eyes glowed. "The magic in them?"

"No."

Naji grabbed my hand and squeezed it between both of his palms. I jolted at his touch, and at first I thought it was just me being moony – but then I realized it was something else, some power coursing through him, seeping out of his skin. Not his blood magic, which was like death curling her cold soft hands around your heart. This was ancient. This was the towering trees growing out of the cold damp ground of the ice-islands. This was the darkness of caves and the richness of desert sand. This was the emptiness of the night sky.

"They aren't actually weapons, you know." Naji said, his voice soft. "People want them to be, because of their strength..." His hands trembled against mine.

"They're the source of all magic," Naji went on, so soft I was pretty sure only I could hear him.

"What?" I stared at him. Behind us, Mama took a few steps closer, leaning in like she wanted to hear.

"You felt it," Naji said, looking over his shoulder at her. "The power. When your crewman died–"

"I don't want to talk about that."

Naji actually shut up. I guess Mama's sharp voice can even scare a Jadorr'a. Or maybe it wasn't Mama he was scared of.

"What's going to happen to you?" I said. "When you hold them?"

He looked at me. "You already know."

I shook my head. "It ain't right. I mean, think about what happened when I... you thought the other thing was impossible, and it wasn't at all."

Naji's eyes loomed dark and empty. Then he turned back to the starstones. I didn't let that stop me.

"There's gotta be something about you," I said. "Cause you're Jadorr'a, cause you can't die, it's in all the stories."

I knew I was babbling; I knew Mama and Papa were giving each other looks over in the corner. "None of the tasks are impossible, that's the thing. You only *think* they are. It's like how I thought it was impossible for me to do magic and then I *did*, and I saved your life on the river, and–"

He lifted his head. The glow in his eyes illuminated the tears streaked across his cheekbones.

"Naji?" I whispered, cause all other words had left me.

"I hope you're right," he said, and then he reached out with his bare hands and scooped up the stones.

Magic flared around us, bright white and stinging like the edge of a flame. Naji screamed. The stones filled with light. For a dazed second, I thought that Jeric yi Niru was right, that they really did look like the stars plucked out of the sky.

And then I heard Papa shout, and I was aware of him and Mama both drawing their pistols, and Mama saying something like *not again*. And Naji stared at me with hollowed eyes and a gaping mouth, the stones growing brighter and brighter. I realized I could see the outline of his bones beneath his skin.

"Drop them!" I screamed. "You've done it! Skin against stone! Drop them!"

The faint presence of Naji's thoughts evaporated out of my head, leaving me empty and alone.

The stones clattered against the floor.

And then so did Naji.

CHAPTER FOURTEEN

I bounded on board the *Nadir*, screaming Marjani's name. Tears streamed down my face. I couldn't stop shaking.

"What is it?" She appeared at my side, one hand holding her gun, the other wrapped around my shoulder. "Where's Naji? Dammit! I knew we shouldn't have surrendered–"

"No!" I shouted, before she could call up the crew to arms again. "It wasn't... Where's Jeric yi Niru?"

Marjani blinked at me.

"Where's Naji?" she asked again.

"He held the stones," I said. More tears welled up behind my eyes. "He held the stones and now he's... now he's–"

"The stones?" Marjani shook her head. "Ananna, what are you talking about?"

"The starstones!" I shouted. "My parents had the starstones!"

"What?" Marjani stared at me. "And he... Oh, Ananna...is he..." She swallowed. "Is he dead?"

I shook my head.

Marjani closed her eyes and let out a long relieved sigh.

"But there's still something wrong with him. He won't get up. Jeric yi Niru!" I wiped at my eyes, suddenly ashamed of the tears, and turned toward the deck. "Where *is* he?"

"Here, first mate."

He slunk up behind me. When I glanced at him his face twisted up into a mask of sympathy and he said, "Oh, my dear, I'd offer you a handkerchief, but it seems–"

"Stop it." I dug the heel of my hand into my eyes. The salt stung. "What else do you know about the starstones?"

Jeric gave me his slow, easy grin. "I believe you're in need of an Empire magician, not an Empire soldier."

I slapped him.

"Uncalled for," he said.

"You're a noble," I said. "Nobles don't sign up with the Empire's navy unless they get to be officers. But you ain't no officer."

The smile vanished from Jeric's face.

"Right now I don't give a shit what you did that got you condemned to sea. But I've half a mind to think it might got something to do with starstones." I pulled out my pistol and pointed it at his chest. "Am I right?"

"Will you shoot me if I say no?"

I curled my finger around the trigger.

Jeric grinned again, although this time it wasn't so easy. "You're cleverer than I gave you credit for."

"What else do you know about them?"

"You said the assassin is still alive?" Jeric's eyes glinted. "I've heard of people surviving this long after touching the stones, but I've never met one. Of course, I've also heard that they never come back the same."

Fear prickled cold and sharp down my spine, ice in the heat. I didn't know if Jeric yi Niru was lying to me or not.

"Could you help him?"

Jeric shrugged.

"Come with me," I told him. Then I turned to Marjani. "I'm going to bring Naji back on board and you need to tell Queen Saida to let my parents go."

Marjani opened her mouth.

"Just this once. They'll be back. I know Papa. She can do whatever she wants to them then. But please. Just let them go today."

Marjani got real quiet, and then she gave me a short little nod, and that's how I knew for sure that the queen's fleet had been following behind us as we gave chase, all set to interrupt our parley and take my parents prisoner.

I grabbed Jeric yi Niru by the arm and dragged him to the rowboat. He stumbled along with me and didn't say anything as we climbed in, just gave me that steady stare of his – though this time it was shot through with wariness. My pointing the pistol at him had been a bluff; it was just as likely he got sent out to sea for seducing some courtier's wife. Sometimes you gotta take a gamble.

The boat splashed down, cold seawater cascading over my lap. I didn't care. I didn't care about anything except getting Naji back on board the *Nadir*, and then to someplace that could give him care.

"I'm putting you in charge of the stones," I said. "We're bringing them back with us."

"Mercy, why?"

"My reasons are my own," I snapped. It was because of the curse – I didn't know if Naji touching them this time had worked or not. I wanted to cover all my bases.

"And how exactly do you plan to get them on board the ship?"

"They've got a box. Papa's crew was able to transport 'em fine that way."

"I imagine it's safe to assume they're not in the box now."

I glared at him.

"I'm sure you know what my next question is." He paused, eyes glittering. "How do we get them in the box?"

"I don't know. That's why I brought you."

Jeric settled back and didn't say anything.

Naji was still stretched out when we got to the *Tanarau* holding bay. Mama was sitting over him with a bucket of seawater and the big pink conch shell she used on fevers and nightmares. She had peeled his shirt away and set the shell on his scattershot scar.

His tattoos glowed.

The starstones were glowing too, although they were dimmer now, casting long, pale shadows. Mama looked up at me when I walked in, her face foreign-looking in the light of the starstones. Her eyes flicked over to Jeric yi Niru.

"If those stones knock you out, don't expect me to treat you," she said to him.

Jeric didn't respond, not even to give her one of his mocking smiles. I knelt beside Naji and pushed the hair out of his face. I concentrated real hard, trying to see if I could peer inside his thoughts, to see what he was feeling. But I couldn't.

His skin was cold to the touch, but when I pressed my fingers against the side of his neck I could feel his pulse fluttering soft and light.

"Do you know if he'll get better?" I was afraid I would start crying again.

Mama didn't answer, just handed me a little silk bag filled with the glass vials she kept her spellstuff in, the bits of coral and the sand from Mua Beach and the dried seaweed harvested off the coast of the ice-islands.

"I mixed up some salts," she said. "Lay them under his nose twice a day. Maybe it'll work."

Not maybe! I wanted to scream.

Behind me, Jeric yi Niru cleared his throat.

"I don't want to hear your opinion on the subject," I shouted. "Grab the damn stones and take them to the rowboat."

"I wasn't going to say anything." He paused. "And I'm afraid I can't just *grab the damn stones*."

"Find a way."

He sighed. Then he looked at Mama. "What's the thickest fabric you have on board? A carpet would be best."

She gave him a dark look.

"I'm not taking the carpet with me. We just need a way to set them back in their box."

"Of course," Mama said stiffly. Then: "Anything you see in the holding bay, that's the best we got." She pointed off to the corner. "Got some Empire rugs there, that thick enough?"

"Ah," Jeric said, winking, "a pirate with taste."

"Shut up, Jeric." I threaded through the treasure and peeled one of the rugs away from the stack – a small one, the sort they lay in front of shop entryways. Jeric took it from me and slid it under the first starstone like he was scooping up a spider. When he lifted the carpet off the ground, he sucked in his breath and clenched his teeth, and his eyes widened with strain. The starstones pulsed, twinkling like stars.

When he was done he slammed the lid down over them, blinking out their light. Then he collapsed against the wall, breathing heavy.

"Don't ask me to do that again," he said.

Mama got one of the big *Tanarau* fellows to carry Naji to the rowboat. I followed behind with the box of starstones. It was lighter than even an empty box of that sort should be, as though it held negative space. Naji was limp as a rag doll in the crewman's arms, his head lolling back. Papa's crewman took Naji over in a *Tanarau* rowboat and I stayed close by in my own, not letting Naji out of my sight.

Jeric yi Niru didn't say a word as we crossed back over to the *Nadir*.

••••

Naji slept for seven days.

He didn't move, didn't roll over, didn't moan like he was having nightmares. He just lay there, tattoos glowing. Queen Saida put him up in one of the garden houses, which she said were always used for convalescence – I let her cause she called off her fleet when we headed back to Arkuz, and Papa and Mama and the *Tanarau* went free. And when I insisted, she brought in one of her palace wizards to hang the garden house with protection spells, just in case the magic cloaking Naji from the Mists weakened while he was sleeping.

The garden house was one big empty room full of sunlight and the scents from the garden. Sheer curtains hung over the windows to keep the bugs out and at night I could hear noises from the jungle, the rackety screeching of animals, and noises from the palace, too, music and laughter, women's voices trailing out into the night.

I did what Mama said, and put the salts under Naji's nose. Still he slept on. Queen Saida sent in a physician and then a wizard. The physician showed me how to drip water into his mouth so he wouldn't die of thirst, and the wizard told me it wasn't necessary.

"The magic's keeping him alive now," he said.

"That don't make sense."

"Of course not," he said. "It's magic." He sighed and pressed his hand against the scar on Naji's chest, the scar that covered his heart.

I stared at him, my face blank, still not understanding.

"Magic is tied to the human body. Some people have a little, some people have a lot."

"Some people have none at all," I said.

The wizard smiled. "Fewer than you would expect." He sighed. "The stones make the magic inside us swell up, multiply. It chokes out everything else, all the light of life." He paused. "Your friend is quite strong. Most blood-magicians are. But even so, his survival is... unusual."

"Will he ever get better?" My voice quivered like I was about to start crying but I told myself: no, no you will not cry in front of strangers. In front of anyone.

"I don't know, sweetness." The wizard leaned forward and looked at me real close. He was old and wrinkled, but his eyes were bright and kind. "I'll read through my books, and see if I can find anything, alright?"

I nodded, even though I knew he wouldn't find anything.

After a while I took to laying my hand on Naji's heart the way the magician did, so I could feel it beating faint and far away. I sang old Confederation songs to the beat of his heart. The song for lost love. The song for strength and for health. The song to stave off death.

For seven days, I didn't leave the garden house. Marjani brought me food and sat by my side, unspeaking. Queen Saida paid her visits and offered condolences. The magician returned with books and scrolls, none of them with any information to help.

Jeric yi Niru came on the fourth day, stepping into the garden house without knocking. I mistook him for Marjani at first, confused by worry and sleeplessness and the fuzzy sunlight pouring in through the curtains.

"The hell do you want?" I said when I realized my mistake.

"To come see," Jeric said. "I spoke with the palace magician. In all my studies, I never heard–"

"Get out!" I hurled a leftover breakfast plate at him. My aim was off. It banged against the wall and clattered to the floor. "He ain't some experiment for you to poke and prod."

Jeric yi Niru lifted his hands in the air. "I never thought a *pirate* would let her emotions get in the way–"

I sent a coffee cup flying through the air. This one shattered across the floor into pieces.

"Get *out*," I shouted.

"Don't you understand?" Jeric asked. "The starstones were my treasure. I studied them for years at the courts, long before you were even born. The magic in them – the *power* – if the assassin was able to survive their touch, I may be able to–"

I was on my feet, my knife in my hand, my hand at his throat. Jeric yi Niru stopped talking, just stared down at me.

"You want to stop this line of thinking," I said.

Jeric yi Niru didn't say anything even though I could tell from the expression on his face that he wanted to.

"I ain't interested in helping develop Empire weapons, which I'm assuming is what you're after–"

Jeric sneered. "I don't care about the Empire. Why is that so hard for you to understand? The Empire banished me to service on the sea. I don't want to help them. I only wish to examine Naji to help myself."

I glowered at him and dug my knife a little deeper into the skin of his neck. Three drops of blood appeared, and Naji's magic suddenly flooded through me. I hadn't felt any connection with Naji since he fell, but now there was a rush of coldness in my thoughts, a black-glass desert, a song in a language like dying roses, calling out for help.

I dropped the knife and stumbled backward across the room. Jeric laughed at me, but when I fixed my glare on him his laugh dried up like saltwater in the sun.

"I'm not letting you touch him," I said, shaky. "I can see that." Jeric lifted his hands like he was surrendering. "I only thought I'd ask."

"The answer is no. Now get out."

He didn't. He just watched me from across the room. I forced my concentration on Jeric, trying to ignore the terrifying, icy rush of Naji's thoughts.

"When you're older," he said, slowly and carefully, "you'll understand what it is to have a life's devotion."

I stared at him, taking deep breaths.

"You were right, by the way." He gave a short nod. "I was sent to sea because of the stones. There's a Qilari merchant who made his home in Lisirra. He owned a pair. I befriended him just so I could study those starstones. But studying wasn't enough. I wanted to own them."

"They really were your treasure," I snapped. "Thief."

"You have no room to talk, Ananna of the *Nadir*. No room at all."

He was right about that. I took a deep breath, bracing myself against Naji's thoughts, wishing Jeric would just leave.

"But you're right. I did steal them. It didn't take long before the authorities captured me." He sighed, wistful. "I was sentenced, and here we are. I never once touched the stones directly. I was too afraid. And I never thought I'd have the chance again, until I heard you and the captain speaking about them after you captured my ship. That's the entire reason I joined with your crew in the first place."

I stared at him. For once he didn't look mocking or smug.

"That's mad," I said. "Look at Naji! Look at him." I jabbed my finger at his body, unmoving on the bed. Jeric gazed at him without expression. "You want that to happen, go chase down the *Tanarau*. I'm surely they'll be happy to oblige a snakeheart in his suicide attempt."

"I don't want that," Jeric said.

I glared at him. But he didn't say anything more, just turned and left.

I closed my eyes, relieved to be alone except for Naji. Even though Jeric's fresh blood was gone, Naji's thoughts still swirled up with mine, cold and shadowy. I could feel him, distant, indistinct. But alive. Alive.

I curled up beside him on the bed until the thoughts bled away.

On the seventh day, the assassins came.

There were three of them, all dressed the way Naji had been when I first saw him in Lisirra. Black robes, carved armor, swords glittering at their sides. They didn't cover their faces, though.

"Who are you?" one of them asked in Empire when they walked into the garden house.

"Who the hell are you?" I shot back, even though I recognized their clothes. Still, I grabbed Naji's cold hand and squeezed it tight.

The first assassin narrowed his eyes at me. He was from the desertlands, like Naji, though he didn't look like Naji at all. Older and not as handsome and no scar. The other two looked Qilari.

"You aren't saving him, keeping him here," the desertlands assassin said. "He needs our magic."

"And you shouldn't care if he lives or dies," one of his companions added.

I didn't let go.

The desertlands assassin stepped up to me. My breath caught in my throat, and I kept my eye on his sword even though I knew if he wanted to use it I wouldn't be able to get away. But he didn't attack me. He kept his movement slow and steady, and put a hand on my forehead like he was feeling for a fever. I jerked away at his touch, but he grabbed me by the arm with his other hand and held me in place.

"You're scared of me? I'm no different from him." He leaned in close, looking me in the eye. I didn't turn away. I bet he could hear my heart.

He dropped his hand, pulled out a knife. I jerked out my own knife and pressed myself against the wall. One of the Qilari assassins laughed.

"This isn't for you," the first assassin said.

He picked up Naji's hand and cut a line down his arm. A thin trace of blood appeared on Naji's pale skin. I got another rush of thoughts that didn't belong to me – black-glass deserts and cold cold winds. The assassin glanced at me.

"Don't worry, little girl. This wound will heal." Another smile. He dipped his finger in Naji's blood and then licked the blood away, neat like a cat. He closed his eyes.

"Oh," he said. "He failed to mention that."

The Qilari assassins stirred. "Mention what?" one of them asked.

"He blood-bonded." The first assassin looked over at me, still cowering against the wall like a little ship-rat. "With this one, it seems."

The Qilari assassins exchanged glances.

"Ah," one of 'em said. "That explains her unnatural devotion."

"My devotion ain't unnatural!" I shouted, in spite of myself. "And besides, I'd be helping him even if we hadn't shared bl–"

The desertland assassin held up one hand and my voice left my throat and I was filled up with silence. "There's no need to explain yourself. I know about the curse and the foolishness with your kiss."

Something heavy landed in my chest. I didn't say nothing.

"And I know *this* foolishness was one of the tasks." The assassin sighed. "He certainly dawdled long enough."

"What?" I stepped forward, whole body tensed. "What do you mean, *dawdled*?"

The assassin looked at me. "Ah, the joys of dealing with the uneducated–"

"I know what the fuck the word means. I don't understand why you–"

"I commanded him to break the curse," the assassin said. "I thought he did well, managing the first task so easily." He sneered at me. I sneered back. "Unfortunately, the cause of the first task resulted in him taking too long with the others."

The sneer disappeared from my face, and the assassin laughed. The cause of the first task? My kiss? I understood what the assassin was implying, but I didn't believe him. Naji didn't love me back. This assassin was making fun of me. I was certain of it.

I lifted up my knife and lunged at him.

A blur of shadows and the two Qilaris had me pinned to the floor and the desertland assassin had my own knife at my throat.

"You knew that wouldn't work," he said.

"Get off me!"

He lifted the knife up off my skin by a fraction. "You need to step outside now," he said. "My associates and I have work to do."

"Are you gonna kill him?" I asked.

"A true Jadorr'a welcomes death."

"I ain't a Jadorr'a."

"Yes, but Naji is." He pressed the flat side of the knife against the left side of my face – the same as Naji's scar. The metal was cold, colder than ice. "Although I'm not going to kill him. He still has work to do." He dropped his knife. "Now leave."

The assassin grabbed my arm and yanked me back, hard enough that my feet lifted off the ground. He put his mouth against my ear. "You shouldn't care for him so."

"Let me go, you Empire ass."

The other two drew their daggers. I stopped struggling.

"Love is a wound," the assassin said. "Neither life nor death."

I wanted to tell him to shut up, but I figured I better hold my tongue. He smiled at me, showing all his teeth.

"Whatever you're thinking, girl," he said. "Speak. I won't hold it against you."

"Love is a wound?" I said. "Sounds like something a killer would say."

"So you must understand my metaphor well."

His words slammed into me, and for a moment I faltered, thinking about Tarrin bleeding in the desert. Then I kicked him, hard, in the shin. He laughed and dropped my arm, and the two Qilaris lifted me off my feet and dragged me, kicking and struggling, out of the garden house. I slammed my feet into one of them, right in the hip, before the door swung shut and I landed face-first in the soft grass.

"Are you alright?" The voice was speaking Jokjani. I spit out dirt and looked up. One of the palace soldiers, his eyes wide with fear. "They wouldn't let me go inside. I tried—"

"Ain't your fault."

The soldier pulled me to my feet. I smelled mint.

A few moments passed, and the smell grew stronger, drowning out the rainy scent of the garden. Bright blue light seeped out of the house's windows. The soldier positioned himself between me and the house, gripping his dagger tight, and I wanted to tell him he didn't have to do that for me, but I was too tired to try and get the words right. Plus it reminded me of Naji, and I was afraid if I spoke then I would cry.

A chill crept into the air.

I stepped away from the garden house and sat down beneath a banana tree. I kept seeing Naji stretched out on the bed, unmoving. I kept hearing his faint, slow heartbeat. And then the scent of mint flooded through the garden. It plunged me backward in time, till I was facing down Naji that first night, when he could've killed me easier than a bug, but he didn't.

Don't cry, I told myself. You're a pirate. Don't cry.

But I did anyway. The palace guard came and patted me on the shoulder like I was noblewoman crying over a suitor. I snarled at him until he went away.

The assassins stayed in the garden house for a long time, long enough that the afternoon rains came and went, that the sun sank into the horizon and turned the sky orange, that the soldiers changed places, the first one scuttling off into the palace and leaving another man, older, more grizzled-looking, in his place.

I didn't move from my spot beneath the banana tree.

The assassins came out of the garden house one at a time, their robes swirling around their feet, the armor gleaming in the thick orange light. They ignored the soldier and walked up to me.

"We need your help," the desertlands assassin said.

I glared at him. "Need my help how?"

"You don't seem to understand much of anything, do you?" he asked. "Perhaps if I inserted more profanity–"

"Just answer my damn question! What do you need my help for?" My heart was pounding. "Is Naji dead?"

"Your blood-bond." The assassin looked like he'd just swallowed a scorpion. "It seems we have use of it."

"What?"

He grabbed me by the wrist and pulled me up close. "It's not a difficult concept to grasp. We were unable to pull Naji out. We may be able to do so with your blood. It seems your bond was helping keep him alive."

I stared at him.

"I'm not explaining all this to you, girl. I saw he had enough of you in his blood when I cut him – I was testing for the curse but got *that* nasty little surprise."

"Not so nasty," I snapped, "if it means you'll get to save him."

The assassin scowled at me and dragged me back into the garden house. I let him. I didn't think it would work, but I let him.

"Stand here," he said, lining me up at the foot of Naji's bed. The floor was covered in rust-colored markings, and the air smelled like blood. One of the Qilari assassins bolted the door shut and they both stood behind me. I could feel their eyes on the back of my neck.

The desertlands assassin pulled out his red-stained knife. "Hold out your arm," he said.

I was shaking. I didn't want to let him cut me, but I didn't want Naji to die, neither.

"I know you want him to wake up," the assassin said, sneering a little. "I saw it when I cut him."

"Are you going to kill me?"

"Would you let yourself die to save him?"

"Ain't nobody wants to die," I said, and I knew it wasn't a proper answer.

The assassin moved up close to me in a blink. Another blink and he'd stretched my arm out over the bed. I thought maybe I should struggle.

Another blink and he cut me.

The cut was long and deep and this time Naji's thoughts flooded over mine so deeply I stopped being in the garden house and started being in the black-glass desert. It was empty except for the wind. I shivered in my thin Jokja dress and called out Naji's name. My voice echoed out across the emptiness. I took a hesitant step forward, and my knee slammed into something invisible, and invisible hands grabbed my arms and pulled me back.

A voice whispered on the wind. Not Naji's. It belonged to the desertland assassin. *Look for him*, he said. *Stop shouting. It won't do any good.*

"I can't look for him!" I shouted, struggling against the invisible hands. The Qilari assassins. I knew it and didn't know it, all at once. "I can't move."

With your mind, girl.

I stopped struggling. The wind swirled around me, icing over my bare arms and my bare cheeks. My bones rattled in my skin. The cold was worse than the Isle of the Sky had ever been. But I forced myself to concentrate, to reach out with the fingers of my mind.

I found him.

I found his thoughts, warmed by blood, thin blood, weak blood. He was thinking about food and water. He was thinking about me.

The invisible hands yanked me so hard my head spun round and around and then I was back in the garden house, sagging between the two Qilari assassins. The desertlands assassin was leaned over Naji, tracing blood – my blood, I knew – in patterns over the scar on his chest. My blood was all over the bed. It dripped down my arm, stained my clothes.

"He was thinking about me," I said, dazed.

"Shut up, girl." The desertland assassin didn't even glance up at me from beside Naji's bed, and the two others dragged me over to the corner. I slumped down on the floor, still dizzy and confused. In my head was an image of myself, standing on a boat, looking out over the ocean. And I was beautiful somehow, like all my insides had turned to light.

He was thinking of me as he lay dying in a world between worlds.

And it was real. I could feel it. I *knew* it.

I leaned against the wall, taking deep unsteady breaths. The Qilari assassins were singing, the desertland assassin was chanting. Their eyes glowed pale blue in the darkness. My spilled blood steamed and smoked, and it smelled like mint and the ocean.

After a while I couldn't see much of anything but the blue of the assassins' eyes and the ghostly trace of magic-smoke.

And then I heard someone say my name.

The singing and the chanting stopped. The smoke lingered in the air. I could feel the walls of the garden house shifting and squirming just outside my vision.

And then a warmth flowed into my thoughts, familiar, barely there–

"Ananna?"

"Naji!" I pushed myself up to my feet, tottering in place. All three of the assassins turned and glared at me.

"Not yet, girl," hissed the one from the desertlands.

"No," Naji said, his voice rough and faint. "No, it's fine, I'm here–"

The assassin turned back to him. The glow faded from the Qilaris' eyes. I stumbled forward, my arm aching, my head spinning. "Naji," I said. "You're alright–"

"Not exactly."

I knelt beside the desertland assassin, who made no move to send me away. He just stood there glaring. Naji was stretched out on the bed the way he'd been all week, but now his eyes were open and his fingers fluttered against the sheet.

"Naji," I said, because I couldn't say what I wanted to. I buried my head into his shoulder. The scent of medicine and magic lingered in the room, and although the smoke was drifting away the air still seemed thick. Naji laid his hand on top of mine.

"You're here," he said.

"I had to save you. These buddies of yours ain't worth a damn." I blinked, trying not to cry. I was aware of his hand touching mine. "Besides, where else would I go?"

"I don't know. I thought you might take off with the *Nadir*, plundering."

I tried to laugh, but it came out strangled-sounding. "Thought? How could you think anything? You were…" I didn't know what to call it. Dead?

"I was trapped in between here and the Mists," he said. His hand was still on mine. "The Order found me, sent Dirar to bring me back." He glanced over at the desertland assassin and nodded. "Thank you."

Dirar scowled. "It was lucky the girl was here."

I didn't say anything.

"Yes," Naji said. "I suppose you'll be alerting the Order of my blood-bond."

Dirar huffed and crossed his arms over his chest and didn't answer. Naji chuckled. I didn't understand what was going on. I wasn't sure I wanted to.

"By the way," Naji said. "It worked."

I stared at him for a long time.

"One more," Dirar said. "I suppose you plan on taking another four months with this one? Or maybe you'll just go for another four years. Why not?"

Naji's eyes took on that brightness that replaced his smile. "It worked," he said again. "Can you feel it?"

"No," I said, except as soon as I spoke I did: a lightness in his presence I hardly noticed. Missing weight. Missing darkness.

"You do," Naji said, his eyes still bright. "Come here."

"What?"

"Lean close," he said. "I have something to tell you."

Dirar stomped over to the garden house door with the other two assassins. All three of 'em stared at us. But I leaned over anyway, tilting my ear to his mouth. He put one hand on my chin and turned my face toward his.

"It worked," he said, and then he kissed me on the mouth, his lips dry from sleep.

CHAPTER FIFTEEN

I kept watch over Naji for two weeks, long after the other assassins left. We had to move him to a room in the palace, because the garden house was destroyed by the magic-sickness, its walls turning into thick ropy vines, the bed transforming into an enormous moon-colored flower. I stayed away from the place where the garden house had been.

But tucked away in the palace, Naji did get slowly better. The color returned to his face. His tattoos stopped glowing. He ate every bite of food Queen Saida had brought to him.

Sometimes he kissed me.

Some days I would lay my head on Naji's chest, the way I had when he was asleep. I listened to his heart beat strong and sure. He let his hand drift over my hair and down the length of my spine. It was nice. I was afraid to say something about it, though, afraid that if I opened my mouth it would all disappear.

When he felt good enough to stand up, I walked with him around the perimeter of the palace garden, the way he had with me on the Island of the Sun. He pointed out flowers to me, identifying them by name, telling me what sorts of magic properties they had, but all the while his hand was on the small of my back, and I didn't remember one word of what he said.

Jeric came to visit. He knocked on Naji's door while I was there, and when I answered, he scowled at me and said, "I'd hoped you'd be gone."

"Go away," I said.

"No." Naji's voice was bright behind me. "No, Ananna, it's fine. He can stay."

Jeric gave me a smug smile and pushed into the room. Naji was sitting on the bed, the sunlight making his hair shine. Jeric gave a scholarly little bow and said, "That one–" He pointed at me, "–gets over overenthusiastic. I only wanted to ask you about the starstones."

Naji nodded. I was all prepared to chase Jeric away, but when he started asking questions Naji didn't seem to mind answering them. I guess it was Naji's university background, and all the studying he had to do for the Order. He told Jeric what it felt like when his skin touched the stones, and his theories about how they had affected the magic in his body. Jeric nodded all the while, scratching notes down in a little leather-bound book, and after they got to talking both seemed pleased with themselves. I sat in the corner and listened, because it was interesting, even if I didn't always understand the technicalities of what Naji said, even if the thought of the starstones scared me a little, still.

Jeric only visited once, but he became a lot easier to deal with after that. Like Naji'd given him a gift.

One afternoon me and Naji went to see Queen Saida in her sunroom. Marjani was there, dressed in a long golden dress that suited her, her hair woven with ribbons and shells. Saida looked a proper queen in Empire silks, Jokja metals in the bangles on her wrist. She stood up when me and Naji walked in.

"You've recovered!" she cried out. "Marjani told me the news, but I'm so glad to see you walking about." And she actually crossed the room to greet us. She kissed both of Naji's cheeks and beamed at him.

"Thank you, my Light," Naji murmured, bowing his head.

Queen Saida turned to me. "And I heard you were most instrumental," she said. "The Jadorr'a told me about it when they thanked me for my hospitality. I told them: no Jokja has ever feared a Jadorr'a." She laughed. Naji's eyes crinkled into a smile.

"And what about the third task?" Marjani asked from her seat by the windows. It was raining, gray-green light pouring in around her. "Have you figured out what that means yet?"

"Ah yes!" Queen Saida said. "The third task. I can ask the palace magicians to look into it for you, if you'd like."

I thought about how worthless her palace helpers had been when it came to finding the starstones, but Naji only nodded and said, "Yes, I would appreciate that. Thank you."

Afterward, me and Naji walked together in the garden, the way we usually did. I linked my arm in Naji's and he didn't say nothing about it, so I figured it was alright. I'd been refraining from dipping in his head ever since he woke up. It had been startling to see myself in there, beloved – though I was still afraid of what might happen if I didn't find myself at all.

The rain had slowed down to a slow shimmering drizzle. The sun came out and refracted through the drops, filling the air with diamonds. Me and Naji sat down at one of the pavilions near the fence. The jungle was quiet from the rain.

"Why'd you tell her to help you?" I asked.

"So I can cure my curse."

"You want to get rid of me that easy?" I tried to keep my voice light, but it trembled anyway.

Naji looked at me with eyes as dark as new moons. "No."

I looked down at my lap.

"Surely you'd like to run off and have your adventures," he said, "without having me tag along complaining about the vagaries of the ocean."

"What's a vagary?" I said. "And I wouldn't mind none anyway. Having you with me." With that last part, I blushed and slurred my words on purpose.

Naji leaned over and kissed me, one hand cupping the side of my face. "I wouldn't mind either," he said softly, "but I prefer not to feel as though I'm dying every time you loosen the sails."

I laughed at that, and his eyes lit up. I'd been seeing that more and more. It got to the point that I could fill in the blanks, and every time he did it was like his whole face was smiling. Funny that I hadn't seen the crinkle back on the Island of the Sun. When I thought about it, I knew it had been there.

Naji kissed me again.

Something squawked over in the garden.

"What the—" I pulled away from Naji and sure enough there was that big white seabird that'd flown into his room before we found the starstones. Another note was attached to its foot.

The bird cawed and flapped its great white wings.

"It's that bird again," I said.

Naji took my hand in his. "I saw it," he said. "When I was under."

"What? Really?"

The bird hopped forward and stuck out its leg. Naji slipped off the canister and dropped out the note and the map, the same as before.

Naji of the Jadorr'a:

I never received a reply to our last missive, although Samuel assures me that you did read the note. I plead you not to dismiss this one as well – we are not seeking your harm. Nor do we have interest in your skills as a murderer-for-hire. The King of Salt and Foam merely wishes to thank you. That is all. If you are concerned, you may bring guards and weapons, magic or otherwise, as you see fit. I guarantee you will not have use of them. Regards, Jolin I.

Naji lay the note down in his lap.

"What do they got to thank you for?" I asked. "You sure nobody knows anything about them?"

Naji sighed. "I told you, they're completely unknown to the Order and to Saida's scholars – I asked about the court and about this Jolin I both. Nothing." He hesitated. "However, I did see that bird when I was trapped in the liminal space, circling the sky, over and over, dropping down sheets of parchment..." He turned to me. "Ask one of the palace clerks for some ink. I'm going to send them a response."

"You don't even know who they are!" I snatched the note off his lap and flapped in the air. "This could be the Mists. A trap–"

"It isn't." He pulled the note away from me. "I'll fetch the ink myself."

I scowled at the bird, who just cawed at me.

Naji disappeared into the palace. Part of me wanted to follow behind him and find some way to stop him, but I just sat there glaring at the seabird to see who would blink first – me, as it turned out. Whatever Naji knew, whatever Naji thought – some of it was seeping into my brain. Not all of it, but enough that I let him be.

Naji emerged twenty minutes later with a pot of ink. When he saw me staring at the seabird he laughed.

"Write your damn note," I told him.

"Ananna." He sat beside me and pulled his black quill out of his shirt. It occurred to me that despite everything that had happened to us he'd never once lost that quill, and then I thought about how thin Jokja cotton was and

I wondered just where he kept the quill at all, cause I'd never seen it.

"Naji," I said.

"I want to visit this…" he glanced down at the note. "This King of Foam and Salt. Things don't appear in the liminal space unless they're important."

I sighed. "You want me to sail you to… to wherever. The middle of nowhere. The place where Mistress Hariri shot me."

He touched my cheek with the back of his hand. "This has nothing to do with the Hariris."

"Fine," I said. "But I don't know if I can convince Marjani to come with." I gave him a sly smile. "Maybe you can be Captain Namir yi Nadir again."

"I doubt it." He stared at me, his eyes all dark and intense. He was gonna get himself killed.

The way he almost did picking up the starstones.

But that was different. That was the *curse*. This was just some nonsense he saw while he hovered between worlds.

I listened to the *scritch scritch scritch* of his pen against the back of the seabird's note. When he finished he slid the parchment back into the tube and then slid the tube back onto the seabird's leg. He kept the map, at least.

Then the seabird spread out its wings and dipped its head down low, almost like it was bowing, before taking off into the gray-blue sky.

I knocked on the door to Marjani's bedroom. A guard stood nearby, gazing at the wall in front of him in such a bored way that I knew really he was keeping tabs on me. Don't know why: Queen Saida was off in some diplomatic meeting, according to the whispers around the palace, and it's not like I was up to any mischief.

The door swung open. Marjani blinked when she saw me.

"I need to talk to you," I said.

She pushed the door open wider so I could come in. Her room was bigger than mine, with lots of open windows and expensive-looking furniture and a bed that looked like it had never been slept in.

"Is the ship alright?" she asked, soon as the door was shut. "The crew?"

"What? Oh, yeah, they're both fine. Crew all came back from the Aja Shore and picked up their work shifts right where we left off."

Marjani smiled. "I'm glad to hear that."

"Actually, I kinda wanted to talk about the ship."

"You want to leave."

That gave me pause, the way she knew right away, and for a moment I just stared at her. She didn't look like Marjani much anymore, with her pretty dresses and the makeup around her eyes, but I realized it was just that she didn't look like the Marjani I knew, and that she had been *this* Marjani long before she met me. I wondered if she thought the same thing about me. I hadn't been in men's clothes much since we came to Jokja, either.

"Yeah," I said, "I want to leave."

She gave me a quick smile.

"Do you?"

The smile disappeared, and there was this long pause as she looked out the windows. "I don't know," she finally said. "I miss it, you know, but when I was sailing I missed all this."

I knew she really meant that she had missed Queen Saida, but I didn't say nothing.

"Where do you want to go?" she asked.

I took a deep breath. "We got coordinates to someplace out in the ocean. Naji – he's got some *feeling* about them, though–"

"You don't agree," Marjani said. "You don't want to go."

"Yeah, but... the thing is, I looked at the coordinates and they're... well, they're about the same place where we had that battle with the Hariris."

She stared at me. "Violence," she said. "It's a cure for his curse."

"It's the middle of the ocean!" I said. "More likely it's some Hariri trick."

Marjani tilted her head at me. "Do you want me to go so you can stay here?"

"No! I ain't no coward. I just... it's your ship, you're the captain–"

Marjani's face changed. Just for a second, when I called her captain. I got the feeling she missed it all more than she let on.

"Besides," I said, "if we do gotta fight the Hariris, I need to have you around. Don't think I could lead the ship into battle the way you could."

She laughed. I could tell it was cause she was flattered. "Well," she said, "how can I say no to that? Not that I think you're going to have to fight the Hariris."

"We won't be out long," I said.

"You say that." She shook her head. "I'll go. I do miss it terribly. Saida may not be too pleased to hear it, but…" Her voice trailed off and she toyed with the end of one of her locks.

"Tell the queen I'll bring you back safe," I said. "Pirate's honor."

Marjani looked at me and laughed, but I knew I had my captain back.

We made sail three days later.

Queen Saida'd had her navy repair the boat after our trip to the Aja Shore, but Naji was still too weak to do magic, so we had to sail the old-fashioned way, with no guarantee of favorable winds. In truth it was nice, cause it gave the crew something to do besides sitting around on deck drinking sugar-wine and playing dice. And I didn't have to deal with Jeric begging for more information about the starstones – Marjani kept him busy down in the armory, tending to the pistols and ammunitions and making sure everything stayed dry.

A storm blew through a week in, threatening to knock us off course. I crawled up in the rigging myself, to help keep the sails straight. Ain't nothing like it, swinging from rope to rope while the water soaks you to the bone. It ain't pleasant, but it was something I'd missed.

The whole time Naji was up near the helm, a rope

knotted round his arm so he wouldn't get tossed overboard, and whenever I glanced at him he'd be staring straight at me, his eyes flickering in and out, his face twisted up in pain. I'd locked him out of my head for the time being, but seeing that expression hurt me in a way that had nothing to do with my body.

That storm was the only one we faced, though, and for the rest of the trip the seas were smooth as glass, the winds brisk and warm. Two weeks passed. I checked the navigation every day and compared it to the map the seabird had left us. But it was hard as hell, cause the map just led us straight to the middle of the open ocean.

"You sure this is correct?" Marjani asked me one afternoon when she was up at the helm. I had the maps spread out on the deck beside her, pinned down with rum bottles and sea rocks.

"Sure as anything," I said.

Marjani frowned. She'd been in good spirits when we started out, but now that we were out on the open sea she was constantly gazing off to the east. Off to Jokja.

"Does Naji know anything?" she asked.

I shrugged.

"Go ask him."

"He probably ain't well–"

"Go ask him." She gripped the wheel a little more tightly. "I trust him more than I trust that map of yours."

I couldn't much blame her for that, seeing as how the map had been given to us by a bird. I left her to her steering and made my way down to the captain's quarters, where Naji was laid up recovering from my swinging around the rigging. I knocked but didn't bother to wait for an answer, and when I walked in he was stretched on the bed, his hands folded over his chest.

"Marjani wants to know if we're going the right way," I said.

He turned his head to look at me, his hair falling across his face.

"Are you navigating?"

"Course I am."

"Then of course we're going the right direction."

I scowled at him, though inside my whole heart lit up like a bonfire. "Yeah, but we ain't sailing to land. Some tiny spot in the middle of the ocean... that ain't easy to get to. You know she's talking about using magic."

"I know what she's talking about." Naji sat up and patted the bed beside him. I stared at him for a few seconds.

"I want you to sit beside me," he said.

"What for?"

He laughed, one of those short sharp Naji laughs. "We aren't lost," he said. "I've gone to Kajjil, to follow our path on the underside of the world. We're quite fine."

I blinked at him, confused.

"My trances," he said.

"Oh."

"It's how we learn things in the Order. Come, sit."

I sighed and sank down on the mattress beside him. He put his hand on my knee. I glanced at him and he flicked his head away real fast. The air crackled with something like magic.

He kissed me. I was starting to get used to his kisses, but this one went on longer than usual, and his hands trailed down over my shoulders, and tugged on my shirt, tugging it up over my shoulders.

"Oh," I said, pulling away from him, flustered and embarrassed, sure he would take one look at me and call the whole thing off.

"Are you on shift?" he asked. "You said you had taken the mornings–"

"Yeah," I muttered. "I was helping Marjani out some, but it wasn't my official time–"

He kissed me again.

We sank down to the bed. I wrapped my arms over my stomach, afraid *now* would be the moment that he left. But he didn't leave. He slipped out of his own clothes, and his tattoos were flat and dark against his skin, tracing all over his chest and down to the tops of his thighs. The scar from the spell fallout was red and new-looking, not like the scar on his face.

He climbed into the bed with me. I couldn't believe it was going to happen, but when I let myself peek at his thoughts I felt only this hot red flush, and I knew he wanted me.

He kissed me all over, on my neck and my jawline and my shoulders. He touched me in that certain way and I felt him everywhere, the movement of his body and the warmth of his breath. It hadn't felt like this the other times I'd been with someone. I hardly felt anything before; now, all I had was feeling.

Naji buried his head in my shoulder, his breath hot on my skin, and dug his fingers into the blankets.

Afterwards, he kissed me long and deep and rolled over onto his back.

My chest filled with this warm honeyed feeling. And I knew it wasn't gonna go away. I could feel his thoughts bumping up against mine, telling me it was for real, it had always been for real.

I kissed along his chest and asked him what we were looking for. I figured he'd know from his trances.

"Sentries," he said.

"You just got that out of the letter."

"Well, of course, that's what I'm working off here."

I rolled on top of him, pinning him to the cot. He gazed up at me. "I thought you saw them in Kajjil," I said. "Or the seabird. Or something."

"I saw the albatross when I was under," he said. "It didn't speak to me. And Kajjil doesn't work that way. I don't see people. I track them."

I sighed. "I still think it's a trap."

Naji pulled me down and kissed me, his hand running up and down my spine.

"Stop it." I pushed away from him. He frowned. "You're distracting me!" I said. "Marjani's probably pissed enough right now—"

"Do you really care?"

I glared at him. He knew I did, although not enough to leave. My thoughts were spilling out of me.

"We're just gonna sail around in circles till the crew has the doldrums and we've eaten up all the food and then the Mists is gonna *attack*—"

"It's not the Mists," Naji said. "I know that for certain."

I looked at him long and hard. He was telling the truth. Or what he thought was the truth.

"Who posts sentries in the middle of the ocean?" I asked.

"Someone who lives in the middle of the ocean," Naji said, and he drew me close to him and kissed me again. This time I let him.

CHAPTER SIXTEEN

Next morning, I was up at the helm, guiding the *Nadir* through those smooth glassy waters. I'm not crazy about steering on the best of days, and that morning I was tired and distracted with thoughts of Naji. Plus the morning sun was hot and bright in my eyes. All I wanted was to be down below, my clothes in a heap on the floor, Naji's mouth at the base of my throat.

Old Sorley came bounding up to the helm with his hat in his hands.

"The hell do you want?" It came out a lot gruffer than I meant.

"Madam First Mate," he stuttered, looking down at his feet. He'd been some kind of servant before he got nicked off the street and forced onto an Empire boat. "You told us to come to you if we saw anything odd."

I tensed my hands around the helm but kept my eyes straight ahead. "Yeah? You see something weird?"

"Yes, madam."

A pause.

"Well, what is it?"

"It's... well, it's probably nothing..."

I glowered at him.

"Sharks!" he squeaked. "It's sharks!"

"Sharks?" I squinted out at the horizon, light flashing up into my eyes. "Don't let anybody fall into the water, it'll be fine. Not like we're in danger of sinking."

"No, you don't understand..." He crushed his hat into a tight little ball between his hands. "They ain't normal sharks. I can't... it's a bit hard to describe, madam, I'm sorry–"

I felt bad for him. "Show me."

He nodded. I called off for Jeric yi Niru to take the helm. He came over no questions asked, the way he usually did these days, though he gave me one of his insolent little nods. Some habits you just can't break.

I followed Sorley across the deck to the port side. Sunlight was everywhere, bright and glittering.

"There," Sorley said, pointing with his crumpled up hat.

I didn't have the words for it.

There were sharks, to be sure. About sixteen of 'em, lined up four by four, swimming alongside us without breaking formation.

And they were wearing *clothes*: vests made of seashells, all strung together so that they looked like scaled Empire armor. The sharks skimmed across the water, tails switching back and forth in time.

"What the hell?" I said, cause what else do you say? Then I turned to Sorley: "Go get the captain." I thought for a moment, then added, "And Naji."

He didn't hear me, though. He was leaning over the railing, waving that stupid hat around. "Hey!" he called out. "I brought her! The first mate! Captain's not on duty."

"What are you doing?" I grabbed at him. He ignored me. I glanced over my shoulder – a bunch of the crewmen had gathered behind us. They were all spooked.

"The hell's going on?!" I shouted. "One of you, go get the captain." Nobody moved. "Now!"

They scattered, as though "one of you" meant "all of you". When I turned back to the railing, Sorley was staring at me, and down in the water, one of the sharks had broken formation.

"Pardon me!" the shark called out. "But does this boat bear Naji of the Jadorr'a?"

I screamed. Kaol help me, but I screamed liked I'd just been sliced through with a damned Qilari blade. The shark dipped its head in the water and splashed around foam.

"A thousand apologies, my dear, I didn't mean to frighten you–"

"Why are you *talking*?" I screamed. I turned to Sorley. "Why didn't you *tell* me?"

He looked cowed. "I didn't think you'd believe me."

I took a deep breath. A talking shark. I leaned back over the railing.

"Are you from the Mists?" I asked, watching closely for a spray of smoke or a smear of light.

"No, I'm from the waters," the shark said. "I am Lorens, member of the eighty seventh Guard Infantry, sentry to the Court of the Waves and sworn protector of the King of Salt and Foam."

My mouth dropped open a little.

"We were sent here to guide you to the rendezvous point. Assuming you are, in fact, carrying Naji of the Jadorr'a. The young gentleman said you were." He splashed water in Sorley's direction.

"Are you gonna kill him?" I asked. "Naji?"

The shark looked affronted. "Madam, never! We are in his *debt*, you must understand–"

"Ananna?"

I stepped away from the railing and whirled around. Naji came barreling across the deck, Marjani close behind. "What's wrong?" he asked, putting his hands on my face and pulling me close. For once in their lives the crew didn't hoot and holler when he did it.

"What's going on?" Marjani asked.

"Sharks," I said.

She stared at me like I'd gone mad. "Sharks," she said. "*Sharks* have got the crew off the sails?" She frowned. "It's like they've never been at sea before."

I tried to figure out a way to explain it to her without sounding mad, but I couldn't. Naji stepped up to the railing. Turned around again.

"They want you," I said. "They can, uh–"

"They what?"

"This is getting absurd," Marjani said. "Ananna, just tell me what's happening."

"I'm not–"

"Are you Naji of the Jadorr'a?"

It was the shark again, his rough rasp of a voice calling up out of the water. Marjani shrieked and stumbled up against me, one hand on the butt of her pistol. Naji, though, leaned over the railing. "I am!" He sounded unconcerned, like he spoke with sharks all the time.

"We are in your debt," the shark said.

"Why?"

"What is going *on*?" Marjani whispered.

"I ain't got no idea."

Marjani shoved me toward the railing. The other sharks were all facing us now, their heads bent low into the water. The head shark hadn't bothered to answer Naji's question.

"You must come down below!" the shark said.

"Below what?" asked Naji. "The water?"

The shark nodded.

"I'm afraid that isn't possible, not if you'd also like to speak with me. I won't be able to breathe–"

"We've made arrangements."

I grabbed Naji's arm. "Don't do it," I whispered. "It's a trap."

Naji wrapped his arm around my waist. "May I bring some companions?" he asked.

"What?" I hissed.

"Of course." The sharks all bowed again, splashing water.

"Are you insane?"

"We shall send the device to the surface shortly," said the head shark. "You may bring down as many of your crew as you like. In shifts, of course."

Naji waved his hand. "No need." He squeezed my waist again. I scowled at him.

The sharks disappeared beneath the water.

"What are you *doing*?" I shouted, smacking him in the chest. "You're gonna get us both killed!"

"Yes, I agree." Marjani stepped forward, hand still on the butt of her pistol. "I'd prefer you not get my navigator *eaten*, thank you."

"I'm proving to you – to both of you – how undangerous I think it is," Naji said. "Ananna, I want you to go with me."

I peered up at him. He really did think it was safe; I could feel it creeping into my own thoughts. But that didn't mean I agreed with him.

Naji's eyes glazed over, like he was thinking. "Something about this," he said. "It feels... right. Pieces falling into place."

I wanted to hit him.

"You can come too," Naji added, turning to Marjani. "If you're truly concerned about Ananna's safety–"

"That wouldn't be wise," Marjani said quietly. Behind her, the crew shuffled and mumbled to each other. She was probably right. Captain and first mate disappearing beneath the waves with a bunch of talking sharks? Hell, I'd be hightailing it out of here too.

Frothy bubbles appeared on the surface of the water, followed by a low whining noise that reminded me of the Hariri clan and their machines. I yanked out my knife. The boat began to rock.

"All hands to stations!" Marjani screamed. "Keep her steady!"

The crew scrambled to attention.

Sea foam sprayed over the railing. Naji stepped in front of me.

Ha, I thought. Showing me how safe it is.

And then there was a hiss like the biggest snake you ever heard, and a big glass box erupted out of the sea, showering the *Nadir* with water and sea foam. Me and Naji and Marjani were soaked through.

For a minute the box floated in the open ocean, glittering a little in the sunlight. Then the top of it popped open.

"Naji of the Jadorr'a!" shouted the shark, who'd showed back up without his sentries. "You and one other must come inside the transport."

Naji pressed himself against the railing. "Will we be able to breathe?" he asked.

The shark nodded. "We tested it on air-breathers. There are some among our number."

Naji turned to me. "Air-breathers," he said.

"Does he mean other humans? Cause I don't breathe water."

"I doubt it. There are certain sea creatures who only live half in the water." His eyes sparkled. The closest he ever came to smiling. I figured he'd gone and lost his mind. "Please, Ananna," he said. "Come with me."

"Course I'm gonna come with you." I eased my knife back into my belt. "Just don't expect me to be happy about it."

"Me, neither," Marjani said. "If you let her die, I'll kill you."

We were both soaked already, so me and Naji just dove into the water and swam over to the box. My heart pounded the whole time, cause I couldn't quite shake the notion that the Hariris or the Mists were behind this somehow. Plus the thing kept hissing and groaning and the water around it bubbled like it was boiling.

Once we climbed in, I had Marjani toss me my gunpowder. That left me a couple of shots on my pistol, plus my sword and my knife, and Naji's sword and knife and his magic too.

The lid lowered down onto the box.

"You want to kill me." My voice echoed weirdly against the glass walls.

"I want no such thing."

"You know what's going on, then." I looked at him. "But you won't tell me."

"I honestly don't. Which you know, because..." He tapped his head.

"Still like hearing you say it out loud."

There was a big hiss and the box began to lower into the water. I braced my hands against the glass and waited for the water to come rushing in and drown us. It didn't. Just slapped against the outside of the box, blue and green and filled with sunlight.

"I have my intuition," Naji said. "It's surprisingly fine-honed."

I thought about all the times he'd known the Mists was trying to seduce me. All the times he showed up at the last minute to save me from more worldly deaths. All the times he knew exactly what to say to piss me off.

His intuition. Yeah, I guess I could give him that.

We sank lower and lower. The water got darker and the air got colder, but at least we could still breathe. The shark swam alongside us.

"It didn't strike you as weird they wouldn't tell you what's going on?"

Naji glanced at me. "It's a little strange," he said. "But not nearly as strange as a talking shark."

I sighed.

Deeper and deeper. It was dark as night now, no sunlight to speak of, just the endless black press of the ocean.

And then a light glimmered off in the distance, tiny and bright.

"What's that?" I asked, leaning forward. I was afraid to touch the walls of the box, afraid they'd shatter into a thousand pieces.

The light brightened and expanded.

It swelled, looking for all the world like the moon on a cloudy night. A big bright circle amidst all that watery darkness.

The box hissed and screeched.

And then we got close enough and I could see – it wasn't just a ball of light.

It was a city.

"Kaol," I said, my words forming white mist on the glass. Even Naji wasn't so unconcerned no more. He pressed his hands against the side of the box, his eyes growing wider and wider.

The box slipped through the water, churning up bubbles behind us. I could see the buildings were made out of broken-up shells and something rough like sand and what looked to be glass. A fuzzy algae that glowed like a magic-cast lantern grew over everything, hanging off the edges of buildings like moss. And the buildings didn't look like the buildings anywhere on land, cause they twisted and curled out of the ground like seabones, and they merged together and split apart without no definite order. Sea creatures flitted past us, some of 'em wrapped in strips of seaweed that fluttered out behind 'em, and some of 'em were decked out in the same shell armor as the sharks.

Naji and me didn't say a word to each other. I got flashes of his thoughts: wonder, confusion, a little bit of fear. Or maybe it was my thoughts. They were all mingled together.

The box came to a tunnel, encased in shining shells, with words spelled out across the top in a language that didn't look nothing like anything I'd seen before. The tunnel sucked us down to a sort of dock, and the box lifted up, water streaming over the sides. We weren't underwater no more.

"What's happening?" I asked.

The box lid hissed open. Air rushed in, damp and musty.

Naji looked at me and I looked at him, and then he climbed out.

"It's fine!" he said. "There's air, a place to stand–"

"I can see that," I snapped, since I could spot him, a little wavy from the cut of the glass, but definitely standing. I climbed out, too, though I kept one hand on my pistol as I did so.

We stood in a hallway as big and empty as the desert. It was all made out of glass, too, except this one didn't flood with sunlight and rainbows. It didn't flood with anything, thank Kaol, although every time I thought about all that ocean water crushing in on us I took to shaking.

Naji and me stood on the platform and waited. Our box bobbed in the strip of water that flowed in through an opening in the wall, and I could feel the magic sparking around us.

A shark's fin appeared in the water. Part of me wanted to grab for Naji's hand, but I grabbed for my pistol instead.

A shark lifted his head up out of the water. It wasn't the same one that brought us down, and he wasn't wearing no armor, neither, just a circlet of seabone around his neck.

"Follow me," he said. "Along the walkway."

I couldn't stand it no more: I took Naji's hand in mine. Like a little kid, I know, but swords and pistols can't save you from drowning.

Naji dipped his head politely and together we followed along with the shark, our footsteps bouncing off the glass. When we came to the end of the hallway, the shark said, "You may open the door. Preparations have been made for your arrival."

I murmured an old invocation to the sea, one Mama'd taught me years ago, while Naji pushed open the door.

No water. Just air.

It opened up into a big round dome, the way I'd always imagined a nobleman's ballroom to look. Only the floor opened up here, too, a ring of cold dark seawater. The shark's head popped up.

"Our soothsayer will be here soon," he said. He disappeared into the darkness.

"What do they need a soothsayer for?" I muttered.

Naji wrapped his arm around my waist and buried his face in my hair. I was too startled to react, so I just stood there and let him touch me. "Thank you for coming with me," he whispered, and his gratitude rushed into my thoughts, turning all my fear into a weird sort of happiness.

"Thank you?" I laughed. "I thought this was proof that it wasn't dangerous."

"That too."

It's funny, cause even though we were at the bottom of the ocean with only a layer of glass between us and the deep, I still couldn't get enough of his hands on me. I leaned against him, his body warm and solid and reassuring, and thought about giving him my blood the day of the battle. It wasn't so bad, being in his head now and then. It was the whole reason I knew he cared about me.

Water spilled across our feet.

"Naji of the Jadorr'a!" The voice boomed through the big empty room. "Is this your companion?"

I pulled away from Naji. An octopus bobbed in the water, its tentacles curling around the edges of the floor, its skin a rich dark blue, bright against the water's black. He wore a row of small white clam shells strapped to one tentacle.

"Yes," said Naji. "This is Ananna of the *Tanarau*."

"Of the *Nadir*," I corrected.

The octopus heaved itself out of the water. "How lovely to meet you. My name is Armand II, and I saw you," he turned to me, "in my visions as well, in the swirls and mysteries of the inks." He looked at me expectantly.

"Uh, that's good."

"I'm afraid the King of Salt and Foam is not a two-way creature, like myself." Armand lurched forward, dragging across the floor, his legs coiling and uncoiling. "But we have made preparations."

He opened up one of the clam shells and pulled out a pair of glass vials filled with a dark, murky liquid. "It will not harm you," he said.

I got this slow sinking of dread, but Naji took one of the vials and held it up to the light. He opened it up and sniffed. Looked at me.

"It's water-magic," he said.

"So? You'd expect sand-magic down here?"

Naji brushed his hand against my face, his touch gentle, almost as soft as a smile. "Forgive her," he said, turning to Armand. "Her profession requires a certain amount of wariness."

"As does yours, I imagine."

Naji looked at the vial again. "Less than you might think."

"What's it gonna do to us?"

"You will be able to breathe water," Armand said.

I frowned. Of course. And Naji was right; that was old sea-magic, the sort of thing Old Ceria would know how to do. It wasn't impossible. It was dangerous, I suppose, but then, so's all magic. So's cutting open your arm and giving your blood to the man you love.

"I'll give it a shot," I said. I took off my shoes and my coat, though I figured I shouldn't meet the King of Salt and Foam, whoever he was, in my underwear. I left my pistol cause there was no point having it underwater. Then I took the vial from Armand, unscrewed the lid, and shot the stuff back like it was rum. Immediately my lungs started burning, and I gasped and choked and clawed at my throat. Naji pushed me in the water.

Release.

The water filled up my lungs and then pulsed out though gills that appeared on my neck. The lights from the city swirled and bled into one another, bled into the darkness of the sea.

It was beautiful. And I'd never even have to come up for air.

Another muffled splash and then Naji was beside me, barefoot and coatless, his hair drifting up in front of his eyes. I laughed, bubbles streaming silvery and long between us, and for the first time in a long time I wished I could do sea-magic myself, so I could swim through the water undeterred by breath, and Naji could come with me, and we could swim and play and entwine ourselves together.

"This way," Armand said, graceful now that he was underwater. He propelled himself forward, toward the blur of lights, and Naji and me followed with slow easy breast strokes.

The King of Foam and Salt held court in a big curling palace that looked like more bones. Everything glowed with the light of that weird algae.

I've never been to court before. In Jokja Queen Saida didn't hold court, just met with petitioners in her sun room. Court's an Empire thing, and the Empire don't like pirates. But I bet the Emperor's court had nothing on the Court of the Waves.

It was full up with all manner of sea life, rows of little clams and a whole school of flickering fish that turned to us like one person when we swam in. There were big sharp-toothed predators and slippery sparking eels and the rows of shark sentries, swimming ceaselessly in circles around the room.

And then there was the King.

He wasn't like any fish I ever saw. He reminded me of the manticore, cause he had a long curling shark's body and the wide graceful fins of a manta ray and the spines of a saltwater crocodile, all topped up with a human face with pale green-gray skin and flat black eyes and hair like strips of dark green seaweed.

He was coiled around a hunk of coral when we swam in, and as we approached he rose up in the water, his full length taller than any human man. Naji stopped and bowed his head best he could in the water. I figured I should do the same.

"Are you Naji of the Jadorr'a?" the King asked, his voice booming through the water like the blast from a cannon.

"I am."

"And who is your companion?"

"I'm Ananna of the *Nadir*." Water flooded into my mouth when I talked, only to pour back out through the gills in my neck.

"And how do you know Naji of the Jadorr'a?"

I didn't want to talk again, cause of the way the water rushing through my head made me dizzy. But everybody was staring at me, especially the King with his flat black shark eyes.

"I saved his life," I said

The King smiled, showing rows of teeth. Exactly like the manticore.

"Well, I am grateful for that, Ananna of the *Nadir*." He swam toward us, his tail flicking back and forth in the water. "I suppose you'd like to know why you are here."

"Yes," said Naji. "Your Grace."

The King of Salt and Foam stopped a foot away from us. I kept picturing his teeth sinking into my arm, into my belly – but no. He was like the manticore, right? He wouldn't hurt us. His shark-sentries hadn't hurt us–

"You created this," the King said to Naji. His manta-ray fins swooped in and out, like they were trying to gather the city up in his arms. "All of this."

Naji stared at him.

"It was your magic, the soothsayer told me." The King nodded. "You cast wave after wave of magic into the sea, and from that magic we were born."

"That's impossible," Naji whispered.

"But it isn't," the King said. "Look at all this. Our city, our people. We can feast you in our hall, we can entertain you in our gardens…"

I wondered how an underwater city could have gardens.

"All of this came about because of you," the King said. "The soothsayer saw it."

Over in the corner, Armand bowed.

Naji shook his head. "No, no... My magic... it doesn't create, it destroys..." His voice trailed off. He was shaking, I realized, the water bubbling around him. And his skin had gone pale and sickly-looking, even in the soft glow of the algae. I pushed over toward him, wound my arm around his, touched his scars.

"You told me blood-magic can do whatever you will it to do," I whispered, cause he was wrong, his magic had saved me from a gunshot wound.

Naji shook his head. "No," he said. "No, I never willed–" He stopped and looked at me. His eyes widened. "Your blood," he said.

"What?" Water swooshed through my head. I did my best to ignore it. "What about–"

"Your blood mixed with my blood..." His hands were on my face, his touch muted by the water. "We did this. Together. And I think..."

Lightness passed over his face like sunlight. He drifted away from me and floated up toward the ceiling, his mouth hanging open in something like surprise. Tiny white bubbles spun around him.

"Naji of the Jadorr'a?" The king flicked his fins at the courtiers and the school of fish flashed forward and swarmed around Naji, brought him back down to the floor. "Is he hurt?" the King asked me. "I don't understand what he's saying."

I looked at Naji out of the corner of my eye, caught up in all those flashes of light and silver. "I helped him," I finally said. "Whatever he did to make all you…"

And then I understood too. The battle with the Hariris. The magic we created. That *violence*, it all spilled into the ocean. This was all the magic-sickness. This was clams growing out of the side of the *Tanarau*, this was blood staining the walls of the *Ayel's Revenge*, this was Queen Saida's garden house collapsing into jungle plants in the middle of her garden. All that left over magic sank to the floor and brought forth this city, this whole civilization, with a king and a court, with soldiers and soothsayers. Life.

The third piece of the puzzle.

Once I understood what had happened, I felt the curse dissolve away. There was a sharp and sudden crack, like what I felt when I kissed Naji back on the Isles of the Sky, and then there was only a lightness, an absence of weight. This was northern magic, after all, unknowable and strange – we might have created life during the battle, but the curse had stayed in place until this moment, when Naji learned, when we *both* learned, that the third task wasn't impossible. Completing the task wasn't what broke the curse, it was learning that the impossible wasn't really impossible at all.

Naji burst out of the school of fish, his clothes and hair fluttering around him. "Thank you," he said to the King. "Your hospitality is most kind." He seemed back to himself. My head was reeling from what I'd just figured out. It's gone, his curse is gone.

The King looked confused. "No," he said. "I am thanking *you*."

He lowered himself to the ocean floor, and then so did all the rest of the courtiers, until everyone, every fish and clam and eel in the Court of the Waves, was bowing to me and Naji.

Naji's face was full of light. He wasn't smiling, but he was happy, and his eyes were gleaming, and his hand looped in mine and squeezed tight as we kicked our feet there in the water. I pressed against him and held his hand as tight as I could. Music was pouring through the hall – not like the music up on land, but this soft creeping echo, like the reedy melody of a flute.

"Is it true?" I murmured to him, wanting to feel his body close to mine, wanting to hear him say it even though I already knew for certain, even though I could feel that the weight of the curse had drained away from him. "Is it broken?"

"It's broken." His hand squeezed mine. The King rose back up, solemn-faced and grateful, and the rest of the courtiers followed. The water churned from their movement.

"You're free," I said.

"Yes," Naji said. His hand gripped mine so tightly my fingers ached. "Free of the curse."

The King was smiling at us. Water rushed into my head and out through the gills in my neck.

"We broke it," Naji said. "I didn't know until I understood, but we broke it."

CHAPTER SEVENTEEN

The King of Salt and Foam gave us gifts: sacks of pearls, vials of Armand's potion that granted breath underwater, hard pink shells lashed together into strange clattering sculptures. They were brought in by a school of fish, all those tiny silvery bodies buoying up the gifts as they swam beside the King.

"The art of our society," the King told us. We were in his garden – turned out it was all seaweed and coral and glowing algae, beautiful and haunting. "We shall erect statues of your faces, Naji of the Jadorr'a and Ananna of the *Nadir*. Our children's children will not forget what you gave us."

"I thank you deeply," Naji said, bowing his head low, all serious and respectful. When I tried to do the same thing I almost turned a cartwheel in the water.

"Come," the King said, "swim with me." And then he began to slice through the water in his graceful, fluttering way, bubbles forming at the tips of his fins.

Naji and me paddled along beside him.

"I would like to know the story," the King said.

"The story?" I asked. Naji kicked me, hard and on purpose.

"Yes. The story of how this all came to be." The King stopped and floated in place, his seaweed hair drifting up away from his shoulders. "I know it was your magic–"

"And Ananna's," Naji said.

The King gave him a polite smile. "Armand saw *you*," he said firmly. "He saw the spells you cast into the sea. You were trying to defend your vessel, I know." The King fluttered his fins. "Armand saw that as well. But what we know of magic – it is all intention, yes?"

"Technically," Naji said. "But when a great deal of magic is cast, the way it was when I – when Ananna and I – were working to defend our ship... it sometimes takes on a... a life of its own."

The King gazed at him with flat black eyes. "Our life," he said. "Our lives."

"Yes." Naji bowed.

"So we really are creatures of magic."

"Magic and the sea," Naji said. "And yourselves, given the time."

That was a nice touch, I thought. You could tell Naji was used to dealing with royalty.

The King nodded. "I don't entirely understand," he said, "but I will set my scholars to studying the phenomenon."

Naji frowned a little, but I thought that was reasonable enough. Why wouldn't they want to know where they came from? 'Sides, the King was a fish. Couldn't expect him to understand everything about the land, just like we can't be expected to understand everything about the sea. Any pirate in the Confederation and any sailor on the up-and-up could tell you that.

"Regardless of our origins, you are welcome back to my kingdom any time you wish," the King said, and he gave one of those bows, deep and sure-finned in the water.

"I will visit as often as I can," Naji said, returning his bow, and I knew he meant it.

Armand appeared at the entrance to the garden, accompanied by a pair of shark sentries.

"Ah," the King said, "it's time."

"Your water-breath will wear off soon," Armand said. "We should wait in the air-hall."

The King turned to us. "Are you certain you wouldn't like to stay longer?" he asked. "You can stay in the air-hall. I'm certain we could provide food for you."

"We need more than food, I'm afraid." Naji smiled, polite as could be. "We can't go long without fresh water – ah, that is, water without salt."

"And we want to make sure our ship's still waiting for us when we get back," I added.

Naji's voice flashed a warning in my head, but the King only nodded. "I look forward to your future visit," he said to Naji. "I will investigate this matter of saltless water. And remember, all you must do is come to these coordinates. We will know it's you."

Armand rippled in the water like he was impatient. "I don't wish to be rude, your Grace," he said, "but if the water-breath were to wear out here in the open, the effects would be disastrous."

"Ah yes, of course, Armand." The King bowed one last time.

We swam out of the garden and through the city to the big empty hall where that hissing glass box sat waiting for us. The potion kept working all through the trip, and for about five minutes or so after we arrived in the big empty hall. When it did wear off, though, it wore off quick as it had come on. One minute my breath was churning through my head and the next I had that tightness in my lungs that meant I was drowning. I pushed myself out of the water, onto the platform. Naji shot up a few seconds later, gasping. It felt weird to breathe air again. It was so thin and insubstantial, like spun sugar. I felt like I couldn't get enough of it.

Naji and me didn't really talk on the ride up, though he held me close like he was afraid I would disappear. I didn't feel all that different now that the curse was broken, but Naji was filled up with light, like the glow of the algae down there in the depths of the ocean.

Part of me was afraid he'd leave, now that he wasn't bound to me, but I told myself over and over that he was bound to me in other ways. I told myself he didn't have to be bound to me at all in order to love me. And the way he held me on the way up, his face pressing into my hair, water pooling at our feet, it helped convince me that I was right.

The *Nadir* was waiting for us when we surfaced. Thank Kaol.

Naji watched us load up the treasure, crewmen carrying it down to the holding bay – we were gonna split it proper, on account of how little actual pirating we'd been doing. Me and Marjani's idea. Naji didn't seem to care at all, and he watched us load up the cargo in happy silence. The only time he spoke was when he leaned over the railing and thanked the shark sentry.

"No," said the shark. "Thank you, Naji of the Jadorr'a." Then he turned to me and said, "And you, Ananna of the *Nadir*."

The shark and the glass box disappeared beneath the waves. You'd never know there was this whole city down there, full of talking fish and a king like an underwater manticore. Naji slipped off into the captain's quarters, and I moved to chase after him, but Marjani stopped me.

"What happened down there?" she asked. "Naji seems–"

"Cured?" I asked.

Her eyes widened.

"Yeah," I said. "The last part of the curse, remember? Create life out of an act of violence?"

She nodded, and I told her about the city and its inhabitants, the overflow of his magic. I told her how my blood, with its little trickle of ocean-magic, had mixed with his, and that's how everything came together.

"So we're done," she said. "We don't have to sail around chasing after his curse anymore."

I nodded.

"Now what?"

"You're captain," I said. "What do you want to do?"

She stared at me for a few seconds. "You know what I want to do," she said softly.

I got a heavy weight in my chest. A realization. "Yeah."

We stood in silence for a few moments. Then Marjani broke off from me and stood next to the railing. The *Nadir* bobbed in the water, held in place by sea-magic. She was waiting to be set free. I could feel it thrumming through her planks and her sails.

"I had a thought," Marjani said. "A few days ago, actually, sitting in the garden room with Saida."

"Well, I'd hope you'd had more than one thought the last few days."

Marjani laughed. "Saida was playing an old Jokja song on the reed, and I was sitting there listening – I never did care for sitting around listening to palace music, but with her it's different. Anyway, I was listening to this song and thinking. Thinking about the *Nadir* and her crew. And you."

The wind blew across the water, slammed against the frozen sails. Everything tasted like salt. I didn't want to go back to Jokja, I didn't want to live in the palace and smell the flowers blooming in the jungle. I didn't want to watch the rains fall every afternoon. Most things are only nice for a little while. Jokja was one of 'em. The sea wasn't.

"It's your boat," I said, voice small enough that the wind swallowed it whole.

"Not anymore," Marjani said. "It's yours."

I didn't speak, didn't move, I just kept staring out at the ocean.

"That was my thought," Marjani said. "When I was listening to that music from my childhood. The thing is, I became a pirate to run away from Jokja. But I don't have to run away from it anymore. And if anyone deserves her own boat, it's you."

"The crew'll never—"

"The crew'll listen to anyone who takes them up to the Lisirran merchant channels and pays them fair. And they've listened to you before." She smiled at me. "They're as tired of Arkuz as you are."

I didn't bother to correct her; she was right.

Another wind-blown pause.

"Don't let some Confederation scummy blow a hole in her side," Marjani said, "that's all I ask."

I nodded out at the sea, a nervous happiness churning up inside me. "I'll try my best, Captain."

She laughed.

"Lady Anaja-tu," I said, correctly myself.

"More accurate." She paused. "Go plot the course back to Jokja. We'll tell the crew about the trade-off once we make port in Arkuz." Then she pushed back away from the railing and hopped up on the helm and shouted, "Get your asses back to work! We make sail for Jokja and then Lisirra!" She gazed across the deck. "You can all quit your bitching, cause it seems we're pirates again."

That got a roar out of 'em.

As they readied the boat to turn back toward civilization, I slipped into the captain's quarters to draw up our route. When I walked in, though, Naji sat up on the bed and said, "Come here."

"Don't have time for that now." I nodded at the navigation maps. "Gotta chart us a new course. We're heading for Jokja and then..." I couldn't help myself; I broke out into a grin. "Marjani gave me the ship! So we won't be staying in Jokja no more. I figured we'd make sail for the Empire merchant channels and then head to Qilar. Ain't been that way in a long time, and–"

I stopped. He doesn't have a lot of expressions, sure, but I can tell happy from sad. And he wasn't happy right now.

"I know," he said quietly.

"You *know*? How the hell... Oh." I frowned. "You were in my head, weren't you?"

"Yes." No apology, no explanation. "Ananna, I won't be able to sail with you to Qilar."

"Why not?" I could feel his thoughts pressing against mine, but I shoved them away.

"Because I will have to stay behind in Lisirra."

The room got drawn and quiet. The curtains hanging over the port holes shimmered in the sunlight as the *Nadir* made her way east.

"Ananna," Naji said, "one cannot just *leave* the Order."

I stared at him. My heart felt the way it had when he didn't smile at me. Like it was frozen.

"But you *did*," I said. "You ain't been a part of the Order–"

"No," he said. "I didn't."

"I don't understand."

He didn't answer right away, and I lunged across the room and made to hit him, though he caught me by the wrist and sat me down on the bed. "I don't understand!" I shouted again. "You haven't been part of the Order for going close to a year now! I ain't seen you take no commissions or meet with any of them–"

"That's not true," he said softly. "You saw me in my trances. I didn't take any commissions, no, because I was cursed. It was a... hindrance."

I went limp. All the anger just collapsed out of me and turned to sorrow.

"I'm so sorry." He reached to touch my hair, but I slapped his hand away. He didn't try to touch me again. "I didn't think we'd break the curse, and in truth, some days I didn't... I didn't *want* it broken, despite the pain, because I didn't–"

I stared down at my knees, heat rising in my cheeks. "You should have told me."

"I know."

"So now what?" I asked. "You go back to... to wherever, to your castle in..." I didn't know where the Order was located. Lisirra? Or the capital city? Who gave a shit?

"It's not a castle," Naji said.

"Whatever! I won't ever get to see you again."

"That's not true," he said, and he pulled me close to him. "You're a *pirate*, Ananna, you can sail to wherever I am, and I can come to wherever you are."

I was hot with anger and I thought about how he wouldn't once smile for me and then I thought about how he kissed me like I was the only person in the whole world. I thought about the light in his eyes whenever he was happy. I thought about how he shied away whenever I touched his scar and the way his hands traced the tattoos on my stomach.

"I love you," I said.

He blinked.

I don't know why I said it. It was true, but I was also furious with him. I guess I just wanted him to know what he was leaving behind.

"I love you, too," he said.

My face got real hot, then, and it wasn't just the anger. "Then don't leave me!"

"I'm not," he said. "I just can't... I just can't *stay*."

"What!" I shoved him away. "That's what not staying means, you idiot. *Leaving*."

"Ananna, I'm bound to the Order. If I try to leave, permanently, they'll kill me. A permanent death."

"As opposed to an impermanent one?"

"Yes," Naji said, his eyes serious. "I work blood-magic, remember?"

He reached out to touch me, but I jerked away from him. He said my name again, and it was full of all this sadness and longing, but I refused to look at him. I gathered up the maps and the divider and carried them outside, up to the helm. The air was calm and I could weigh the maps down with some bottles of rum if need be.

Anything to get away from Naji. At least for a little while.

Marjani glanced at me but didn't say nothing when I stretched my maps out on the deck of the ship. The wind blew my hair into my eyes, and I cursed, trying to get the divider to slide across the map.

"I got Jeric to cast the fortune," Marjani said. "Looks like the air'll be clear from here to Arkuz. How long are you thinking it'll take? We had that storm on the way out..."

I was grateful to her for giving me the ship to talk about so I wouldn't have to think about Naji. "About a week and a half, looks like." I smoothed my hand over the paper. "We should have enough supplies. I haven't checked the stores in a while. Have you?"

Marjani didn't answer. And I realized with a start that the entire ship had gone silent: there was no creaking of the masts, no thwap of water against the boat's side.

For a moment, my heart froze.

"Marjani?" I whispered, and I twisted around to face her.

A man was standing at her side, one hand grabbing her arm and the other holding a knife under her chin.

The knife looked like it was made out of starlight.

The man's feet ended in mist.

"No!" I jumped to my feet and drew out my sword.

"Ah, that got your attention." The way he talked reminded me of Echo, cold and empty. He kept his knife at Marjani's throat and she stared at me, shivering, although her hand was creeping up to her pistol. "And you know what I want."

He grabbed Marjani's hand and twisted it around behind her back. Marjani let out a muffled scream.

"Let her go!" I shouted. "She don't have anything to do with this."

"Of course she does," the man said. "She denied my offers as well." But then he shoved her away from him so that she stumbled up to my side. I didn't waste a second:

I swung my sword at him. It sliced through his shoulder and came out at his waist. All he did was laugh.

Marjani pulled out her pistol and pointed it at him. He laughed again.

"The ship is mine," he said. He jerked his head toward the crew, who were doing their work all neat and orderly with faces as blank as masks. "They aren't as protected as you–" he jerked his head at me. "Or as knowledgeable as you–" At Marjani. "But I can't *captain* her to the assassin until you tell me where he is."

My heart jolted. He doesn't know. Naji's charm was still working. He doesn't know Naji's on the boat.

"We don't know where he is," I said. Marjani stayed quiet, just kept her gun trained at his chest.

"Lies." And he reached back his hand and slapped me hard across the face, hard enough that I stumbled back and slammed against the railing. I was stunned that he could touch me. My fingers grasped for the charm. It still hung around my neck. He laughed. "I'm not *Echo*, child. Echo is only a piece of me." He leaned closed. "I can smell him all over you. His *magic*. His filthy little *dirt-charm*." He sneered at me. "You don't protect him as well as he thinks."

"Shut your mouth." I darted forward and grabbed Marjani and pulled her close to me. She gripped her hand in mine.

The man slid toward us. His mist curled around my bare legs. One of the maps had blown over beside us and the mist smeared the ink into long unreadable streaks.

"I've sent Echo to you so many times," he whispered. "Both of you." He grazed his fingers against my cheek and his touch burned with cold. When he touched Marjani she flinched away. "Did you not believe her? All those things she offered?"

I spat on him.

He laughed and wiped the spit away. "That's no way to treat a lord, my dear."

"You ain't no lord."

"But I am. Of course you know that. *He* told you." He smiled again, only this time there was something strange in his smile, like part of his face didn't work. The left side. Like it was scarred–

I knew what he was doing. Giving me what I wanted. Showing me Naji's smile.

"Ananna, be careful," Marjani whispered. I barely heard her.

"Stop it!" I screamed, and I sliced my sword through his belly this time, and all that came out of him was mist.

Where's Naji? I thought, and then I remembered. He wasn't cursed any more; he wouldn't know I was in danger–

Our blood-bond. He knew Marjani gave me the ship, he should know about this.

Maybe he didn't care. Maybe he wanted me to die, then he could go back to the Order and never think about me again–

I didn't really believe that.

The man reappeared right close to me, close enough that I could feel his breath on my skin. "Couldn't tempt you with ships and lovers and power," he whispered. "Couldn't even tempt you with a smile. But there are other ways, of course." And his mist crawled in through my nose and my mouth, crowding into my brain.

"Don't listen to him," Marjani said. Her voice sounded far away even though she was still pressed up against me, her hand in mine. "He's doing something to you. Don't listen–"

The man turned to Marjani. She gazed up at him. I gripped my sword tighter. The mist was still in my head, turning my thoughts cold and hard. She was going to betray Naji. She didn't love him the way I did. It wouldn't even take much. One sentence. He's on the ship. In the captain's quarters.

"Don't even try," Marjani said, gritting her teeth.

The man laughed. "Don't you want to see what I can offer you?" And he pressed his hand on Marjani's forehead. She screamed and jerked away.

"I know what you can offer me," she said. "Slavery and imprisonment."

"You're not as easy to fool as your first mate," he said. "She at least let me show her what I had to offer. I believe she even *considered* it, one bright day."

I felt myself turning hot. A pang of guilt pierced through the fog. How could I think Marjani would hand him over? Cause he was right. *I* almost had.

"Yes," the man said, turning back to me. My whole body turned to ice. "You did almost give him up once. Because he had hurt you. And he's hurt you again, hasn't he? I can smell it on you." He buried his nose in my hair and breathed in deep and my whole body crawled with revulsion. "He could stay, you know," he said. "Sail with you through every ocean in this world, blowing your enemies away with spells and blood magic. Never go back to the Order lair again." The man gave me a lazy grin. "He just doesn't want to."

"And could you give me that?" I shot back. "Naji at my side?"

"I could," the man said. "But then I wouldn't be able to take my revenge, would I? Besides, do you really want a man at your side who doesn't love you?"

I trembled. Behind him, Marjani said, "Ananna, don't you dare listen to him. He's spinning a web–"

"Shut up!" The man whirled around and struck Marjani in the stomach. I lunged at him with my sword, which did nothing, and for a moment or two Marjani stared stricken at him, like she couldn't believe he had hit her. And then she pulled out her pistol and shot him through the heart.

The man roared with laughter. "How many times will you two try to kill me? You know it won't work–"

Light flowed across the deck of the ship.

It knocked me and Marjani over, stunned us both. Naji, I thought. He came after all–

"Yes," the man from the Mists said. "He did come. Hello, Naji of the Jadorr'a."

My whole body turned cold. Marjani grabbed my arm. "Don't be stupid," she said, voice slurring a little. "Don't be–"

I scrambled away from her. Naji was floating above the deck, his body contorted in pain. And the man was laughing.

"Stop it!" I shouted.

The man looked at me. "I knew that would draw him out," he said. "Putting you in enough danger. *Frightening* you enough." He laughed.

"Why didn't you kill him?" I shouted at Naji, who just screamed and writhed in the air.

"Because even the people of the Mists have charms of our own." The man smiled at me. Then he walked up to Naji and pulled out his starlight knife. Naji moaned. My heart damn near stopped beating.

Charms of our own.

"Ananna," Marjani said, her voice faint behind me. "Don't rush into this."

The man dug the knife into the left side of Naji's face. Naji screamed and kicked. Blood splattered across the deck of the ship. Magic surged through me, a rush like the sort you get before battle. Marjani grabbed my hand and pulled me back.

"Think," she said roughly, her mouth close to my ear. "He has a charm. Something the other one didn't have."

"The knife."

"Yes. But it's too obvious. Something on the knife." Marjani jerked her chin toward the man, the man and Naji. More blood splattered across the deck. My stomach lurched. "Look at the hilt. It's wrapped in enchanted silk. I've seen that before."

"You've been to the Mists?"

"Of course not. It's not Mists magic." She shoved me forward. Naji's pain was starting to intrude onto me. It started in my head, but now it was a stinging in my face, a ghost of a wound lining my left cheek. "Get that charm off the hilt."

I ran toward Naji and the man. I didn't let myself think about what I was doing. I just ran forward and plunged my hand through the man's back. A half-second of resistance and then it slipped through as easy as it had the day I punched Echo. The man hardly had time to react when my hand shot out the other side and I grabbed hold of the knife.

Naji gasped and landed with a sickening thump on the deck of the *Nadir*.

The man whirled around and snarled at me, his teeth like daggers. A *pop* of a pistol and his chest turned to mist. Marjani. It wasn't enough to disperse him back to the Mists, but it gave me enough time to see that the hilt of his knife was wrapped in stiff silk that smelled of the sap from the trees of the ice-island. I yanked on the silk, balled it up and tossed it in the sea.

"I beseech your help!" I screamed. "Waters of the ocean! Please accept this gift–"

The man from the Mists growled and snarled again. He looked less and less like a man and more and more like a beast from a temple painting. His eyes glowed with starlight. His skin was gray and pale, the color of mist.

"What are you doing?" he howled.

"Waters of the ocean!" I shouted, tears streaming down my face. "I beseech your help! Take this man away from the *Nadir* and her crew!"

Naji lifted his head and stared at me. His eyes were so dark they looked like holes in his face. His mouth opened and closed. I could feel him – fear and panic and despair. I pushed it all away.

"Waters of the ocean!" I screamed. "Please!"

A shadow fell over the boat.

For a long terrible moment the entire world seemed to freeze. Then the *Nadir* tilted backward, and a dark ocean wave rose up against the bright sky, the water throwing off dots of light.

"Hold on!" Marjani screamed. "Knot a rope around yourself! Ananna!"

I didn't move. The wave wasn't for me. It wasn't for anyone human.

A wall of ocean water crashed over the ship. For a minute all I knew was water and salt and light. I couldn't breathe. When I opened my eyes I saw Naji floating through the murk, his hair streaming out from around his face, his eyes on mine.

I screamed his name. Nothing came out but a stream of golden bubbles.

And then the ocean slipped away.

I slammed down onto the deck. The whole world was lit up in white sunlight. I squeezed my eyes closed and pressed my back against the wood. Crewman shouted and sputtered, their feet pounding against the wood. The sails snapped, the masts creaked.

"Ananna?" It was Marjani. "Ananna, wake up. Are you alright?"

I lifted my head and blinked at her. She was soaked, her hair plastered against her face. Behind her, the crew scrambled and crawled across the deck, rubbing at their heads.

"Where's Naji?" I asked. "Where's–"

"Over there..." Marjani pointed. Naji was sprawled across the deck, his chest heaving. "The man from the Mists is gone." She gave me a short smile. "Didn't know you could work water-magic?"

I pushed myself up. My head spun. The ship was undamaged from the wave; the masts stood straight and true, the sails fluttered in the breeze. Everything was wet. That was all.

Marjani helped me to my feet. My body ached, but I ignored the pain as I limped over to where Naji lay. I wasn't sure if it was my pain or Naji's anyway.

"Ananna," he said when he saw me.

I knelt beside him and pressed my hand against his forehead. The ocean had washed the blood off his face, but the cut was still there, a dark jagged tear that would add another scar to the lines of his features.

"I saved your life again," I said. "I'm sorry."

Naji laughed, though it came out choked and short.

"You didn't catch the curse again, did you? Cause I'd feel right bad about that."

Naji shook his head, wet hair flopping over his eyes.

"Good to hear." I stroked his hair, squeezed the saltwater out of it.

"That was... impressive," he said.

I shrugged. "Just gotta know what to ask."

His eyes brightened. For a minute a tightness pinched in my chest. I thought about the man from the Mists smiling for me like he was Naji. But he wasn't Naji. Because this was Naji's smile.

"Are they gone for good?" I asked.

"I don't know," Naji said. "But you scared him worse than I ever could."

I laughed, heat creeping up into my cheeks.

Naji lifted one trembling hand and tucked it against my face. "Thank you," he whispered, and then he drew me down for a kiss.

CHAPTER EIGHTEEN

We sailed into Jokja water a few weeks later, on calm seas and high winds. A trio of royal ships were waiting for us, the Jokja flag fluttering against the bright blue sky.

"What the hell?" I asked. Me and Marjani were up at the helm, looking out for the sparkle of Arkuz on the horizon. Marjani smiled.

"Saida," she said.

"You sure? I dunno, I usually see navy ships, I either fire the cannons or run."

Marjani laughed. "I don't think either of those actions will be necessary."

We sailed up alongside the closest of the navy ships. The crew lined up along the railing and shouted and waved. Marjani shouted and waved right back.

The captain showed up, his green sash rippling like the sea. He gave us a wave. "We're here to accompany you back to land!" the captain shouted, his voice rising and falling on the wind.

"Why?" I shouted back. "So you can arrest us?"

Marjani smacked me on the arm.

The captain shook his head. "By orders of the queen!" he shouted back. "She wanted to see you safely returned, and your boat docked with the royal fleet."

When I looked over to Marjani she was glowing.

"Royal fleet, huh?"

"That's why I'm handing her over to you," Marjani said. "I don't imagine this ship sitting well next to a bunch of Jokja schooners."

I laughed at that, but really my stomach was turning somersaults at the thought of Marjani giving me the ship. She hadn't made it official yet, hadn't told the crew or nothing. I still didn't see how this could go too well.

It took another hour to sail to the Azende Palace docks and get the ship tied down. Just as we were finishing up, a pair of palace guards showed up on deck and snapped their blades into a salute the way they did up at the palace.

"Can I help you?" Marjani asked.

"The Queen sent us," the older guard said. "We're here to watch over your ship."

"Don't need you," I said. "Some of the crew'll be happy–"

"Ignore her," Marjani said, and she had that glow again. I wondered if that was what I looked like every time Naji came around. I hoped not. "We'll be happy to make use of your services." Then she turned to me. "Go tell the skeleton crew they have free run of the city. But," and she touched me lightly on the arm, "they have to be back here at sunset, same as the rest." She smiled at me, and the rest of that sentence hung unspoken on the air. For the exchange.

I sighed, but I did as I was told. The crew was certainly happy about it.

Marjani was waiting for me on the dock along with Naji and another pair of palace guards.

"Let me guess," I muttered, "more accompaniment."

"Life at court," Marjani said. "You'd get used to it, I imagine."

"It wasn't this bad before."

Marjani shrugged.

We made our way through the palace gardens and into the queen's sun room. She was pacing in front of the big open windows when we walked in, the sunlight setting all her jewels to sparkling. When she saw Marjani she cried out, lifted up her skirts, raced across the length of the room, and caught Marjani in her arms.

"Jani," she murmured, burying her face in Marjani's shoulder. "The fortuneer said you were drowned – she saw a wave crash over your boat. I sent out men to look for you, but we hadn't heard – and the sentries were only there on the off-chance–"

Marjani cupped Queen Saida's face in one hand and kissed her, gentle and soft. Saida gazed at her, tears sparkling on the ends of her lashes. For a moment, no one in the sun room moved.

"I really thought you were dead," Queen Saida whispered. "And it was like when you left before, only worse, unending–"

"I'm not dead," Marjani told her.

"It's going to be like this every time you–"

"I won't be leaving again," Marjani said.

Queen Saida pulled away, stared at her. "I thought you were a… a pirate now."

Marjani smiled. And then she shook her no. "No, I was never a pirate. Not really." A long breathless pause. "I'm staying."

My guts twisted up when she said that, not cause of her making me the new captain but because I wanted Naji to say those words to me more than anything, "I'm staying", and he wouldn't, I knew he wouldn't. I glanced at him out of the corner of my eye: he stood very still, his face a mask even though it was uncovered.

"You're staying?" Queen Saida trembled. "You're really staying?"

"Really. I'm really staying."

"Oh, Jani, this is marvelous news!" She threw her arms around Marjani's shoulders and kissed her. "I'll tell the kitchens right away. We should have a feast–"

"I doubt the kitchens will be able to prepare a feast in the next few hours," Marjani said. "And even if they could, it would be far too much work–"

Queen Saida ignored her; she just turned to one of her pretty attendants and said, "Send Najala up to meet with me. I want to discuss the menu."

"Of course you do," Marjani murmured, low enough that only I could hear her.

"Aw c'mon," I said. "Not many of us get feasts thrown in our honor."

"Yes, I suppose that does make the two of us members of a very particular club."

I laughed. Marjani just shook her head.

But then Naji caught my eye, and my good mood evaporated. His expression was like the night sky during a full moon, dark dark dark, but in some ways bright enough to cast shadows.

I could feel Marjani looking at me. I knew she knew something was wrong. But she didn't say anything, and Queen Saida was calling her away for preparations, and I slipped out of the sun room and down to the garden.

Naji knew not to follow.

The feast wound up being postponed, cause, like Marjani said, the kitchens didn't have time to prepare everything to Queen Saida's liking. All that meant was that Naji and me couldn't stay for it. He needed to leave, needed to go back to the Order, back to Lisirra. And truth was I didn't much want to stay in Jokja any longer anyway. Partly because seeing Marjani and Queen Saida made me sad, but partly too because of the way I'd missed the sea so bad during all my times on land. Papa used to talk about it with Mama, the way the sea meant more to him as he got older. Mama always said it was because of the sea's magic, that he was finally feeling it.

And maybe I was finally feeling it too. I'd saved Naji with the sea's magic. I'd saved him, just so he would have to leave me again.

I stayed out in the palace garden all afternoon, listening to the jungle creeping up along the other side of the fence, chatting with the guards as they changed positions, taking cover underneath the banana trees when the rains came. Naji never came around. I told him not to, in the whispers that still bound us together by blood and magic. I told him I wanted to be alone for a while, to think. And he honored that.

Although in my thinking I did, at one point, see just how well we were connected. I thought maybe it would come in handy, once he left and I sailed off to the merchant channels or the ice-islands or Qilar. It was during the rainstorm, and I was stretched out in the grass, rain beating against the wide, flat banana leaves. Everything smelled like soil. I closed my eyes and reached out with my thoughts. It didn't take long.

He was in the palace library, pouring over some old Jokja text. I saw him like I was standing in the doorway, but he didn't look up, didn't greet me, at least not in the physical. Instead, I heard his voice in my head.

I thought you wanted to be alone.

I am alone. So are you.

For all I knew he was still reading that stupid book, but when I thought that he smiled. Just for a second.

Not so alone, he told me. *You're here.*

Not really.

Your thoughts are. It's the same thing.

No it ain't. Except I didn't say it, exactly, nor did I think those specific words. I just... disagreed with him.

We can do this across the seas, he went on. *You do know that, right? We won't really be splitting apart–*

Out in the garden, I sat up, knocking my head against the banana leaves. Rain soaked through my hair, though my clothes. The image of Naji in the library was lost. His voice in my head was a whisper: *Ananna? Where'd you go?*

I shook my head, trying to knock him out. It didn't work. So I focused on the sound of the rain as it pattered across the garden, and in a few minutes I was alone again.

Won't really be splitting apart.

I curled up beneath the banana tree, tucking my chin onto my knees. I knew he was right, but–

I just didn't want to think about it. I didn't want to think about anything.

At sunset, I walked down to the *Nadir* alone. She was waiting for me in her place at the docks, her sails drawn up tight, her pirate colors fluttering like they were the Jokja flag. In the golden light of day's end, she looked like something out of a dream, like something out of one of Echo's visions.

Almost too perfect for me.

"Ananna!" Marjani leaned over the railing and waved at me. "I was starting to think you wouldn't show up."

"Got lost in the garden."

She laughed. I wondered if Queen Saida was gonna be on board, surrounded by her attendants. If there was gonna be a line of guards watching as Marjani told the crew I was their new captain.

But there wasn't. It was just Marjani standing there in a simple blue dress, and the only person by her side was Naji.

His eyes crinkled when he saw me, and at first I wanted to ignore him, pretend he was just another scummy among the crew. But when he held out his hand I took it, and I let him drew me close and kiss me softly on the mouth. And I knew then that I'd missed his touch.

"Alright, men," Marjani hollered. "I made you all come back here for a reason."

"We leaving?" called out Bashar. "Finally sailing off to Lisirra like you promised?"

"*You* are," Marjani said, and the crew whooped and hollered without thinking on what she might've meant by that.

"In fact, you can leave tonight," she said, and the cheers picked up again. "Assuming that's what your captain wants."

That got their attention. Finally.

"And what do you want?" somebody called out.

"I'm not your captain anymore," Marjani said.

Silence. My palms were sweating, and I wiped them on the edge of my dress.

"You saying he is?" Bashar asked, pointing at Naji. "He ain't no captain. He don't know his way around a boat–"

"I'm saying she is," Marjani said.

Every eye on that boat turned to me. The silence was even thicker than before, so thick I choked on it like Otherworld mist. I realized, standing there, that I'd expected to be jeered, but this silence was worse.

And then Jeric yi Niru stepped out from the knot of crewman. "Annoying though she is," he said, "I couldn't imagine a finer captain."

I glared at him.

Still, his words broke some spell, and the crew started cheering the way they had when Marjani said we were setting sail for Lisirra. I didn't quite believe it at first, that they were cheering – well, not for me really, but for the idea of me as their captain.

"So are we setting sail tonight, Captain First Mate?" Jeric asked me.

"Don't call me that." I stepped forward and looked out over the crew, all of them staring back at me, waiting to give an order. And I knew I could order them to take me anywhere but Lisirra, all the way to the underside of the world if I wanted, and Naji couldn't do a thing about it.

Except he could. Even if he didn't blow the ship off course he could slip into the shadows or go through the trance-place and I'd never see him again.

"We'll set sail tonight," I said. I could feel Naji staring at me, but I didn't say nothing. "We'll set sail tonight, and we'll set sail to Lisirra."

Lisirra was as hot as I remembered, that dry baking heat that soaked into my skin and made me feel like I was home. Naji and me walked side by side through the streets of the pleasure district. It was the middle of the day, and everyone was tucked away in the shadowy coolness of the buildings, the way the *Nadir* was tucked into the Lisirran dock under a fake name and the promise of a few sheets of pressed silver.

Every now and then Naji's hand touched mine. Every time it did my body shivered with happiness.

Naji took me to an inn. The Snake Shade Inn. The one we'd stayed at after I'd started up his curse. This time, though, the innkeep didn't recognize him for what he was. When he handed us the key to our room, he looked at us like we were nothing but a pair of pirates.

Upstairs in the room, Naji undressed me slow and soft, starting with my boots and jacket and then undoing my dress with all the precision of a clockmaker. He stood behind me as he pulled my underclothes off me, and then he pulled my naked body close to him and kissed my neck and whispered in my ear, "I'm not leaving you."

I twisted around to glare at him. "I don't want to talk about that."

He gazed at me for a few seconds. Then he tapped his finger against his temple, tapped it against mine.

"That ain't the same!"

"I know," he said softly, "but it's there."

He set me down on the bed and stood in front of me as he peeled off his own clothes. His tattoos gleamed in the light streaming through the windows. The scar on his chest looked a million years old. The scar on his face from the Mists lord's knife did not.

He crawled on top of me and kissed my mouth and neck and my stomach. He kissed every part of me. Every time he kissed me he told me that he loved me, and after a while I knew I had to believe him.

We stayed in the inn room for a long time. The sun dropped in the sky. The light in the windows turned golden and rich and syrupy. I laid my head against Naji's chest and listened to his heart beating.

"I'm not leaving you," he said again.

"Don't." I was gonna start crying. I could feel the weight of it, lurking there right behind my eyes.

Naji rolled over so we were facing each other. Ran his fingers over my lips. "I'm not even talking about reading your thoughts," he said. "Even if we couldn't do that, I still wouldn't be leaving you."

I scowled up at the ceiling.

"Would you want to stay in one place?" he asked.

"What?"

"Say I bought you a house in Lisirra," he said. "The garden district, maybe. And you lived there. And I could travel through the shadows to come see you–"

"Like the Hariris?" I frowned.

"You wouldn't like that?"

"I like being on a boat."

Naji brushed my hair away from my forehead. "I know," he said. "It's part of you. The ocean. The water. You can't stay in one place. Even if you wanted to."

I thought about those first few days after I ran away, how badly I wanted to be back out on the sea.

"I ain't a sea witch," I said.

He laughed hard enough that the bed shook. "Don't you dare try to tell me you still believe that."

I scowled. "It was just cause of your blood-bond."

"It was not and you know it." He kissed the tip of my nose. "If ever there was someone who was a part of the ocean, it was you."

I didn't say nothing.

"You have to follow the currents all over the world. It's who you are." He kissed my forehead, my cheeks, my throat. "And I have to follow death all over the world at the Order's command. It's who I am."

I frowned.

He rolled me onto my back and sat up and traced two paths over my belly with both hands. "Here I am," he said. "And here's you."

The two paths crossed each other.

"I can make that happen," he said. "I can make that happen anytime you need me."

For a long time I didn't answer. I just stared at him, at his beautiful face and his beautiful scars.

"I need you all the time," I said.

"You do now." He kissed my forehead. "And so do I. But after a while we won't. And you'll be glad to be rid of me."

"I won't stop loving you!"

"Did I say that?" His face darkened. "I said you'll be glad to be on your own. And you will."

I couldn't imagine it at first, but then I thought about it and I could. I wasn't like Marjani, who could give up a life on the sea in exchange for a life with her love. Because Naji was right: Marjani wasn't a part of the ocean. I was.

And now I had a boat of my own, and a crew of my own. And we'd sailed to Lisirra with no trouble. They listened to me like I was Papa, like I was important. And when you got down to it that whole trip Naji'd just been a distraction, really. Keeping my mind away from the boat.

I threw my arms around his neck and kissed him deep and sure.

"Do you really want to see me smile?" he whispered into my neck. "I know the Otherworld lord tried..." His voice trailed off.

I hesitated. "I know how you look when you're happy."

"It's not the same as a smile. I know that." His fingers ran over the bridge of my nose. "After it happened," he said, "after the blood-fire burned me, I would spend hours in front of a mirror Leila had given me, trying to find my face." He dropped his head to the side and didn't look at me as he spoke. "And one day I was going through my expressions, trying to find myself again."

He paused, ran his hand over the tattoo on my belly.

"And I smiled. People used to like my smile. Women, you know." He sighed. "And I'd never seen anything so monstrous."

"You're not a monster," I said.

He looked at me.

"I know that now."

I smiled.

And then he did too.

It didn't look like a smile at first. It looked like a snarl. One part of his face twisted up and the other twisted down. His teeth gleamed.

But I looked at his eyes, where the brightness was. And everything changed.

For the first time, I understood the difference between leaving and not staying. It was the difference between a snarl and a smile.

"Thank you," I whispered, and I kissed his scars, those ridges and lines that twisted his face up into something beautiful. I kissed the place where the man from the Mists had cut him. I kissed over the smooth skin of his neck, the soft tangle of his hair, his lips.

When I pulled away, the smile disappeared from everywhere but his eyes.

"We'll see each other soon," he said.

And he was right.

ACKNOWLEDGMENTS

I'd like to kick off the wave of thanks with my editor, Amanda Rutter, who first suggested that we split the megabook that was the first draft of *The Assassin's Curse* into a duology. For this reason I was able to preserve the original story and didn't have to edit away any of my favorite characters. Amanda also deserves thanks for all her tireless support for both books in the series.

As always, I want to thank my parents and Ross Andrews, for all their love and support. Thanks to Amanda Cole and Bobby Mathews, my friends and beta readers and general writing support system. Indeed, special thanks goes to Amanda for reading the first draft of this book and helping me see its strengths and weaknesses.

Thanks to my agent, Stacia Decker, as well, for her help with early revisions of the book, as well as all her ceaseless hard work in general. The rest of the Angry Robot crew – Mike Underwood, Lee Harris, Darren Turpin, and Marc Gascoigne – deserve special mention too.

And finally, I would like to thank everyone who read, reviewed, and wrote to me about *The Assassin's Curse*. You all helped make the experience of releasing my first novel a overwhelmingly wonderful one, and I sincerely hope that you enjoy *The Pirate's Wish*.

ABOUT THE AUTHOR

Cassandra Clarke is a speculative fiction writer and occasional teacher living amongst the beige stucco of Houston, Texas. She graduated in 2006 from the University of St Thomas with a bachelor's degree in English, and in 2008 she completed her master's degree in creative writing from the University of Texas at Austin. Both of these degrees have served her surprisingly well.

During the summer of 2010, she attended the Clarion West Writers Workshop in Seattle, where she enjoyed sixty-degree summer days. Having been born and raised in Texas, this was something of a big deal. She was also a recipient of the 2010 Susan C Petrey Clarion Scholarship Fund.

Unlike many authors, Cassandra does not have a resume of peculiar careers. She worked at a Barnes and Noble once – that's about as exciting as it gets. In her spare time she enjoys drawing, painting, crocheting, cooking, and quilting, because she is secretly an old lady.

She will see literally any movie as long as it's in a theatre. She watches television. She doesn't play many video games though.

cassandraroseclarke.com
twitter.com/mitochondrial

EXPERIMENTING WITH YOUR IMAGINATION

"A rollicking adventure yarn with plenty of heart – *Emilie & the Hollow World* shouldn't be missed."
Ann Aguirre, USA Today *bestselling author of the* Razorland *and* Beauty *books.*

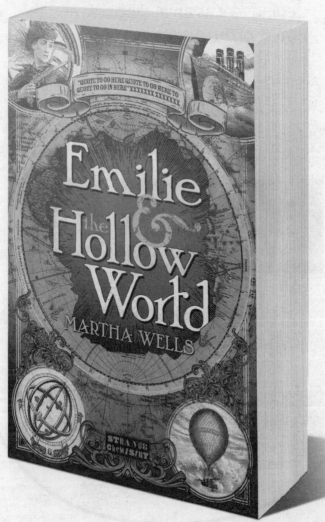

EXPERIMENTING WITH YOUR IMAGINATION

"Mars, monsters, and mysteries: *Zenn Scarlett* is a thoughtful and thrilling science fiction adventure that's perfect for readers who think they've seen it all!"
E C Myers, author of Fair Coin *and* Quantum Coin

EXPERIMENTING WITH YOUR IMAGINATION

"An enjoying, compelling read with a strong and competent narrator … a highly satisfying adventure."
SFX Magazine

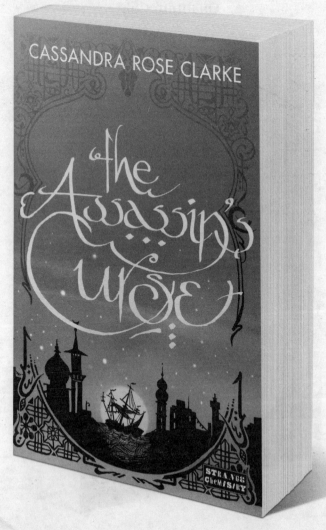